DO YOU BELIEVE?

A *Novelization by*

TRAVIS THRASHER

HOWARD BOOKS
An Imprint of Simon & Schuster, Inc.
New York   Nashville   London   Toronto   Sydney   New Delhi

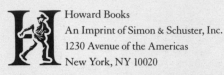 Howard Books
An Imprint of Simon & Schuster, Inc.
1230 Avenue of the Americas
New York, NY 10020

First Howard Books trade paperback edition March 2015

HOWARD and colophon are trademarks of Simon & Schuster, Inc.

For information about special discounts for bulk purchases, please contact Simon & Schuster Special Sales at 1-866-506-1949 or business@simonandschuster.com.

The Simon & Schuster Speakers Bureau can bring authors to your live event. For more information or to book an event, contact the Simon & Schuster Speakers Bureau at 1-866-248-3049 or visit our website at www.simonspeakers.com.

Interior design by Renato Stanisic

Manufactured in the United States of America

10 9 8 7 6 5 4 3 2 1

Library of Congress Cataloging-in-Publication Data

Thrasher, Travis.
    Do you believe? / Travis Thrasher. —First Howard Books trade paperback edition.
        pages ; cm
        1. Clergy—Fiction.   2. Life change events—Fiction.   I. Do you believe? (Motion picture)   II. Title.
    PS3570.H6925D6   2015
    813'.54—dc23   2014048995

ISBN 978-1-5011-1198-3
ISBN 978-1-5011-1219-5 (ebook)

*I believe in Christianity as I believe that the sun has risen:
not only because I see it, but because by it I see everything else.*
—C. S. Lewis

PROLOGUE

A pastor prays.
A soldier surrenders.
A criminal flees.
A woman prays.
A medic doubts.
A mother winces.
A grandfather navigates.
A child cries.
A murderer passes.
A friend grieves.
A nurse awaits.
A doctor scorns.
All while God watches over them, wanting one thing, asking
for one simple thing . . .

We are all searching. I believe this without a doubt.

Faith, of course, is my life, my love, my passion. But you don't have to be a pastor to long for meaning.

It's late as I write this and I think of the windy city surrounding me. This great beating heart, hanging on the edge of an even greater lake. There are ten million people here. Ten million souls. Each of them searching for some sort of meaning in their lives.

But how many actually find it?

I know the reality. Some believe they find it in a dead end they wander into. They allow themselves to settle in. Others drive down highways headed to nowhere for their entire life. Some of them are running away, others refusing to ask for directions.

It's easy to run or even ignore the truth. You can miss it, even when it's right there in front of your eyes.

Like the cross on top of the hospital. The one I see every day on my commute to the church. Countless people pass underneath that cross every day. But how many notice it? And for those who do, what does it mean to them? Ask me and I'll tell you it's about forgiveness and redemption. Because I know that's what it's supposed to mean.

At least that's what I would have said a month ago.

But what does the cross *truly* mean? And why do we all seem to forget it? And how might God—assuming there is a God—go about trying to get us to remember?

I'm remembering everything now, and how it all started that one night at that very hospital, underneath that very cross.

LACEY

S he wasn't supposed to still be there.

The lights of the city passed her by in a blur. They no longer made Lacey happy, but then few things did anymore. Chicago used to hold such promise, but now those shimmers felt like lights on a neighbor's Christmas tree. She could see them but she knew there were no presents for her underneath. She couldn't even get inside to touch them.

Lacey faded, then came back, then faded again. The siren in the ambulance continued to blare. She wasn't dead, right? They had stabilized her, she thought. She didn't know. Half of her felt like she was floating and the other half was freezing in this uncomfortable bed on wheels. She did know that her neighbor had come into her apartment at the very worst time possible. Of course, Lacey would never tell anybody else this, but you don't usually talk about your suicide, right? Or in this case, your *attempted* suicide.

"Dispatch, EMS Eighty-One to UC Trauma Center, hot response."

Even though Lacey had an oxygen mask covering half her

face, she could see the paramedic speaking into the com link. He was a good-looking guy, dark-haired and fit and maybe possibly a little over thirty. It was nice to open her eyes and see him hovering over her.

"On board is a priority-one critical Caucasian female, mid-twenties," the man continued to report. "Experiencing acute respiratory difficulty. Airway constriction still allows for oxygen. Pushing one hundred percent at fifteen liters a minute. I'm gonna pass on the trache unless you advise me otherwise."

"Affirmative, Eighty-One," a female voice answered. "Let's try not to cut her if we don't have to."

Cut her, a voice inside Lacey screamed in alarm. *I would've done that myself if I wanted to go that route.*

The uncomfortable stretcher she lay on shook gently as the ambulance raced down the street. She wanted to tell the paramedic that she didn't want them to go to all this trouble. She didn't mean to get everybody into a panic over the allergic reaction to her dinner. She thought of Pam and already felt bad. Her poor neighbor had found her nearly unconscious, unable to breathe, on the couch with four boxes of Chinese food nearby on the glass table. She had blacked out just as Pam dialed 911. Lacey wasn't even able to swallow that last full bite of General Tso's chicken.

The paramedic glanced down at her and smiled.

"We're almost there, okay?" he said. "You'll be back to your old self in no time. Just keep breathing."

She nodded and tried to smile even though the mask probably hid it.

My old self.

Ah, the irony of his statement. It was a cliché, really. "Back to your old self in no time." The reality was she didn't want to go back to her old self, that she didn't *like* her old self. Her old life. Her old everything.

Time was all she had, but unlike that song, it wasn't on her side. It hadn't been for quite a while now.

That song reminded her of her father. She pictured him now and felt the regret in her soul. This was followed by a snapshot of Donny, which replaced that regret with anger. Sometimes the pictures blurred, and sometimes the emotions blurred with them. Regret, anger, hurt, fear, isolation . . . There were too many, and none of them were good.

The ambulance turned and started to slow down and Lacey assumed they had arrived.

She couldn't help feel a wave of disappointment.

All that energy and courage it had taken to do the unthinkable. And now this.

Now she was here and she would be starting over at square one. But it wouldn't change the past twenty-five years. Nothing could change that.

The only person who could change things was Lacey. That's exactly what she had tried to do tonight.

Maybe she would have to try again once she got out of there.

ELENA

Everything can change in a minute when you're working in
the ER. A steady night can turn into a nightmare very fast.
A rush of adrenaline can come at any moment, even though you
might be prepared and ready and think you've seen it all. For the
staff at the University of Chicago Medical Center, just like the staff
of any hospital in any thriving city, the truth is you've never seen
it all. Every sunrise and sunset bring chances to be surprised and
shocked and thankful for the life you're living.

Elena Wilson checked the vital signs for the recently admitted
patient now unconscious but stable in her bed. She wasn't surprised
to see the young woman on the stretcher at this time of night. It
was a pretty young woman, and Elena figured she'd overdosed or
tried to take her own life. But she didn't have time to try to con-
template what happened. Her role was to make sure this young
woman made it through the night. Whatever happened before
this could wait. Making it to tomorrow was what mattered now.

She had barely seen Bobby when he brought the stretcher in
and she took over. Elena occasionally managed to see him during
work hours whenever they had to bring someone in. Once Bobby

had finally become a full-time paramedic, they both were grateful to be working in the same industry, to be helping people on a daily basis, and to know the stresses that life could bring. In a hospital full of so many people and colleagues and sharks, Elena was glad to have Bobby around every now and then. Sometimes the only chance they had to see each other was in the hospital, passing each other by in their revolving and seemingly never-ending shifts. Occasionally she felt guilty about this, and about their boys, who didn't see their parents together often.

But you do what you have to do.

This was what they had to do at the moment. Elena told herself that over and over again.

It seemed like it took the doctor forever to get there, but she knew the doctor on call right now. It wouldn't surprise her if it would be another ten minutes or more. Dr. Farell was just that sort of guy.

In the small treatment space, which resembled the other dozen down this white-washed hallway, Elena stood and stared at the young woman named Lacey. She was so young and full of potential and life. She wondered what had gone wrong and why Lacey was here. What decisions had brought her here. Maybe, possibly, it was just an accident. But Elena doubted it.

I don't believe in accidents. And I don't believe in miracles.

The door opened and she could smell the strong cologne even before turning. Dr. Thomas Farell picked up the paperwork without any sort of greeting. Another nurse followed him. The doctor usually liked to have an entourage around him. Or at least one that laughed at his jokes and hung on every word he said.

"Eating Chinese takeout with a severe food allergy. I'd like to try 'suicidal' for two hundred, Alex."

Dr. Farell spoke as if he were standing at a podium in front of a thousand adoring fans who listened to each word he said. The word *grandiose* filled Elena's mind whenever she was around him. He was only in his forties but he acted like a sage in the health industry, someone who had seen and done it all. His cynical attitude and cavalier demeanor only made things worse, especially when dealing with patients like this one.

"EMT's already pushed five mg epinephrine," Elena said.

The doctor began to examine Lacey. "Anybody bother to tell them that's a lot of adrenaline for a girl this size?"

"They had trouble maintaining her airway," the other nurse said.

"That's why it's called *anaphylaxis*. My guess is she couldn't care less whether we save her."

"How can you make an assumption like that?" Elena said, unable to help herself.

Sometimes she wondered if doctors like Farell even cared whether they *could* save patients like Lacey. She knew to him, they were just that: patients. They weren't people, not in his eyes. They were numbers and they were work and they were inevitabilities.

To Elena, they were still souls, like anybody else. Souls trying to figure it out in this world. Dr. Farell had obviously already figured things out.

He shot a glance her way, finally acknowledging that Elena was even there. The look on the doctor's face said it all. Smug, dismissive, short.

He grabbed the loose arm of the young woman and revealed what he had been looking at earlier. She could see the red beneath a set of bracelets. It was a series of scars on her wrist. There were way too many to argue with. Elena was sure that each one of them told the same sad story.

"Do you have a better theory you'd like to share, nurse?"

Dr. Farell knew Elena. They had been working at this hospital together for over four years. The way he seemed to spit out that word *nurse* was enough for her to back down. He used it like a judge spelling out a sentence for a convicted criminal.

Elena shook her head and then went back to work. It wasn't the first time the doctor had quickly shut her up.

It was an ironic life when men like Dr. Farell were paid very well to take care of wounded souls like Lacey. But that was the world today. It wasn't fair and sometimes it wasn't right but Elena had long ago decided there was nothing you could do about it.

Nothing at all.

All she could do was be there when this young woman woke up. Maybe to offer some kind of help. Or maybe just a few words of hope.

I love throwing a stone on the smooth surface of a calm lake. The ripples spread out in every direction, moving, then breaking. The stone disappears, but its effects continue to disturb the water all the way to the shore, where I stand.

At the time, I didn't realize the impact that call in the middle of the night would have. As a pastor, I'd gotten many of them. In my mind they were just part of the job.

The call had come from the Newtons, an older couple in the church whom I knew well. Teri had called me, asking if I could take them to the hospital. You might think she'd just call the hospital, but J.D. wasn't having a full-fledged heart attack. He was just having chest pains, enough that they were concerned. J.D. was closing in on seventy with Teri probably about ten years younger. She didn't want her husband driving, and she struggled driving at nighttime. So I hadn't hesitated. They lived only ten minutes from us.

It took about an hour for J.D. to get checked out. I decided to wait outside the hospital, reading on my iPhone in the sanctuary of my Prius. Sometimes hospitals overwhelmed me simply because there was so little I could do there. Yes, I could pray, but sometimes it felt as if there had been too many prayers left unanswered in this building in front of me.

God has a plan, I have always believed that. But I also know that in some cases—or what recently has felt like many cases—we don't get to see that plan. I think that's what Heaven will be. An eternity of recognizing the plans we never got to see and seeing the answers to the prayers we thought went unheard.

I put my phone away the moment I saw Teri guiding J.D. back to my car. They were a cute couple. I know that word can often be used for infants and elderly folks, but they really were *cute*. I know they were a good-looking couple when they were younger. J.D. had made it a point to show me a few Polaroid pictures at church one Sunday evening. They showed the couple when they were much younger. To say his wife was mortified was quite the understatement.

"Sorry to rush you out here, pastor," J.D. had told me as I greeted them on the curb.

"Everything okay?" I asked.

"False alarm," he said in a bit of a growl. "My pacemaker thought the battery was running low. Pretty sure I could've driven myself."

"No worries, J.D. Better safe than sorry."

Teri smiled. "He still thinks he's seventeen . . ."

"Whereas she's convinced I'm a hundred and seventeen," J.D. replied. "Personally, I like my fallacy better."

Teri gave her amused husband a not-so-amused look, a kind that I'd seen my wife give me plenty of times.

"You think this is funny?" Teri asked him. "We've lost enough already. I'm not ready to lose you, too."

That was enough to shut both J.D. and myself up. Women have a way of doing that with men. And in most cases, it's probably necessary.

Moments later, as I drove them home through the streets of

Chicago, still busy even at this hour, the silence felt a bit thick in my small car. I didn't press them. Death was nothing to joke about. I had seen enough of it to know this firsthand.

J.D. decided to break the silence.

"You realize we're both gonna die eventually, right?"

He said this with his head turned, facing his wife in the backseat. I couldn't see her expression, but I could tell she wasn't amused by his tone.

"I do," Teri said. "But if you were a gentleman, you'd let me go first."

I couldn't help laughing at that. J.D. continued to keep the smile on his wrinkled face.

"Duly noted," he told his wife.

I stopped at a light, scanning the intersection. It suddenly dawned on me that I'd turned down a street I usually never drive down in order to get to the Newtons' home quicker. And that was fine, but the hospital was near Washington Park, and it's not the best neighborhood in the city.

I wanted to get out of there as quickly as possible.

That's why the sight on the sidewalk next to us surprised me.

It was a girl—had to be a teenager—walking by herself alongside a brick building. On the corner was a liquor store. Farther down the street was a bar, one of those that stayed open twenty-four hours. There were no stores or apartment complexes or restaurants nearby. I had no idea what the girl was doing on this block.

For a second I began to think that maybe she was selling herself, but then I noticed something even more surprising.

She was pregnant.

She didn't look at our car and she kept to herself. J.D. and Teri kept talking, so they didn't notice the young girl. But I did. For a minute.

Then the light turned green and I moved on down the street. Away from the intersection and the dangerous neighborhood and this figure walking alone.

Part of me wanted to ask her if she was okay, if she needed help, if she needed a lift. But I already had the Newtons in my car. And hey—it was cramped enough with three people. So I simply watched that figure slowly disappear in my rearview mirror.

I simply kept driving, doing what anybody else probably would have done.

I think about that girl right now and I know something.

I used to think the most important thing was watching those ripples expand from the center of the throw. But I don't think that anymore.

Now I know that the most important thing is deciding to throw the rock in the first place, to not worry about what happens and the impact it will have. You'll never be able to see that fully. But there will always be ripples that follow. Always.

JOE

The little girl was obviously sick. Anybody in the waiting room could tell.

Joe Philips had been watching the girl for a few minutes, fascinated and amused. Her face was flushed but she didn't seem to care. It was nice to see a girl—maybe five or six years old—keeping herself entertained using a purple pen to draw a pretty butterfly in a small notebook. She sat a couple of seats down from him and was alone. The woman who had been sitting next to her—surely her mother by the looks of it—had stepped away for a moment.

Probably checking to see if there are any doctors actually working at this time of night.

The air in the hospital felt stuffy enough that Joe took off his jacket, but the girl didn't seem bothered in her heavy, oversized coat. The coat didn't look like something bought new for the girl. It looked ratty, a used garment that the girl could grow into. Joe knew coats like that very well. Whenever he could find one at Goodwill that fit his massive frame, he'd take it.

"That's a nice butterfly," Joe finally said.

She looked over at him, but didn't appear nervous like some

kids did when talking to him. Joe knew the muscles and the tattoos that he couldn't hide sounded off warning sirens to kids. But this young girl didn't appear to be daunted. Maybe it was because there were several other strangers in this waiting room.

"I love butterflies," she said. Then she pointed at his arms, obviously noting the colorful ink on them. "Do those wash off?"

"Afraid not." He smiled, impressed that she wasn't intimidated to ask a question about his tattoos. "What's your name?"

"Lily."

She looked like a lily with a wide smile that spread out over her face and expressive dark eyes. A strong, vibrant flower that was so full of colors and opened up so easily.

"Cool name," he said. "Mine's Joe."

"*I* like my name. It's *different.*"

He couldn't get the grin off his face. This little girl was spunky. He liked her even more. Even with a stuffed-up nose and watery eyes, she still looked full of spirit.

" 'The modest Rose puts forth her thorn; but fairer still I hold the Lily white; who shall in tenderest Summer's love delight. . . .' "

She didn't ignore his quote but rather seem entranced by it, looking at him with curiosity.

"What's that?"

"It's a poem," Joe said. "By a man named William Blake."

"How do *you* know that?"

Feisty. I love it.

He gave her a nod. It was an honest question.

"Where I used to live, I had time to do a lot of reading."

A lot of soul-searching, too.

The girl closed her notebook for a moment and then got off her chair to come sit down next to him. His presence and the paint on his arms didn't alarm her in the least. Joe started to ask her about her mother but approaching footsteps answered that question.

"Lily! What-Are-You-Doing?"

There she is.

A woman rushed through the waiting room as if Lily were standing in the center of a highway. Her tired eyes appeared momentarily awakened when she saw who her daughter sat next to.

"Sorry," Joe quickly said to the woman, but she didn't even acknowledge him. "Please don't be upset. It wasn't her fault."

Lily was still small enough for her mother to lift her up into her arms. The woman took a few steps back from Joe, the anger and anxiety obvious on her care-worn face.

"It's fine, it's not that," the mother said in a breathless and beat-up tone. "I just . . . She's sick and I can't get anyone to even take a look at her."

Those words pressed a button inside of Joe. This woman didn't have to say anything more. They had been there since Joe arrived, and he'd already been waiting twenty minutes. The girl looked weak and sick even though she still acted like she was enduring it. The mother, however, looked frightened.

Not just of me. For her little girl.

"Just a minute," Joe said, standing up and leaving the mother and daughter in peace.

He would have bet a hundred dollars (if he actually *had* that kind of money to bet) that Lily and her mother didn't have insurance. He would also bet that if things were different—if Lily happened to have a different zip code and a different set of parents and maybe even a different outfit on—someone would probably be seeing her right this very moment. Of course, they probably would have come in much sooner. And they would have gone somewhere else, to some stuffy family practice in the suburbs, not to the county hospital late at night.

The guy he had greeted when he signed in looked bored out

of his mind, sipping a Diet Coke and watching whatever he was watching on his computer screen. Joe stepped up to the counter and smiled, trying to be courteous and polite.

"That little girl over there is sick," he told Mr. Diet Soda guy.

"That's generally why people come in here."

Ten years ago a comment like that would have resulted in the guy eating his soda can. But Joe kept his cool. He'd learned to do that the hard way.

"She obviously has a fever. She needs to see a doctor."

"But it's not above a hundred and three," smart guy said. "So the severity algorithm puts her on the lower-priority list."

Then the guy gave him a shrug. An *oh-well-what-you-gonna-do* sort of shrug. With this smirk on his skinny smirky face.

"It's how it works," he said.

Really?

He leaned over a little more so Diet Soda guy could get a real good look at the man he was talking to.

"So why don't you input something that'll put her *next* on the list. Unless you want the whatever-algorithm to put *you* ahead of her."

Joe's eyes didn't waver, and his body didn't shift. He knew what he probably looked like to this scrawny male nurse. And right now, Joe liked it. He enjoyed seeing the fear in this snotty little guy's eyes. Smarts could get you through a lot of fancy doors, but they still didn't get rid of those life-and-death fears everybody carries around with them.

"Are you threatening me?" the man behind the counter asked, both in disbelief and worry.

"Yes."

Joe's response came quick and sudden. The nurse's response was slow to come and uncertain in its words.

"I'm gonna call security."

The guy reached for the phone as Joe just shook his head and smiled.

"They won't get here in time," Joe told him.

He was bluffing, of course. He wasn't going to harm this puny little soulless man. But he did want to instill the fear of God in him.

"Trust me," Joe said in the meanest tone he could muster.

He'd been a reformed man for a while, but that still didn't mean people were going to mess with him.

The guy behind the counter, sweat beads suddenly forming on his forehead, didn't take any time to debate the situation. He swallowed and then cradled the phone. Then he turned and called back behind him.

"Gina? Can you take that little girl over there into room three?"

The know-it-all look was gone. Instead, the nurse looked back at Joe with defeat.

"Dr. Singh will be with you in a minute."

Joe turned around and saw Lily and her mother staring at him. They, along with everybody else in the waiting room, had seen and heard the exchange. But the others didn't matter to Joe.

For a brief moment, he locked eyes with the mother. Her apprehension was gone now. The world-weary look was still there, but something else was there, too. And as a nurse opened a door for Lily and her mother to go through, Joe could see the woman mouth silent words to him as they passed.

"Thank you."

He smiled and nodded.

Joe felt better than he had felt in a very long time. And that was saying something.

ELENA

She found her husband in the cafeteria near the coffee vending machine, waiting for his cup to fill. He saw her coming and offered the cup to her. Elena was more than happy to take it.

"How's she doing?" Bobby asked.

"Should be fine," Elena said, still frustrated at the doctor's arrogant response to Lacey's condition.

Bobby pressed the buttons for another cup of coffee for himself. "She's lucky someone called 911 when they did. Are you gonna be home tonight?"

She shook her head and gave a familiar *guess again* look at Bobby. "Maribel's decided it's time for the flu, so I'm working a double."

She thought of Rafael and Michael and wished she could check on them before going to bed tonight. Elena didn't know what they'd do without the assistance of her mother, who ended up spending more time with her sons than she did.

"Again?" Bobby asked.

"Hey, you're the one always saying we need extra money."

The gray was starting to show on her husband's hair even though he was only in his mid-thirties. She wondered if it was simply due to age or whether it was stress. Elena knew from other EMTs that the job easily led to burnout. That or worse.

"No," Bobby said. "I'm the one saying we should spend less so we don't need the extra money."

"Good luck."

She took a sip of her coffee and knew the clock was ticking for her to get back to her shift and her patients. There was always a sense of urgency for her at the hospital, and somehow that dark and restless cloud had managed to hover over all other aspects of her life as well. Parenting, marriage, her emotional well-being, the tiny spiritual life she tried to have. Everything felt urgent and Elena felt in control of none of it.

"How's Prince Charming?"

Elena smiled. "Oh, he's his wonderful self."

They often spoke about Dr. Farell since both of them knew him and his inflated ego.

"He with you all night?"

She tightened her lips and nodded with glaring eyes. She took another sip of coffee and then gave it back to her husband.

"I gotta run."

"I'll see you later," Bobby said.

She gave him a peck on the cheek and then headed back to the ER.

Things could be worse. She could be here alone trying to figure out what to do with her life. Or she could be working here while her husband traveled the country or spent his hours in some office building somewhere. Even though their paths might not even cross during the day—Bobby's days as a paramedic were always different—they still lived in the same universe. Small moments like this, even though they might be short and trivial, were still something. Just like the passing moments she had with her nine-year-old and seven-year-old sons.

Elena was trying to force herself to appreciate the small things in life simply because the big things always seemed to pass her by. Men like Dr. Farell lived in a world full of grandiosity. Elena and Bobby were swimming with the unimpressive. And that was okay because at least they had each other to swim alongside.

Even that's started to change lately.

She swallowed the thought as quickly as she had the coffee. As she walked in the hallways, she passed a nurse guiding a woman with a young girl. She went to pick up a clipboard, curious to see what their story was. The mother and daughter looked like they could use some help. And Heaven forbid Prince Charming offer them any. Hopefully the ladies would be spared from that doctor and his smile and false charm.

Hopefully Elena would be, too, for the rest of the night.

watched J.D. and Teri walk back inside their two-story house, and knew the demons that followed them. I'd done my best to help them through the difficult times, and with their grief, but I also knew that grief didn't simply vanish. I could only imagine how they sometimes felt living in a house too big for two souls. I knew the rooms were weighted down with silence. In a small way, I understood that silence better than they realized.

Sometimes you grieved the soul that left you behind, like the Newtons did. And sometimes you grieved a soul unseen, like Grace and I did. That child we had tried for and failed to conceive never left our minds.

I drove back home using a main boulevard rather than side streets. *Drove* might not be the word. It felt like I floated, my head lost in thoughts like always. Sometimes I prayed during times like this, but I didn't feel like praying. Yes, pastors sometimes didn't feel like praying, and this was one of those times.

A prayer, however, was waiting for me at a red light. A prayer in the form of a man carrying a cross.

At first I didn't know what I was seeing. My car was stopped alone at the traffic light. The man himself was large and imposing, but the cross he carried was even larger. The way he lugged it with both arms made it obvious it was heavy. He wore grubby and worn clothes and stopped right in front of me.

The look he gave made me wonder if he was crazy. His eyes were wide and seemed to stare me down like oncoming tractor trailer lights. The African American looked serious and stranded. He simply watched me.

The light above us turned green, but the Old Testament prophet didn't move. He was carrying a cross, and was likely certifiably crazy. I was ready to put my car in reverse and tear down the avenue the other way. Yet for some reason I waited and watched what the big guy was going to do.

He moved and shifted so he could come alongside my car. He waited for me to roll down my window. Even before I could get it down fully I heard the man speaking in a deep bass tone. A voice thick like black coffee.

"Whole world's runnin' to its destruction. Devil's dug a big hole, and people are fightin' each other for the chance to be the first to jump in."

I waited as the man looked intently down at me.

"Tell me, son. Do you believe in the cross of Christ?"

It was a simple question, and quite an ironic one. I couldn't help but smile.

"I'm a pastor."

He didn't need any more of an answer, did he? We didn't need to converse about the cross because both of us obviously knew about it. I'm not sure I quite understood the whole carrying-a-real-cross-in-the-middle-of-the-night thing, but I wasn't going to fault the guy for it. Even if he looked dangerous. I knew danger came in all shapes, sizes, colors, and forms.

"You haven't answered my question," the stranger said, his

eyes peeling me open with their intensity. "I asked you: do you believe in the cross of Christ?"

It was strange to be on the receiving end of this. It had been . . . well, I couldn't remember the last time someone had witnessed to me. I was usually the preacher, the evangelist, the one praying, the one telling others about God.

I think my smile had started to fade.

"Of course . . ." I said, my voice trailing off.

It wasn't that I was uncertain of the answer. I just didn't know where he was going, and why he was asking me this in the middle of the street in the middle of the night.

He didn't appear to be even close to letting me leave.

"Listen to me. Believin'—*true* believin'—ain't just knowin' about it, or preachin' about it . . ."

The stranger pointed at the cross in his arm.

"No, true believin' means acceptin' that Christ carried this cross, was nailed to this cross, died on this cross . . . all for you!"

The man who sounded like some kind of southern preacher working his magic and getting "Hallelujahs" and "Amens" from the crowd only had my silence as his audience. I didn't know what to say.

Something in me wanted to sink into my seat. I didn't know why. I couldn't move, couldn't speak.

"If you truly believe that, then I ask you . . ." the man continued on, moving closer to me, luring me in with that expression of wonder and awe. "What are you doin' about it, son?"

I wanted to say something but couldn't. I was speechless. Not because of the surprise of what he said. No. It was how he said it. With a terrified and urgent tone.

I might have answered, but just then something else interrupted us.

The crash of glass made us both look the other way. I know

now that there was nothing random about it, that the stranger who came into my life the next moment was brought there for a reason. This unlikely soul wasn't just wandering in the night. He was running up to me and inadvertently holding up a mirror.

He wouldn't know it, of course, and neither would I.

Yet I know it now.

PRETTY BOY

No goin' back now.

N Pretty Boy could feel his heart beating, but was glad nobody else could. The smashed window sounded louder than it should've in the silence of the night. They were mostly alone on this Chicago street. Nobody was going to pay them any attention, especially since it was just a plain white delivery van anyway. It wasn't like it was a Porsche or a Rolls or something like that.

They were far enough away from their home in Englewood, so the four of them didn't need to worry about angering a rival gang down the street. Used to be they were divided by neighborhoods. But once Chicago started getting rid of the projects, everybody was split up. Now there were rival gangs on streets next to each other.

The killin' never stops bodies crumble obituaries drop.

As always the thoughts in his head came out like lyrics in a rap song. He couldn't stop them from coming. They just had to go somewhere. That soul inside. It spilled over into mixtapes and freestyle sessions and when it was just him they echoed inside his mind. Especially when he got nervous.

Pretty Boy stood watch on the sidewalk as the guy leading this foursome took his ice pick and cleared shards of glass. His name was Kriminal. And like his name, there was nothing subtle about him. Pretty Boy often joked that Kriminal was the beast while he happened to have inherited all the beauty. But there was a lot of truth in that.

"Come on!" Kriminal shouted at them.

Kriminal had spent a lifetime giving Pretty Boy orders, but that's what big brothers did.

40 Ounce jumped at the order and climbed in the back door Kriminal had just opened. The three of them were all from the same neighborhood. Little B was the only one who stuck out. They liked giving him a hard time for not being black, but the short, Hispanic guy had more ghetto in him than the other three. He'd been taken in by them after his mother and sister were shot a few years ago. You couldn't help loving Little B. He was like that stranded puppy you couldn't leave on the side of the street.

Pretty Boy jumped in the passenger seat of the van while he watched Kriminal remove the plastic cover on the steering column and then start hot-wiring the vehicle. The clock was ticking. They needed to get out of here fast. Pure, one hundred percent adrenaline rushed through every bit of him. This felt different from the times he'd just watched. Even watched the shootings. This time *he* was part of it. This could get him jail time.

And the reason there's the reason for this and that's the deadly slope we're headin' down.

Soon the van rumbled to a laugh, yet they didn't drive off. Pretty Boy sat, waiting to feel the van moving. So why weren't they going? What was Kriminal's hesitation?

A figure approached the van on the driver's side. Pretty Boy looked out the front windshield to see a small car waiting with its headlights on at the intersection. The car wasn't moving, even though the light above him was green. The big black guy approaching them didn't seem a bit apprehensive about coming close to the van.

The idiot was carrying a giant cross, too.

That guy's gonna get popped.

Kriminal cursed in disbelief and stared at the guy. The voice that spoke through the window Kriminal had busted open was loud and booming and deep.

"What you're doin' is wrong," the stranger said.

Come on K let's just get out of here let's go now.

But right on cue, Kriminal took out his 9mm semi and pointed it at crossman's face. Close enough so the muzzle touched the man's forehead.

Kriminal had once told him that he liked a 9mm because it held seventeen shots over a typical revolver, which only held six. But at this close range, it would only take one single, simple shot.

"Back on up, Old Creepy. Unless you want your time card punched."

I'm not ready for murder it was just supposed to be stealing a car a van a worthless van nobody's gonna make a big fuss about but not murder not this K.

The killing didn't scare him. It was the aftermath.

The big guy with the gun aimed at his skull smiled. Pretty Boy couldn't believe what he was seeing. The guy was actually smiling.

"I'm ready," the stranger said. *"Are you?"*

Pretty Boy waited to hear the gunshot. He'd heard enough in his life, but didn't want to hear this one. Kriminal had told him stories, but Pretty Boy didn't want to see it with his own eyes. He could imagine the short, blunt strike. One was all it would take. This close there was no debate. No chance.

Don't do it don't do it come on.

The gun didn't go off. For some reason, Kriminal was being nice.

Bet he would've done it if it was the Adidas Boys.

Crossman didn't change his expression or his stance. He just kept looking at Kriminal without blinking.

"You know what I'm gonna do?" the stranger said.

"Why don't you tell me?" Kriminal asked.

Pretty Boy could tell his brother sounded amused now. So did the two chuckling in the backseat.

"I'm gonna *pray* for you. All of you."

More cackles could be heard.

"Yeah, you do that, old fool."

Kriminal pulled his hand back into the van and revved up the engine.

"That's right, I'm a fool," the man outside said. "A fool for Christ. Paul and me. Me and Paul. Nothin' but fools. Ain't no hole gonna swallow me . . ."

The van peeled away before they could hear any more jibberish from the man on the street. Pretty Boy assumed he was some crazy, homeless person. They always turned out crazy once they'd been on the streets for too long. They began to see things. The drugs and alcohol usually turned them into fools. Yet Pretty Boy had never seen one carrying a cross.

Or so unafraid of dying.

The van headed south toward their neighborhood. The mood continued to lighten with the guys in the backseat cursing and laughing at the crazy guy they had just seen.

"Was that old dude '730' or what?" 40 Ounce barked out through the laughter.

They were excited that it'd gone so easily. Grabbing this van was nothing. Nothing at all.

But what comes next hey K?

Kriminal kept his focus on the driving while Pretty Boy ignored the grade school levity in the back.

"What was that thing he was carryin' around anyway?" Little B asked.

"A cross, you fool," 40 Ounce said.

"Thing looked heavy."

"Thing looked stolen," 40 Ounce cracked again. "Probably got it from a church. They'll show up Sunday and find it gone. Fool'll be roamin' round preachin' on the side of the road."

Pretty Boy looked in the mirror, but nobody was chasing them. Nobody would, either. This was a simple job that they were out there to do. And yet that man. In a second—if Kriminal had made a different choice—it would have all been different. Kriminal could've been in a bad mood. He could've gotten all riled up like he sometimes did.

The streets they passed felt deserted and alone as Pretty Boy stared down them.

"You awful quiet," Kriminal said. "What're you thinking?"

His big brother was always there. Sometimes looking out for him, sometimes showing tough love, sometimes beating the tar out of him. He was afraid of Kriminal but at the same time didn't know another soul he was closer to.

Owin' my life to same old story plunged through the knife . . .

He didn't worry about his brother's question. Not now that the rush inside him was wearing off. Pretty Boy felt a wave of both relief and dread filling him.

"That man was ready to die," he told Kriminal. "You look at his face—his eyes? What if he was right? You know? What if we're going up against God Himself?"

The words amused Kriminal. He was in good spirits tonight. He smiled.

"You tellin' me God works for Nefarius?" Kriminal joked.

The others laughed. But Pretty Boy only shook his head, still thinking about the guy's expression. Fearless. Bold. Uncompromising.

He didn't look crazy, even though his actions certainly seemed like it.

"Forget it," he said without looking back at his brother. He felt a sinking feeling and wasn't sure where it came from.

It wasn't from stealing this van. It was more. A fear inside that something was out of control. That this road he was heading down with these guys was all wrong and that eventually he'd end up floating and breathless in the belly of the dark lake not far from them.

He wanted—no he needed—to get out of there. His songs were gonna do it, too. The music scene in Chiraq was real and the drill music kept coming and everybody told him he could do it.

Everybody but Kriminal.

Pretty Boy thought of his mother for some reason. Then of his grandmother.

You know why.

He wanted to erase the thoughts and the memories, but the crossman back there had brought them back. His mother with her demons and his grandmother with her cross and her Bible verses and her God.

Her God.

It was a fairy tale, but he could still remember the words G-Ma loved to say. Before all hell broke loose and they were left alone.

Like the sidewalks and the streets and the shadows they passed. All alone.

Only one road goin' no lookin' back showin' Pretty Boy stacks blowin' yellow brick roadin'.

Yeah.

He stared ahead and kept the thoughts tied up.

No lookin' back.

Amen to that.

JOE

He was still waiting when the tired woman and her sick little girl walked back into the room. This time the mother didn't avert her gaze or appear concerned about Joe. Instead she walked directly to him.

"Thank you for your help," she gushed in a waterfall of words. "I just wanted to say I'm sorry. For earlier. I was just—I didn't mean—"

"Don't sweat it," he told her.

He knew her concern. He'd be concerned, too, if someone who looked like him was talking to a little girl like Lily. The world was a sick place. Joe had met some really sick fellas.

"Everything okay with her?" he asked the mother.

"Yeah. A sinus infection. They gave us an antibiotic. Thankfully they had some samples to give us."

Joe suspected she meant they didn't have the money to pay for a prescription.

She looked around the mostly empty waiting room. Joe could tell her eyes went to the clock on the wall. It was past midnight.

"You okay?" he asked her.

She gave him a nod, her mind obviously thinking, her arms covering Lily as she stood behind her.

"You got a place to stay?"

"We're fine. We've got a car." Her words echoed the strain on her face.

"A car?"

"Shelter's closed . . ." she said, by way of explanation.

The girl still looked pale and not well. Her eyes were tired now. She needed a comfortable place to sleep, and she needed it now.

Joe was still waiting to see the doctor, but this was more important. He tried to act nonchalant.

"If you don't mind me saying so, I don't think that's such a good idea. She needs to stay warm."

The mother gave him a nod, yet she seemed to be out of answers and not sure where to even look for them.

Wonder how long they've been on the road.

"Listen," Joe said. "I know this is gonna sound crazy, but I only live a couple of blocks from here. If you want, you can spend the night there."

The woman didn't say anything. Joe understood. He got looks like that daily. Whenever he went somewhere, people looked at his outward appearance. He looked rough and couldn't soften it up no matter how much he tried. God had built him this way. Some of the scars and the colors he carried around with him—well, he'd managed to get them himself and he couldn't get rid of those, either. But few saw the new creature he was inside.

All he could offer was a friendly smile.

"I know what I look like. But that's not who I am . . . Not anymore."

The mother still didn't say anything. Lily looked up at him with a weak but pretty smile.

"You can have the place to yourself," Joe added. "I've got somewhere else to stay."

"Look, I appreciate the offer," the woman said, shaking her head. "I really do, but I don't think—"

"It's okay, Mommy. Joe wouldn't hurt us. He's our guardian angel. Aren't you, Joe?"

He grinned and nodded, then waited for the mother's answer.

Something broke inside of me. Maybe it was because of those thugs breaking into the van that night, but I think it was before that. I think it was the words of a man I didn't know, a man I still don't know.

Do you believe in the cross of Christ?

He didn't ask me once, but twice. But that was maybe because I hadn't given a sufficient answer.

But it wasn't that question that haunted me. It was the follow-up question.

What are you doin' about it, son?

I had then watched him brazenly walk across the intersection toward the van the gangbangers were stealing and have a conversation with the driver. I couldn't tell what was happening and I didn't want to know, either. I waited and wondered about calling the cops, wondering if I even had time to call the cops, but then the van drove off into the night. And the black man carrying the cross did the same, walking over to the sidewalk and then continuing on his way.

It felt like I had come across some guardian angel who wanted to give me a message. Who *needed* to give me a message.

This prompted me to do a U-turn and head back the other way. Because . . . I don't know.

Because of something I saw earlier.

I think it was a hunch. But then again, the more I look at it now, I believe it was the Holy Spirit at work. I'll agree that as a pastor, the part of the Trinity that I've understood least is the Spirit of God. I understand in theory what the Bible has said about it, but there have been times I just haven't understood. I've wondered. Yet I think at this moment, after the prophet-angel spoke to me on the side of the road, I felt a stirring in my soul. Maybe it was the spirit. Or maybe it was just my guilt at having driven by without doing anything.

I still don't know to this day.

Maybe it was time to start *doin'* something.

So I started with driving back to the hospital, back along the same streets I had driven down with the Newtons.

Near the area where I had seen her, I slowed down and scanned the sidewalks and alleys. For fifteen minutes I drove at about five miles an hour, cars passing me and even blaring their horns, wondering what in the world I was doing. They didn't know I was looking to help. Looking for someone who might need somebody.

I even prayed to God that I might find her. He heard my prayer and answered.

I found a figure in an alley next to a dumpster. It was just a figure reaching over the dumpster—it really could have been any-body. Anybody who needed a helping hand. But I stopped my car and rolled down the window and when the figure popped back out of the dumpster, the dirty face revealed the truth.

It was the young girl I'd seen earlier walking down the side-walk. She was still alone. Still pregnant. And still had that look of desperation on her face.

"Are you okay?" I asked.

It was such a moronic question. Of course she wasn't okay. Nothing about this situation *looked* okay, yet I was simply trying to be friendly and nonchalant. I didn't want to scare her by saying "you look at the end of a long and desperate rope, hungry, pregnant teen girl." So I asked the foolish question.

The look she gave me said the obvious.

What do you think, moronic middle-aged man?

"I'm just peachy," she said.

I took that as a good signal because it showed there was still some fire deep inside of her.

The girl started looking back at the dumpster, already done with me for the moment, not even embarrassed about continuing to scavenge through the garbage.

"Look, I know you don't know me," I called out to her, hoping she could hear me. "But . . . is there anything you need?"

Again, asking the dumb and obvious question. But again trying to sound innocent and helpful and most of all *safe*.

"What are you, some kinda freak?"

She was tough. I knew right away this girl wasn't someone to be messed with. Despite what she might look like.

"No, look, please," I started to say. "I'm just someone who wants to help."

I didn't look threatening. That's one thing I don't think I've ever managed to do in my life. Part of being a pastor—part of what people had told me over the years—was that I had a friendly face and a warm disposition. A lot of people had told me I was easy to talk to, that I listened to them when they spoke, that I looked like a nice guy. I once joked to my wife that I didn't want to look like a nice guy, that I wanted to look like the dangerous and dark hero that came in and swooped women off their feet. But that wasn't me. I was Matthew, the nice guy. And at this moment of my life, I sincerely hoped this girl could see that.

Don't most serial killers look like the nice guy next door, too?

I tried to toss that thought out. Maybe this young woman didn't know that unfortunate truth about our world. Hopefully she didn't.

The teen paused and stared at me for a long time, considering my comments. Maybe she was weighing her options and trying to figure out what to do.

I waited. Maybe the spirit was still at work there. And if so, maybe it would help stir this young girl's soul as well.

TWENTY MINUTES LATER, I needed that same spirit to try to calm my wife down.

Grace has always been the anchor in our relationship. I know how cliché that might sound, but living with me has probably been a bit like agreeing to set sail on the Pacific when the captain doesn't really know where he's headed.

I haven't always been a pastor. And there are many days when I wake up and wonder what I'm doing and where I'm heading and if I'm really going to stay a pastor, simply because I worry a little bit about *everything.* Then Grace comes along-side me, and sits and holds my hands, and tells me everything's going to be okay.

On this late night, however, hours after I left the house un-expectedly to take the Newtons to the hospital, I had woken her up with another problem on our hands. Well, really, it was on *my* hands, and she was trying to figure out what in the world I had been thinking.

"You can't just do this," Grace said in disbelief, standing in the entryway to our living room.

"The girl needs a place to stay."

Grace opened the blinds and could see the Prius parked in our driveway, still running, the headlights on. The girl's name was Maggie. She was sitting in the passenger seat waiting. Waiting and surely wondering what was going on.

"Then *take* her somewhere," Grace ordered. "But not here."

I started to try to make my case, but Grace stopped me before I could even try.

"You promised. This is our home, Matt. I need a refuge, too. A place *outside* the storm."

I didn't need to ask what she was talking about. I knew it well. Too well, in fact.

I thought back to our ten-year anniversary last year. How a celebration had gone downhill. That had been when I had promised Grace. I had to keep that promise, too.

I exhaled. "I know, I know. I should've called first. But we can't just turn her away."

Grace only shook her head and looked away. This had been my decision and it was now my responsibility. I didn't want the girl in my car to have to wait any longer. I knew I needed to do something about this quickly.

"I'll figure something out, okay?" I said to Grace.

She moved away from me before I could give her either a hug or a kiss.

The first thing I did next was see if Maggie wanted something to eat. Again, I didn't really wonder whether she was actually hungry or not. I knew she was. The point was to see if she was comfortable enough letting me buy her dinner. The White Castle we passed was enough to do the job.

It took us about ten minutes to reach the motel. It wasn't in a bad area of the city and it didn't look too run-down. The Starlite Motel was very close to our church, and I knew some others who had stayed there.

As we parked, I thought about how this might look. The middle of the night. A forty-year-old guy checking in with a pretty and pregnant teenage girl carrying a small pink knapsack. The woman who ran the place knew I was the pastor of the local church, but the guy at the front desk didn't. I might get some looks and some judgments. I might also get a visit from the cops. So I decided to get the motel room on my own while she waited in the car.

I wasn't surprised to find Maggie already finished with her four sliders and fries. I wanted to ask her when was the last time she ate, but I didn't. A hundred other questions filled my mind about her. Especially *what in the world is a young woman like her doing on the street?*

But it was late and it wasn't the time to suddenly get a biography of this girl. She needed a place to stay. A *safe* place to stay.

I opened her door but made it a point to stay outside.

"Look—I've paid for two nights," I told her. "I'll be back tomorrow or Monday and we'll figure something out."

She brushed back the thick, curly hair that hid her innocent and unblemished face. She was still trying to figure me out, still trying to be careful about every step she was taking. She hadn't really said much to me since agreeing to get in the car. I didn't blame her, either. Yet she finally offered up a window into her thoughts.

"You lied. You *are* a freak."

"What do you mean?" I asked.

"Nobody helps people just to help them."

There was an adult tone in her voice. It didn't match that face and her age. But for some, being a child didn't mean they were treated like one. For some, God had other plans.

"Yeah," I said, knowing her sense of disbelief. "Well, I'm a Christian."

"So are most of the people who ignore me."

She took the keys and then walked into the motel room. I pulled the door shut and then heard her lock it. I stood there for a moment, just staring at the worn and weathered handle.

God, please be with this young woman. And be with the child she's carrying.

The drive back home felt longer than usual. Maybe it was because I was driving at a snail's pace. Not worrying about getting home to dark silence. I was more worried about Maggie.

An hour ago you didn't even know her name or if you'd ever see her again.

Yeah.

But now Maggie was my responsibility, which was fine, but this was the sort of thing Grace and I had talked about.

It was another weight to carry. Another burden to pray over and wonder about. And God knew that I had enough of them already. My church alone had enough troubled souls inside it to tend to.

Hello, Matt. James 1:27 calling your name. Seriously. It's almost as popular as John 3:16.

I uttered the words aloud. Sometimes it was good to do that. Not to prove I could memorize Bible passages but to hear them in a fresh and unique way.

"Pure and genuine religion in the sight of God the Father means caring for orphans and widows in their distress and refusing to let the world corrupt you."

I didn't think the world had corrupted me just yet. It tried. Yes, Lord, it tried daily. It beat me down and tried to break me. But this didn't mean I needed to forget one of the most obvious and easiest requests that God ever gave his children.

So there was Maggie in her distress. I prayed that I could do something for her and the life she carried. But for now, I had made the first step. I didn't need to worry anymore. I needed to trust God.

JOE

He carried her bag, which felt far too light, and led them down a sidewalk toward the entrance. The mother followed behind carrying her daughter in her arms.

Joe could see Samantha having doubts about this. He'd finally learned her name. At least her first name. But it had been a start. And so had been her agreeing to come to his apartment.

"I know it doesn't look like Disney World or something, but it's not too bad," Joe said. "And don't worry. I'm gonna leave you with the key. The *only* key."

They had left the hospital without him even getting in to get checked over. But that was fine. He spent enough time in the hospital anyway. It wasn't like they'd tell him something new. It wasn't like he was full of questions and new concerns. He'd be back there sometime. This was far more important.

He opened the door and then guided them upstairs and along a hallway until they reached his place. He opened the door and flicked on the light to reveal the small apartment. Sparse and simple. It looked like a place you had just rented and hadn't fully moved into.

A place you weren't gonna be in for long.

"This is it," he told her, placing her bag down in the doorway.

There wasn't much of an "it" to show off. The living room was also the bedroom. The futon couch was also his bed. There was a small flat-screen television on the wall. A closetlike kitchen with a fridge and stove.

Joe set up the bed and then Samantha set Lily down on it. He found an extra blanket for her to use.

"Sorry I don't have another bed."

She only shook her head. "You keep things very neat."

That was an understatement. He had always vowed in the joint that if he ever had a place again, whatever that place might look like, Joe would keep it in impeccable order. And it wasn't like he had that much to *keep,* but it was first and foremost clean. From the toilet to the burners of the stove to the containers in the freezer.

He could see the woman eyeing his worn-out Bible on the table next to the bed. That Bible had been with him since the pastor had given it to him in prison. Yet Joe was fine leaving it with them. It might do some good for them. It certainly had for him.

It's called the living Bible for a reason.

"Are you *sure* your friend will let you in at this hour?" the woman asked.

He had explained that to Samantha after she initially refused his offer to stay there.

"Positive," he said. "Here's the key."

He noticed the dark grooves under her eyes. But there was a kindness in those eyes. He could tell things like that. She looked like a good soul. Just tired and concerned for her daughter. And yeah, just tired, too.

Joe started to leave but Lily's voice stopped him.

"Don't forget your toothbrush, Joe."

He turned and smiled at the girl on the bed. He had assumed she was already sleeping.

"Good thinking, Lily."

He liked saying her name. *Lily.* Who wouldn't? Uttering it made him happy.

The small things mattered in life now. He'd learned this long ago when every single thing had been taken away from him.

Not everything.

Joe did as Lily said and got his toothbrush, which was set neatly on the rack behind the mirror. Before exiting, he gave Samantha a stern look.

"Lock this behind me," he said.

She nodded.

"I'll see you guys tomorrow," Joe said. "Sleep well."

The bolt sliding into the lock bid him good night.

Back outside to the chilly night, he thought for a moment where he was going to go. Then he headed to the park, a place where he knew he could find some space.

Joe didn't have a car, so he would have to settle on the park. But it was only one night. That's what he told himself.

There was a concrete bench open. Two of the benches he'd checked on were already taken, so he sat down on the end of the bench that stood in the shadows. The other side was under the glare of the streetlight.

So here I am, Lord.

A gust of wind made him tighten up his arms around the rest of his body. He shivered and pulled the collar of his coat up. It was the thickest coat he had but it wasn't really much. He was warm-blooded.

So what plans do you have, Lord?

It wasn't an open-ended question. He really and truly wanted to know. And Joe believed that God would show him, too. God often showed him things in the most amazing ways.

When you've been in the dark for so long, the light can feel so refreshing. You just want to stay there. To keep running toward it with all your heart and soul.

Why'd you bring sweet Lily and her mother into my life?

There was a reason. Joe knew this. Maybe it was simply to give up his apartment for the night. But Joe thought there might be more.

Show me why, Lord. Show me what to do.

The prayer he offered up every morning he woke up and every night he went to sleep.

Going to sleep tonight might be a little tougher to do. But the word *tough* was synonymous with his life. They went hand in hand. He was used to it. He even welcomed it at this point. As long as he was doing the right thing.

LACEY

The room was quiet. Nothing moved inside. Nobody made a sound. The dim light near the entrance was on, but other than that Lacey couldn't see anything. Every now and then nurses came to check on her, but now that it was past midnight they had stopped coming as often.

She had been alone when she finally decided. And after all the commotion over getting her to this hospital, Lacey was alone. Again.

The still. It *still* got to her. She had tried to escape the still over and over again. At the parties and the clubs and the bedrooms. Through the noise and the busyness of life in the city, but nothing had worked. Nothing.

You're just depressed. Are you taking your meds?

So a friend might say.

You just gotta get over it and move on.

So her ex might say.

You need to grow up now and be an adult.

So her father might say.

All the words that could be uttered, and yet . . . she heard none of them. Nobody was there to offer them up. Nobody was in her room and beside her bed.

Because I have nobody.

It was the pure truth. She wasn't saying that to feel sorry for herself. Life was an entire story full of sorry.

That was why she had made the decision in the first place.

Being surrounded didn't mean you had people in your life. Having connections online didn't mean you were connected with others.

A city this big with so many souls could feel so soulless to her. At the end of the day, Lacey found herself alone and unconnected and adrift.

Next time they won't find me.

Lacey wanted to be out of this place, she knew that. Away from all these people who surely judged her, these strangers who checked and probed and prescribed and checked again.

She wondered what her father would say if and when he knew about this. That was the big question. And she didn't want to think about it because it would only depress her more.

The best thing he could do was to be infuriated, to drive out to see her and ground her, to finally show a pulse and a heartbeat.

I didn't do it for him. I'm not here because of him.

She believed it and maybe it was actually true. But Lacey still knew that her only available parent still had way too much influence on her. Even though he wasn't miles away in his body, his spirit was many, many miles away.

The image haunted me. The words convicting.

I'm not sure how long I'd been there, looking at it. Just staring as if it might jump up and attack. Or maybe just run away.

I couldn't sleep. After everything that had happened that night, I had arrived home full of worry and wonder. A lone light had been left on, which was considerate of Grace. I could have simply gone to the bedroom and then spent the next hour with my eyes wide open in the dark thinking through things. But I headed to my office instead.

I thought that I could make some notes for my sermon tomorrow.

But after fifteen minutes, all I had been able to do was to sketch a drawing and write out one phrase.

My paper had a cross covering most of it.

Below it were the words in all caps:

DO YOU BELIEVE?

I kept staring at the cross, thinking of the words and the man who had spoken them. I wondered where he was right now. Then I thought of Maggie and how she was doing.

What can I do? What should *I do?*

I was lost in a sea of thoughts with things I wanted to say and things I thought I might need to do.

Do you believe, Matt?

And I answered with an *of course I do.* Because I was a pastor.

Of course . . . Pastor Wesley.

It wasn't that simple and easy and sugarcoated.

I thought of the big stranger's words again.

"What are you doin' about it?"

I didn't even hear the door open behind me.

"What's that?" the hushed voice asked.

I turned to see Grace. Her eyes were half opened and she was snug in her housecoat.

"My sermon," I said, surprising myself.

There's somethin' I'm gonna do. How 'bout that?

"Feel like sharing?" my wife had asked me.

"No. At least . . . not yet."

She nodded and then urged me to come to bed soon. It was late, and she knew I could stay up worrying and wrestling with my inner demons. I told her I'd be there shortly.

I had suddenly decided to change my sermon. Which was fine. That was nothing new.

But what exactly was I going to speak on?

The cross. Right? But wasn't that what I spoke about or referred to every single time I spoke? Right?

I wondered how long it had been since I gave an honest and open talk about that cross. There was Easter, of course, but those holiday services could be so overstuffed, like the dinner tables that usually follow them.

No, when was the last time I just talked about the cross? The Gospel. Jesus Christ and what He did for me and for you.

DO YOU BELIEVE?

I drew over the outline of the cross and then I underlined those three simple words.

In a sense, they were the ultimate question that anybody could ask us.

Really, the *only* question worth asking.

An idea came to mind. A pretty good one, too.

I decided to do something a little different.

I'm gonna do somethin' a little different, my cross-bearing friend.

I smiled before leaving the office and finally calling it a night.

ELENA

It felt like the car was driving itself. Elena thought that if they ever did start selling those cars that drove on their own, she'd totally buy one. It was a twenty-minute drive from the hospital to their home south of the city, and she had made it so often at the strangest set of hours that she almost tended to sleep-drive. She wasn't sure that was even a term, but at four o'clock in the morning she could have her own terminology as the car moved steadily on empty city streets.

They'd lived in the suburb of Blue Island for a couple of years now. It had been a big deal just to buy their own place, even though they knew they had extended themselves a little too much. It was easy to get a mortgage simply because the rates were so low, so they went with it even though they barely had any money to put down. The debt they'd carried for years and Bobby's ever-changing jobs and school loans all were enough to really cripple them. It still felt like they hobbled around financially. And that was *with* both of them at the hospital.

The house was tucked away in the middle of a street next to similar single-family homes. It was really pretty even though the brick house had been built in 1926. The previous owners had renovated it with hardwood floors and new windows. There were three concrete steps leading up to a small porch on one side of the front, while three new windows looked out on the other side. It had a small second story, and the kids' room and their bedroom were upstairs.

Sometimes when she passed through the more affluent suburbs, she dreamt about what it would be like to have a bigger house. Not a mansion, just a home where you weren't on top of each other. Whenever they had family over, which seemed to be quite frequently, it felt like they were about ready to burst. Thankfully the aboveground pool in the back and the deck that faced it allowed them some space, at least during the hot days of summer.

It'll be a while before we use the pool again, she thought. The November chill had really seemed to settle in. The light coat she wore over her scrubs did little to keep her warm. Elena would be home soon enough and sleep would be pointless, since the kids needed to be up at six.

Pulling into the driveway, the headlights found the boys' bikes resting in the yard. Obviously Grandma had forgotten to tell them to put the bikes in the garage. Or maybe they hadn't really paid attention to her (something that happened quite frequently). She was about ready to turn off the car when she saw the figure on the front steps. Elena jumped. But then she saw the shape of the head and knew.

Carlos.

Her brother was back.

Relief washed over her as she found a bit more energy inside of her to quickly climb out of the car and go over to greet him.

"Carlos!" she shouted out as she rushed to him and made him hug her.

He wasn't big on emotions, but she also knew he was happy to see her.

"I can't believe you're back," she said, trying to see his face in the dim light of the hanging lamp on the porch. "Why didn't you call me?"

The tall, lean figure only gave a shrug. "Sorry. You know me."

She saw his duffel bag waiting on the porch.

"Why didn't you knock? Mom's inside with the kids. Bobby's home, too."

"I didn't want to wake them up," he said.

He spoke in a low, slow tone. Carlos sounded as weary as Elena felt.

She wanted to tell him to stop being crazy, that he was family and welcome in their home anytime, that she needed to give him a key. Bobby had been home since a little after midnight. And Elena was easy to reach.

He knows that, too.

She didn't want to give him a hard time. That was the last thing her brother needed.

"Look at you," she said, moving to get a better view.

The smile on his face was beautiful. She'd missed it. In all the images he sent from Afghanistan, he looked so stern, so adult. She understood a little what it meant to be a Marine—Carlos had certainly tried to tell her and the rest of them what it meant. But she missed that smile. She had missed *him*.

"Is it for real this time?" she asked, afraid of the answer. "They're not sending you back?"

"Deployment's over. My active duty is finished and I'm on Individual Ready Reserve. Meaning . . . I'm a civilian again."

She sighed. "Thank God. *Please* tell me you're not gonna keep the haircut."

There wasn't much hair to even call it a haircut. Carlos laughed.

"What's wrong with my hair?"

"Your head looks like a cantaloupe."

Once a big sister, always a big sister. Even if he ever got married, Elena knew she still could always speak her mind to her little brother. This big, strong man would always be little Carlos. She'd always be trying to protect him, even though the adult in her knew it was a lost cause like so many others.

She found the door keys. "Now come in, come in. You shoulda rung the bell, you know. Bobby wouldn't mind."

"I told you—I didn't want to wake him. Or the boys. I know this is a bit . . . sudden."

"Don't be silly."

MOMENTS LATER, ELENA tiptoed into her bedroom, trying to avoid the crack in the center of the room that always seemed to groan and wake one of them up. The bed linens had been in their closet, stashed away behind clothes and towels. One thing Elena did not have was organizational skills. There just wasn't time to be clean and organized in this house when they both worked so much and spent the remaining time taking the boys around. When she made it out to the family room, she found Carlos in a green T-shirt and his Marine Corps PT training shorts.

"Do you have *any* fat on that body?" she asked him.

He seriously was lean and toned, more so than he ever had been in his life. Carlos had always been athletic, but she still was surprised at how rock solid he appeared.

"I watch what I eat," he said with a grin.

She knew he did more than that. A lot more.

"Fair warning: the kids leave their Legos everywhere, so watch out since you're in bare feet," Elena said as she set up his makeshift bed. "And this couch is brand-new, so try not to drool in your sleep."

"Seriously?" Carlos asked.

"*Yes,* seriously. That baby's leather."

He hopped on the couch and then took the pillow she'd set up and tried to fluff it up.

"Don't worry. I won't be around long."

"Oh yeah?" Elena asked. "You will if I can help it. *Tú eres familia.*"

. Carlos didn't answer. She knew that was okay. There was a lot she didn't know about her baby brother. In some ways he'd gone missing while he was serving in Afghanistan these past few years. The times he had been home, Carlos didn't always let her know. She knew deep down that things had probably been tough for him simply because he hadn't said anything. His silence had scared her the most the past few years.

But Carlos was home now and maybe they'd be able to spend some time with him. To get to know him again. The boys barely knew him, so they'd love seeing the uncle they idolized. The hero that they often spoke about like some character in an action movie.

"Hope you get a little sleep before the wild boys wake up," Elena told him.

His dark skin mirrored the even darker expression on his face. Carlos forced a smile but she knew he was just being polite.

"Thanks," was all he told her before she turned off the lights.

Now Elena knew she wasn't going to get any sleep. Seeing Carlos had been like sipping an extra-large cup of coffee. Her mind raced, wondering how long he'd be around and how Bobby would react and whether or not she needed to take time off work and where he would stay if he ended up staying for a while—

Slow down.

She breathed in. She would climb in bed and try to rest or relax or at least close her eyes for a few moments.

Carlos was finally home.

What did he bring with him?

That was the big question. One that wouldn't be answered quickly. She knew that.

Maybe just maybe . . .

Elena needed to stop all of this. She couldn't afford to over-think things or to get too hopeful. She'd been there before. She had learned the hard way not to go there again.

LACEY

There was nothing about this doctor that Lacey liked. Granted, he had only been around her twice while she was awake, but in those two times he had seemed arrogant and dismissive. The only thing she hated more than a guy who was smug was one who happened to be smug *and* smart. He was a doctor, so yes, obviously he was smart. But he didn't need to treat her like a toddler. Or worse, like some kind of stray pet who couldn't do anything but look up at him with helpless eyes.

A few minutes after eight on that Sunday morning, Dr. Farell had come into her examination bay, whipping the curtain back and getting right to business without even telling her good morning. He carried an iPad that he looked at more than Lacey.

"Conscious, responsive, and alert."

She felt groggy and hungover.

Conscious. Yes. Alert. Not so sure.

But she wasn't going to argue with the doctor. He kept looking at his iPad, making her wonder if maybe he was checking his Facebook account to see what was happening. Perhaps he had a Dr. Farell fan page that she could start following.

And I'm sure he might have four or five people actually follow-ing him.

"Okay, here's how this works," he said to her, still never speak-ing Lacey's name. "I ask you a simple question, and if you want to go home, you say 'yes.' Or just nod your head? Ready?"

His tone was a mixture of annoyed and impatient. She gave him a nod and wondered if his tan was real or fake.

For a few moments, he asked her basic questions. Her name, her date of birth, all standard stuff. Then he asked the big question.

"Your ingestion of a previously known allergen was *accidental,* right?"

They shared a glance.

You know as well as I do the answer to that.

Lacey simply said, "Yes."

Dr. Farell continued to look at the iPad, swiping at it, then swiping some more.

"Okay, you're free to go," he said, finally looking down at her. "In the future, you might want to be a little more careful . . . Unless you're interested in seeing how your name looks on a death certificate."

That was it. No *glad you're better* and no *take care of yourself.* It wasn't like Lacey wanted or expected to have Mother Teresa as a doctor, but this guy could have been a tad bit more sympathetic. She did almost die last night. However she had ended up there, she was still a patient and she still deserved to be treated with dignity and respect.

When was the last time anybody thought of those words when it came to you?

He was just another guy acting just like guys did. Dismissing and judging and then letting her down.

Half an hour later, Lacey was headed home.

Part of hospital policy was that she had to exit in a wheelchair.

She could stand and walk fine, but the nurse forced her anyway. She tried not to look at anybody she passed in the hallway or the nurses' station or even the waiting room to Emergency. All Lacey wanted to do was go back home and forget she had ever been there.

Outside the hospital building, the morning sun hovering over them, Lacey asked the nurse a question she had avoided since he'd arrived.

"Did you call my father?"

"Yes, but we didn't get an answer. Is there someone else who could come for you?"

The nurse was sympathetic. Lacey shook her head and smiled.

"I'm fine. Thank you so much."

She stood up and then nodded at the nurse.

See, I'm fine and there's no problem with me and I really didn't try to kill myself last night. It was just a minor mishap.

Lacey began walking down the sidewalk, unsure if she was even heading in the right direction. She had her phone with her so she'd figure out something.

People on their own always have to figure out something.

That Sunday morning as I went to the motel to check in on the young woman I had just met, I had no idea what was about to happen. I had been working on my sermon for our evening service, the one I always preached, and the message was filling my heart. I felt something different on that day. Something was at work there. Something I didn't know but can see now from afar.

For too long I thought I'd been doing the right thing. But it's easy to see all the signs pointing to the right destinations when you're heading the wrong way.

Suddenly it felt like I'd been turned around. Facing the south. Seeing the sun.

Something needed to tear away. To break off and run free. I don't know what it was. It started when I'd seen the sign of the cross that night. But I believe it was more than that. I believe a door opened and I was finally pushed through. I felt lighter than I'd felt in years.

I think the spirit was slowly starting to bubble the slow-moving blood flowing in my veins. Telling and stretching out the meaning of a bit of everything.

It's time, it said. *It's about time.*

I guess I had waited long enough.

Maybe the sins of my past were finally going to break off like melting ice finally letting a boat set sail.

Maybe I was finally getting out of Antarctica. I don't know.
I still don't know.

I just know that I felt this soaring, swelling spirit inside me
and they said nothing about me but they said all about Him.

This figure I'd been focused on for so long. For my whole life.

Those hands crushed into that wood.

The feet torn through splinters.

The chest that tried to drag air through it.

The face that looked up at a silent sky.

It wasn't just an image, like a painting in some museum. It
bled the colors over my skin. It painted the colors inside my soul.
And every single breath and every single step I'd ever made was
taken because of it. For it. In order to find it.

The cross. Creasing over time and space into the tiny crevices
of every single broken thing I'd ever done.

Jesus seeing all of those things I tried to hide and letting them
hang on His shoulders.

For a moment. The most glorious moment of eternity. The
created falling apart finally set free.

That was it.

That was it for all and for me.

And my eyes had finally seen it and finally understood.

I wanted to run wild and I wanted to tell everybody. To no
longer be a preacher, but to be some kind of signpost pointing
toward the place they needed to go.

It's okay.

That's all I wanted to say.

Jesus says it's okay.

That's all.

*Believe. Ask for forgiveness. And know those hands and feet
and chest and man took it all for you.*

That's everything.

Every single hurt thrown up and at Him.

Every single mess scooped up in hands and tossed forward.

Every single sorrow ever thrown into your face and your future.

Every single everything that broke and bruised your heart and soul.

They all could go there. The cross. This thing that was real and true.

I think my faith had been a little sluggish for quite some time. I think I had forgotten the absolute urgency of telling people about the message of the cross.

That's what I wanted to share on this Sunday night, like some kind of spark setting off the round of fireworks on a New York sort of New Year's Eve.

Bigger and better.

I was ready in some kind of crazy way.

JOE

He started coughing again just before he headed into the McDonald's. He stayed outside, knowing he'd be barking for a few moments. It was loud and obnoxious and usually made heads turn since it sounded so rough. Hey, he was a big guy, and he had a big set of lungs. People needed to relax. But Joe also knew they didn't need him roaring and filling the air with germs while they ate their pancakes and Egg McMuffins.

He could tell it was getting worse. He didn't need to be a doctor to know that. The visit last night hadn't been to see what was wrong. It was simply to help him try to make it momentarily better.

Momentarily.

A term he'd heard a nurse use. He liked it because that was basically what each life on this earth happened to be. We were all souls momentarily living in these flawed and deteriorating bodies, momentarily trying to make connections while living out our lives. It didn't matter if someone momentarily lived to be a hundred years old or if they were a tragedy at twelve. In light of eternity, every single thing could fall under the term *momentarily.*

The coffee tasted extra awesome this morning. November shouldn't have been *this* cold but then again, it had been a while since he'd spent the night outside. Back in the old days, he'd had some extra fuel helping him stay warm. Whiskey has the tendency to do that for you. And he couldn't call what he used to do sleeping. It was more like falling into a drunken stupor.

Seventeen years.

That's how long it had been since he'd taken a drink. Actually, seventeen years and five months and twenty days. He knew it by the day. Not a day went by when he didn't think of the guy he used to be. But now, after nearly coughing up a lung, he couldn't help but think back to the younger version of Joe. The healthier version that he'd tried to destroy in every way possible.

God didn't let Joe finish the job. Instead, God decided to step in and finish it.

To finish me.

This body was just a temporary thing that was giving out a little more each passing day. But Joe knew that and was at peace with it. He was just thankful for every morning he could awaken with it. For every day that God blessed him with.

It's what you do with those days that matter.

He quickly finished the coffee to warm up and get rid of the fog in his head. Then he ordered some breakfast to go and headed back to his apartment.

Joe wondered what Lily and Samantha were doing at this moment. If they had checked his fridge or pantry searching for food, they would have been very disappointed. He didn't spend a lot of time at his apartment. And he never really concerned himself with planning for meals. A lot of his meals were either at the church or with some of the other ministries he helped out with.

When you donate your time and your service, people feed you well. Joe and his belly knew this well.

He knocked on the door and hoped they were still there. It was early Sunday morning, but still—one never knew. But sure enough, the door opened and Samantha stood there making sure it was him.

"Room service," he said, showing her the bag.

The cough came again, and he tried as hard as he could to contain it. He coughed only a few times, holding in his breath and trying to stop it from tickling.

"You don't look too good," Samantha told him.

He offered a simple, friendly smile.

Usually when you sleep on a park bench, you wake up looking a little like this.

"I'm fine," he said as he followed her inside his apartment. "You guys hungry?"

Lily shouted out a yes as she saw the bag in his hand.

"I bet you don't like McDonald's, do you?" he joked as he unpacked the bag. "Now I wasn't sure exactly what you ladies might like, so I got a selection. We have a sausage McMuffin; a bacon, egg, and cheese biscuit; a fruit parfait; some oatmeal."

"You really didn't have to," Samantha told him.

He gave her a look that said, *I thought we were over that now.*

"Joe, guess what?" Lily shouted out beside him.

"What?"

The girl darted into the room where they'd slept and brought back his glass gallon jar full of change and bills.

"I'm sorry," Samantha quickly said, looking embarrassed. "I was just looking for some cereal—something for breakfast—and Lily discovered that."

"It's okay," Joe said, looking at the girl. "That's my 'wish jar.' "

Lily's eyes widened. "What's it for?"

"Well, that's the thing about wishes. You're not supposed to tell or they don't come true."

"Maybe you oughta hide it better."

He couldn't help laughing.

The honesty of a child.

"Yes, maybe I should."

The laugh made him start coughing again, and this time he couldn't hold it down there. He put his hands up to cover it and then he coughed into his arm. It felt like a truck driving through his gut and peeling out of his chest. He couldn't stop it but could only watch it pass by and leave him breathless.

"Are you *sure* you're okay?"

He nodded.

The mom with her girl and nowhere to stay is asking me if I'm fine.

"Don't worry about me. I'll be fine."

Joe wasn't just giving her lip service, either. He meant those words.

He found some plates and offered one to Lily.

"Now whatdya say we eat?"

Lily grabbed the plate. "Yeah!"

The small, square table sandwiched between the kitchen and the family room/bedroom wasn't much but they all fit around it anyway. Joe couldn't remember the last time he'd actually sat down at this table to eat. It had been a while.

It was easy to give God thanks this morning before taking the first bite of his biscuit. He couldn't remember ever having anybody to dine with in this small space. So this was a first.

A very welcome first.

PRETTY BOY

Pretty Boy was the first to wake up, but that wasn't unusual. He liked being the only one awake, to be the first to use the only bathroom they had, to get ready before his grandmother and brother awoke. Both of them got on his case in different ways. G-Ma was the only mother they had so she tried to play the role the best way she could. Kriminal got annoyed with him just because—well, because his older brother was easily annoyed.

This morning he felt different and he knew it should have been because of what they did last night. That *should* be the reason, but deep down he knew it wasn't because of that. They took off with a boring van not worth much last night. He didn't have a reason to feel proud or guilty about that. He still didn't know how to feel about the van or even *why* they'd taken it in the first place. But his thoughts kept going to the guy with the cross, the one who had literally dared Kriminal to shoot him.

It coulda all gone down differently.

He wondered what it would feel like waking up knowing he'd helped kill a man. Not pulling the trigger, but being a witness to the murder. What were those called? An accessory. That's what he would have been. Because he was sitting next to his brother. He was watching but didn't try to stop him. Pretty Boy didn't say a word or do anything.

The van was nothing compared to what *coulda* happened.

Blood on the cross belongin' to the wrong man can't take my guilt ain't got command.

Pretty Boy wondered about writing down those thoughts but let them go. If the lines really were any good they'd come back to him.

The dream of making those mixtapes into some kind of reality was simply a dream, especially since he didn't want to highlight the sex and violence. If there was one thing his grandmother detested it was "the filthy mouth," as she called it. He and Kriminal spoke like anybody else, but around her they had to keep it clean. So the thought of him making rap music like the other Chicago rappers were making it . . . there was no way. G-Ma would come after him. Rolling in her wheelchair and carrying a shotgun in her lap.

He went to the kitchen and pulled some eggs out of the fridge. G-Ma liked having big breakfasts before church. She was still religious about going to church, but then again weren't you supposed to be? Pretty Boy sometimes still took her even though he'd tried getting out of it. But G-Ma needed help with the wheelchair, though sometimes he wondered if she was just using that as an excuse to get one of them to accompany her.

He went to rinse his hands and noticed the trickle coming out of the faucet. It was like the thing was spitting instead of running. It was ridiculous. He shut it off and then he just looked at the small kitchen and the round table in the corner.

A cross hovered above the table on the wall. It had been there for years, ignored like G-Ma's other simple decorations. Her Bible and her pictures of Jesus and His angels. But she grew up in a different era and a different time. When Chicago wasn't referred to as Chiraq, when it wasn't the murder capital of the world, when kids weren't getting killed.

G-Ma said they needed the blood of Christ, but Pretty Boy had seen too much blood in his lifetime.

But none last night.

He stood looking at that cross on the wall a little.

I'm ready, what about you?

Sometimes his skin felt too tight, his soul too restless. Pretty Boy knew something. He wasn't ready. No way. He wasn't even close to being ready. There was a big world out there, a place he could do well in. A place where he could do something, make something, even *be* something. He just needed to get away from this place. Chicago and the black hole inside it. He would've done that already, long ago. But he couldn't, not with his grandmother and his brother still there. He'd never leave them.

But one day he would. He knew this the same way someone might believe in the meaning of that cross.

His father had abandoned them and his mother had died on them and that was the way life went. His grandmother did the only thing she could do. She stayed there and raised them. So Pretty Boy was going to do the only thing *he* could do. And that was stay in this little coffin in the hood until she ended up passing away.

She's gonna probably live to be a hundred and outlive Kriminal and me both.

There was a shuffling in the back room and he knew it was G-Ma. Another reason to get up early was to go back there and help her. Those legs and hips of hers sure weren't going to survive to be a hundred. They'd already given out on her now in her mid-eighties.

Everything eventually gave out. In time.

Pretty Boy just knew it wasn't his time yet. He had a lot more living left to do. A lot more songs to come up with. A lot more heart to seep into some stories. And all of that would be a long ways away from this place.

HIS BROTHER ATE like a horse, just like he usually did. All those muscles and mean energy needed fuel to keep them going. Of course, food wasn't the only thing that did it. Kriminal had help in other ways, too. Ways that Pretty Boy had avoided so far in life. He intended to keep avoiding them, too. Those were the things that made Kriminal unpredictable, even for someone who had been around him for twenty-three years.

"Not hungry?" Kriminal asked as he doused his eggs with more ketchup.

"I get a stomachache watching you eat," Pretty Boy joked.

"Why don't you come up with a rap round that?"

"Will be better than anything comin' out of you."

Kriminal was soon done wolfing down his food. There was a busy day ahead and Pretty Boy was surely going to be a part of it, too. His brother pushed aside the chair and then gave his grandmother a kiss on her head.

"Later, G-Ma," Kriminal said.

The wrinkles and the kind eyes didn't mean G-Ma was a pushover. Hardly.

"How about clearin' off the table before you get on out?" she asked him.

Kriminal looked at Pretty Boy.

Uh-uh.

"I did it last night."

"So you got experience then," Kriminal said.

He started heading to his bedroom. G-Ma let him take half a dozen steps until she stopped him cold.

"Joseph, you'll get back here and do those dishes if you know what's good for you."

Pretty Boy was standing now, grinning as he watched his brother step back into the kitchen like some grade school boy being sent to the principal's office. He threw Kriminal a towel.

"Nice try," he told his brother.

Didn't matter how old they were. As long as G-Ma was around, they were the boys and they lived under her roof, no matter how leaky it might be; they also lived under her rules. Sometimes it got old. But then again, maybe it had kept them out of more trouble.

Pretty Boy thought of all those prayers G-Ma prayed for them. Maybe those had helped. He wasn't sure.

I'm gonna pray for you. For all of you.

The words played in Pretty Boy's mind.

Now we got two crazy people praying for us.

The question he asked, time and time again, the one that always put that big question mark in his heart and soul was this:

Who hears those prayers? And what's ever done about them?

Yeah. That's the question all right. The one that those preachers and those righteous folks and his grandmother and the zealots on the streets never answered. Because at the end of the day, they didn't *have* an answer.

You shoot off your prayers but they stay empty like the shells remaining afterward.

Pretty Boy was tired of the shooting and the praying. There had to be a better way.

JOE

You can get used to a run-down life as long as you don't let it run you over.

Joe believed this. He'd been running for as long as he could remember, but in his youth he'd been sprinting toward trouble. Always heading down the wrong path and always finding sorrow somewhere near its end. But ever since finding Jesus in prison and then finally being let out, he'd been running from those demons. The ones that wanted to tempt and torture him. It wasn't easy, but he managed.

Yet as Joe talked with Samantha while they finished their breakfast, he wondered if she was managing. He didn't think she was. He wanted to help out in whatever way he could, but he also knew he needed to take it easy. To be careful. He needed to be respectful of both Samantha and Lily.

Thankfully, the mother had felt comfortable enough to start telling their story. He wasn't sure if she would. After Lily finished talking about her stuffed animals and how she liked cheese and how she knew all the words of every song in the movie *Frozen,* the five-year-old had gone in the living room to play with a couple of stuffed animals that must have been in her bag. Then Samantha had talked about her husband, who had passed away a year ago.

"I used to believe that was the start of all this, but the truth is we were already broke years ago. Mike kept trying to get us out of debt, but he kept changing jobs and getting laid off and then figuring out ways to blow the money. Investments and get-rich schemes and all those things. He had a big heart like his daughter. But that heart just couldn't take the stress of things, I imagine."

"I'm sorry," Joe said.

He wasn't hungry anymore, but managed to finish his sandwich while he was listening to Samantha.

"Lily had just turned four when he died. I worry sometimes she won't even remember him."

For a moment, she glanced out to Lily, who was having a conversation between her two stuffed animals. Joe could imagine the waters Samantha was wading into with that faraway look. He'd spent many years trying to learn to swim in them himself.

"It was really hard," she continued. "I just wasn't prepared . . . you know, for that much pain, for picking up the pieces, for any of it."

Her voice tapered off, obviously trying to keep Lily from hearing it. Joe's focus never wavered. He remained quiet, letting her talk. He'd grown used to hearing horrific accounts of the broken and struggling in prison. Sometimes you went to someone in prison because you needed protection. With Joe, people would come to him because they needed comfort.

"I had a job for a while, but that fell through," Samantha said. "I borrowed all I could borrow, tried everything I could think of. It wasn't like we had any kind of life insurance or even family to rely on. Eventually the day came—the landlord had enough, I guess. I came home to find all of our things, our whole life, there on the sidewalk in a pile. Clothes, dishes, Lily's toys . . . It was a Wednesday."

Joe nodded. "I hate Wednesdays."

She finally looked back at him, this time with her face brightening.

You look a lot better with that smile on your pretty face.

"I guess I'd never really thought about how it happens to people, you know? But suddenly there I was, without a home. With nobody to turn to. With nowhere to go."

He gave her another nod. He wanted her to know he understood, that he'd been there, but he also didn't want to condescend or say he knew her suffering. He'd been on the streets alone. He couldn't imagine having to take care of a child on the streets, too.

"This is not the way I thought things would end up, I'll tell you that," Samantha said with a sigh.

"Hey, it's not over yet. Take it from someone who knows, things can turn around. God has a way of making bad things turn out for good."

Her shoulders and body and face gave him a gigantic *no-they-don't* shrug.

"What?" he asked. "You don't believe?"

"In God?" she said, pausing and becoming dark and gloomy again. "My husband used to bring us to church *every* Sunday. Look where it got us."

Then maybe he's in a better place. A place where there are no more bad things.

He could have said more, but he wouldn't. Samantha could have said anything and Joe would understand the feelings behind it. Again, she hadn't been stranded by herself. She had a daughter. And Joe knew she was desperately trying to figure out something for Lily first, herself second.

He scrunched up the napkin and then tossed it at her like a grade school boy might.

"So, what, you're telling me these aren't the best egg and cheese sandwiches you've ever had?"

She laughed while she took another bite.

"They're good," she said in a kind way.

"See? Things are looking up already." Joe turned toward Lily. "Anyway, with a little girl like that, you're doing something right."

Samantha touched her long, oily, and unkempt hair and gave him a shy smile. He could tell that she was blushing. A woman like her could be a movie star in the right place and the right life. Now her natural beauty was the only thing she got to carry around, and it was hidden underneath exhaustion and worry and sadness.

Suddenly she looked away and then glanced at her daughter.

"We should go," she told him. She suddenly stood and walked over to her daughter. "Lily, honey. Come on."

"Go where?" Lily asked, not budging a bit.

"You're more than welcome to stay here again," Joe told them. He hoped he hadn't said anything wrong.

Lily raised her eyebrows and grinned, but Samantha only shook her head.

"We can't."

He was going to try to explain that it wasn't a problem, that he would stay out of their hair, that things would be fine, that the apartment could just be a temporary place to be while they figured things out.

Give her space, Joe.

But he shut up and listened to his interior voice. Sometimes it was his own rationalizing he could hear. Other times he truly believed it was the Holy Spirit talking to him, whispering for him to say something at the right time, other times nudging him to keep his mouth shut. This was one of those latter times.

"Okay," was all Joe said.

It wasn't okay, a mother and a young girl like that going back on the street. But a lot in life wasn't okay, and Joe sure wasn't going to change it.

Sometimes you just had to let it be.

HE ESCORTED THE ladies back to their car. It wasn't really a car. You couldn't consider a puke-orange AMC Pacer a car. *How* in the world they had ever gotten this car was the big question. Joe would have normally laughed and joked with the owner of the car. Not to make them feel bad, but *come on*. These things were vintage and up there in the echelon of worst cars ever made. He hadn't even seen one on the road in years.

Keep your jokes to yourself 'cause you don't even have a ride, now do you?

Samantha opened the door without having to unlock it. Nobody would want to steal this thing in the first place. Lily told him goodbye in a casual way that sounded like she'd see him in a few hours.

"You really don't have to go," Joe told them.

"Thank you," she said. "I appreciate everything, but . . . I don't want her getting used to anywhere she can't stay for good. It makes it too hard."

He gave her a nod, then put a gentle arm around her back while she gave him a lukewarm sort of hug. Joe could understand. He was a big guy twice her size. He appreciated her even reaching out.

There were things he could have said. *I'm gonna be praying for you.* Or *here's my number in case you ever need something.* Or even *God's got a plan I know it.*

But Joe remained silent. This woman didn't need guilt or

judgment or preaching. Sometimes the smallest sort of compliment could hurt someone. You just never knew. In her situation, she carried not only the weight of a five-year-old life but the shame of where they were at.

"Take care of yourself," Samantha told him as she climbed in the car.

"You too," he said.

Somehow, the Pacer rumbled to life and managed to drive off down the street. Lily waved at him through her window, her face sad. He waved and smiled and didn't show his disappointment. But his smile faded as fast as their car did.

Joe let out a sigh and felt the ragged tickle in his throat. His stomach tightened and then he wheezed out a few low coughs into the palm of his hand. It was cold out but he felt warm, and now as he coughed he also felt woozy.

It's just 'cause I spent the night barely sleeping and barely warm.

He coughed again and then finally managed to stop. The wind seemed to be picking up, spiraling around him as he stood in place. His hand felt wet, so he looked down to examine it and saw the streaks of blood.

There was no shock or surprise. He'd coughed up blood before. Joe just knew it wasn't a good sign.

Sometimes you couldn't outrun everything. Joe knew this, too. He could just hope and pray and take things one day and one moment at a time.

J.D.

Grief was like the wind. Sometimes it came on strong, some-times it felt completely still, but it was always there. Sur-rounding them. Blowing at any given moment. They couldn't escape it, and no meteorologist could forecast it.

His wife didn't say much on the drive. Sometimes she would make comments just to say something. Mentioning the traffic or an errand she needed to run or something a friend had recently said. But today she remained silent just like J.D. Maybe it was. be-cause they were both tired from last night. Maybe it was from the heart attack scare both of them had had.

He had seen some things in his life. Some horrors. Things that would forever haunt him even on the brightest of days. But still nothing compared. Nothing. There were no words for this drive. For climbing out and walking on the grass. For seeing all the names. For navigating through so many stones.

Some might say that you moved on, that you dealt with things, that God could get you through it, but J.D. would tell them they were wrong. It had been years, and still . . .

He followed Teri, an arm around her. He hadn't worn a thick

enough coat to keep out the cold, but at least the cap covered the few hairs left on his head. Age sure wasn't a pretty thing. But a lot of life wasn't pretty.

He knew you had to hold on to the good moments as long and hard as you could. They were fleeting. They liked to fly away.

They soon stopped at the right place. The same place they had been standing at for more than twenty years. Teri placed the flowers down below the stone. They stared at it as if it was the first time. As if it might talk back.

Beloved Kathleen. Our Daughter, Our Angel, Our Girl

The two of them had made a promise years ago. They wouldn't stop coming here. They wouldn't bury the past and move on. So this was a weekly thing. Coming to remember. To reflect. To pray. To breathe.

My name. If only it could be my name they were looking at.

He couldn't help thinking this. Teri had often said the same thing.

She had been their first and their only and their one. The princess. The smile. The spirit. The ecstatic screams.

Kathleen had been the one to quiet down the noise in his restless soul. To blur the memories he had carried since Vietnam. The story that had ended one saga and began another.

But she was gone, and Teri and J.D. were still there. The girl had closed her eyes but Mommy and Daddy were still watching.

J.D. didn't say anything to Teri. He just kept his arm around her, wanting her to know he was there, that he would always be there. But he also knew that wasn't enough, that it would never be enough.

God . . .

But he stopped himself. He didn't want to. He didn't want to even try.

No amount of praying would bring his little girl back to them. Maybe Jesus and his apostles had healed people, but they weren't around anymore. People had put Jesus to death but he had come back for a short while.

J.D. wished Jesus would come back around one more time. Just so he could ask about Kathleen. Just so he could get some kind of word of hope.

Just so he could make sure that their daughter knew they still loved her and cared about her and remembered her every single day.

This bowling ball tearing down the alley was his heart. The pins it banged into were memories. Yet he could never get a strike. Never.

The concept that God is omniscient still fascinates me. Being able to know everything and see everything . . . Would it be a blessing or a curse? I guess with our Heavenly Father, this is just how things are. Neither a blessing nor a curse but just a fact.

At least a fact that I put my faith in.

I thought of Maggie in her small room at the motel as I drove toward it. I planned on inviting her to the church service that evening, expecting her to say no and to tell me I was crazy once again. Maybe I *was* crazy. Maybe this whole thing called hope is crazy to believe in, but it's a beautiful kind of crazy if you ask me.

It's probably easy to say it's crazy when you're scared and tired and alone.

A part of me still wasn't sure if I could do anything for her. Anything of eternal value, that is. The motel and the dinner and the invite to church were easy. But what could I say to her? What could I do to show I might be safe, that I might be different from some of the people in her life?

Sometimes as a pastor you have to simply ask God to give you the words and the actions and the faith that He can work through you. But I still wasn't sure. I hadn't felt God working through me for a long time. Maybe I was just getting tired of preaching the same message to the same people. Maybe I was just getting tired of waiting for God to show up in some kind of way.

On this day, however, I knew I'd be saying some different things. And something inside me felt different.

It had felt different ever since I'd seen the stranger on the street. I felt convicted in a way I hadn't felt for years. I know that sometimes people don't think of pastors as the sinners unless they're skulking away from some kind of public shame. The difficult part of being paid to preach on a weekly basis is practicing the very words you impart.

I was careful to knock on Maggie's door gently so she wouldn't be alarmed. It took a few tries before I heard it unlock and creak open. The light in the room was dim compared to the sun outside. In the door I saw her tiny figure with the big, curly head of hair sprouting out like a palm tree.

"Good afternoon," I said. "You doing okay?"

Her face came more into the clear, those wide eyes still looking so desperate and alone.

"Yeah."

A teenager's voice wasn't supposed to sound that way. Heavy and exhausted. Short and abrupt.

"I wanted to let you know I'm on my way to church. I wanted to see if you'd like to come."

"It's okay," she said without even considering it. "I'm fine."

"It's a safe place, Maggie. With a lot of good people there. It's not a big church. It's not one of those you'll get lost in."

She shrugged and shook her head. "Really, I'm good here."

"Okay." I waited for a minute, looking down the hallway each way, hearing the sound of cars and trucks in the background. "Do you need anything? Can I get you anything?"

She answered with a no, shaking her head and looking down.

Everything inside of me wanted to pull her chin up and force the girl to look at me. To see that she could trust me. To see that all I wanted was to help her and her child. That was all. That was everything.

But I couldn't touch her, I knew that. I was already walking a thin line here, and I needed to be careful of every action and step.

"You have my number, right? If anything comes up, you just call. Okay?"

"Yeah," she said in a barely audible voice.

"I'll see you later."

I left not knowing when later would be, not sure whether she'd still be there, not clear what the next step should be. So on my way to church I just asked God to show me the way. It wasn't a formal or public prayer. It was just one of my many conversations I had with God.

I heard once that Billy Graham was asked about his spiritual discipline, and he said he maintained it by praying without ceasing and by searching the scriptures. Those words have always motivated me, even though my pauses between prayer times have often been far too long and my quests in life have often been outside God's word.

But in the car in the few moments before arriving at the church, I asked God to help Maggie and to allow me to try to do the same. Whatever way I could. Big or small.

MAGGIE

Nobody was in the lobby of the Starlite Motel, and if they were they probably wouldn't pay attention to her anyway. Maggie sat in the cramped corner facing a desk with a really old computer on it. This was their version of free Wi-Fi. At least she could get online for a few moments.

Shifting in a hard seat she felt like she might fall out of, Maggie took the folded pamphlet from her coat pocket and read it again. It resembled any of the other dozen flyers that were on a display right next to her. Most of the ones in the lobby were for airline shuttles and local restaurants. The one in her hand was a little different.

Family Planning Partners
Serving women since 1973

She had looked at this printed piece for hours, seeing the picture of different women looking happy with their babies. Seeing couples and seeing outlines of a mother with her child. There was a number to call and a website to check out.

A sixteen-year-old shouldn't be planning anything, especially a family.

She wanted to look up the website, but Maggie knew what it would say. Surely there would be advice and questions and answers and lots more faces of happy mothers with their beautiful children. Even young mothers, but they'd surely look happy and content. They wouldn't have bags under their eyes from fear and from sleeplessness. They wouldn't look alone and frightened and completely freaked out.

Maggie sighed and pressed the return button on the keyboard.

Then she deleted the name she had typed in the search line and started typing something else.

Is eight months too late to abort?

She quickly hit return before she could think about it anymore.

The list of websites she could go to seemed endless. But they all confirmed what she already knew. What deep down she already believed.

But maybe . . .

There were no maybes. Not anymore. The time period to have made that choice was months ago.

She wandered onto one page called "Fetal Development" and started to read.

32 weeks . . .

The baby is 17 inches long and weighs 4 pounds. . . .

The diameter of the head is almost 4 inches. . . .

The toenails and fingernails are completely formed. . . .

Completely formed.

The breathless feeling wasn't due to the belly inside her. It was from this paralyzing fear of doing the wrong thing or doing the right thing in the absolute wrong way. Maybe she should have stopped and listened to her parents. Maybe she should have simply been smarter.

Maybe that Gideon Bible back in the room has some answers waiting.

She closed the Web pages and then shifted to stand. Maggie found the nearest garbage can and tossed the family planning flyer into it.

Her parents came to mind again.

Maybe it's time to stop running and to call them again.

They weren't going to break the law, but they also weren't going to let her be a sixteen-year-old mother. Maggie wondered if she'd even see the baby if it was up to her mother and father. Probably not.

Maybe that's for the best.

Walking back to her motel room, her hand found its way to her belly and rested on it. It had become a natural thing to do, even if none of this was natural. But running had felt the same way, too.

Maggie didn't want the supposed best for her. But she didn't want to run anymore. Eventually, there would be no more time *to* run.

The pastor's words filled her mind.

"If anything comes up, you just call. Okay?"

Just call.

Easier said than done.

Yeah, something's come up. It's four pounds with a four-inch head and fully formed fingernails and toenails.

She wondered what the pastor would say to that. Surely he'd be like the rest of the adults in her life. They'd have some plan and some prescription to give to her, then they'd simply want to pass her along to someone else.

Maggie was tired of being passed over and passed around. At least now, out here, she could take action herself. She could make the decisions. She could stop and make the choices she needed to make.

Maybe, sooner or later, she'd figure out what those happened to be.

PRETTY BOY

Anything can be broken and then sold and shipped off. Pretty Boy had known this ten years ago when he first became a teenager. He knew it now. The sounds all around him—ripping and sawing and torching and banging—echoed in the nondescript commercial space that had been transformed into a makeshift garage. It wasn't a huge space, and it was only temporary. They all knew that the best thing to do was to stay in a spot for a short amount of time—maybe a month at the max—before moving on to avoid detection from the cops.

Pretty Boy sat in an uncomfortable, ripped-up chair in the corner of the garage watching the others work. There were a couple of high-end cars already operated on. A Mercedes sedan and an Audi SUV. The latter had been quite the score. It was a day old and they needed to get it out of there fast. In between them was the white van from last night, looking like some lost suburban guy stuck in the middle of Englewood.

They weren't taking apart the van, however. They were welding some steel I-beams to the front bumper and grill, along with adding support beams that extended inside the engine. Pretty Boy had helped with some of it moments ago but now he was just watching the guys work, watching Kriminal overseeing everything.

Kriminal had overseen this operation for several years.

The van was something unique. Most of the time when they took apart cars they started by removing personal items and license plates and destroying them. An acetylene torch helped cut the roof and the floor after the windshield and doors and seats had been removed. It was amazing how easy it was to take apart a car once you knew exactly how to do it.

Pretty Boy wasn't sure how they sold all the parts. Kriminal often referred to the "VINs"—getting rid of the "VINs" and "re-VIN-ing." Those were the vehicle identification numbers, and every car had them. The engine in the car, the transmission, and the frame were all tagged with VINs. Kriminal would replace the VIN completely if they wanted to sell the car intact, but it was easier and usually paid better if they simply sold the different parts.

"So you gonna finally learn how to do this?" Kriminal said to him as he approached.

"Maybe one day," Pretty Boy said, not meaning a word of it.

"Man, you got that dreamin' look again."

Kriminal often talked about Pretty Boy and his dreams. Maybe when he looked distant and maybe when he talked about his songs or made up his rhymes.

Or maybe when I'm lookin' at the corner of a dead end with fewer and fewer doors left to open.

A shout from 40 Ounce came across the shop. Pretty Boy looked over and saw him and Little B doing the usual: playing around and not working. They were standing over a foosball table yelling and laughing and being totally unproductive.

"Gettin' your money's worth with those two?" Pretty Boy asked.

"They're not here for the cars. They're for other things."

He looked at his brother and knew what he was talking about. The van was just a tool, just like 40 Ounce and Little B. Just like the acetylene torch and the Sawzall. Just like the gun tucked away in Kriminal's pants.

I'm nobody's tool nobody's ruling me I get to overrule.

The random nuggets blast like a shotgun. Kriminal continued staring down at him with questioning eyes.

"You sure you're up for this?"

Pretty Boy jerked his head and then stood up. "I told you I was and that's all you need."

"They're wonderin', that's all."

"Who?"

"Little B and 40 Ounce."

He couldn't help letting out a laugh to Kriminal. "They know I'm hard-core."

"I made it clear—they don't get to ask that. *I* do. And I'm askin' now."

"I'm straight."

Kriminal didn't budge but kept facing him. "You still lettin' that old man mess with your head?"

"Nah, I'm cool," Pretty Boy said, acting like he didn't know what his brother was talking about. "Look—I'm gonna split. Head home for a while. Check on G-Ma."

His brother didn't say anything and let him go. He didn't want to face Kriminal and talk to him for too long. Pretty Boy would eventually show all his cards. He didn't have a poker face, not around Kriminal.

Yeah, the old man was still messin' with his head.

He couldn't stop thinkin'. Like it was a sign from God that things were gonna get bad.

The end times comin'. That cross and that old dude and his face and his fearlessness.

He climbed into his car and started it up, a Kanye West song playing on the radio, already halfway finished.

"I'm lost in the world, been down my whole life."

Already halfway finished . . .

Was he just starting up, or was he almost done?

Pretty Boy didn't know, but he felt cold and afraid. Something bad was comin' and something told him to not stop the car. To not stop driving for a long time.

LACEY

Twenty-seven steps.

   She knew the number well. That's how many steps it took to get to her condo on the third floor. Fourteen steps from the entry door to the second-floor landing, then thirteen steps to get to her door. Why there was a discrepancy, Lacey didn't know. She was missing a step. She didn't know how many times she had thought of that missing step, but it came to mind more often than it should.

   Like now, as she opened the door that she had forgotten to lock the last time she was here. Maybe it was because her arms had been holding boxes of Chinese takeout. Maybe it was because deep down she wanted someone to come to her rescue.

   Maybe it's just the randomness of life. Like being here on my own.

   Yeah, maybe. Just like step twenty-eight. It was somewhere out there and she could spend the whole rest of her life looking for it.

   Daylight was fading outside, but it was already mostly dark in her place. The place her father had helped her buy, the place she already felt indebted to him for. Money wasn't the issue but Lacey wished he didn't have this to make him feel better. He had helped her with this condo, with her car, with her college payments. And maybe that allowed him to help justify staying out of her life. *What more did she want?* Maybe that's what he was thinking. Lacey wasn't sure. She probably would never quite know for sure.

She turned on the lights hanging over the kitchen, then she leaned against the counter and found his name in her phone. Soon it was ringing, and soon she got a familiar voice answering in a familiar way.

"This is Rich. Leave a message."

Spoken as if he were rushing through the airport too busy to even leave a voice mail message. Then again, maybe that had been the case.

"Hi, Dad. It's me . . ."

Your little girl who just tried to kill herself last night.

"I haven't seen you in a while, and I was thinking that we could get together."

She paused and wasn't sure what else to say. She didn't like leaving messages. Too many of them went unanswered.

"Just give me a call if you can," she said. "It'd be nice to talk."

Lacey put the phone on the counter and then looked at the couch she'd been sitting on when she was last here. The air inside felt thick, the silence suffocating. It never went away.

She didn't feel like staying there, but she had avoided coming inside here all day. She needed to start living again. Maybe she could call up a friend. Or maybe she'd head out to go try to find some.

Why bother?

These two words were like headphones over each ear. *Why bother?* Over and over again the answer to the ideas she had was *why bother?* Maybe a friend should call *her* up. Maybe someone could come over to her place.

Your neighbor did and saved your sorry life, Lacey.

But that was a fluke. How many times had Pam not come

over, forgotten about things, held parties and neglected to tell her about it.

Lacey knew her father probably wouldn't call back, that nobody would call tonight, and that this closet of a condo would remain dark and seemingly abandoned. No amount of reality television could allow her to try to escape. No amount of distractions could divert her attention from the obvious.

I'm alone.

She opened the fridge and looked inside, then closed it. She turned on the TV but then soon shut it off, too. She wasn't hungry and wasn't interested and wasn't motivated to do anything.

The world moves on.

Sitting back on that same couch, Lacey was jolted out of her doze by the sound of her phone. She couldn't believe it, even when she grabbed it and the caller ID said DAD.

It hadn't even been ten minutes.

"Lacey?"

He sounded more interested than normal. Or maybe more concerned.

"You okay?" he asked.

"Yeah," she said, faking her mood.

"What's going on?" he asked.

"I just wondered if—it would be good to see you."

"Is there anything wrong?"

Life. That's what's wrong. How about that?

"I'm just—I don't know. I get bored in the city. Maybe you could come out here sometime. Or I could even come and visit you."

Her father lived an hour away, forty minutes if there wasn't any traffic. Burr Ridge was west of the city, but it wasn't like he was living on the West Coast.

"Oh," he said. "Well, you know how Violet can be."

Her father was dating a woman named Violet. That was a color, not a name.

"I'm not talking about her," Lacey said.

"You know she'd be here if you came out."

She wasn't sure just how long Violet had been living with her father, but it had been long enough. Long enough to keep Lacey away from a place she had once said she never wanted to come back to. The last couple of times she had been back to her father's home, the experience had been excruciating. All because of the thirty-something blonde that had latched on to her dad.

"Maybe I can pick a time she's not there."

"Lacey . . ."

"Or maybe you can come down here. *Without* her."

"We've already been through this," he said.

No, we haven't even started to go through this. We've avoided it. We've lived with it.

"There are things the two of you need to work out," he said.

"There's nothing to work out," Lacey said, now frustrated like she always got with her father. "It's not like we need couples counseling or something. I know she doesn't like me. I don't really like her, either. But I'm your *daughter*. Doesn't that count for something?"

There was a pause and a sigh on the other line. Then a curse.

"You sure know how to make someone feel like a failure," he said.

"No, that's not . . . I'm not trying to make anyone feel guilty."

A hundred scenes suddenly burst through her mind like some kind of shotgun blast. The words and the silence and the screaming and the cursing and the leaving and the undoing all shook her like they always did. The hurt always washed onshore every time she stood on her father's sand.

"But why do you always take her side?" Lacey continued, not

trying to hide her anger. "Just *once* it would be nice if you would think about how I feel."

She waited but nothing came. Then soon the phone alerted her that the call was done.

Call ended.

But Lacey didn't want it to end. She never wanted it to end. She never wanted *anything* to end. But things just always ended.

Once Mom had left them, Lacey knew that anything and everything could happen.

People always ended everything and they never came back.

For a moment she stood there, holding the phone. Then she put it down on the table, and waited and held it all in to see whether he would call back. Her father lost his temper almost as many times as she did. She took after him in that way. It wasn't something either of them was proud of.

She waited, and waited, then knew he wasn't going to call back.

It's safe now.

The tears came again. She put her arms around her body and tried to hold herself together. But she knew she couldn't. For a while now, Lacey had known this was impossible.

She was tired of everything simply ending without her having a say in any of it.

She was just tired.

PRETTY BOY

———

Deep breath. Exhale. Okay.

The white van had just pulled up and waited now in front of their house. Pretty Boy could see it in the dim light of evening. Waiting with its lights watching. Waiting to head out into the night and do its job.

Still time.

His whole body felt tight, like rods were in his back and his legs.

A shuffling behind him made him turn. It was Kriminal putting on his jacket.

"Guess it's time," he feigned in the tough-guy voice.

His brother just looked at him for a second. "Pretty Boy. Come here."

He didn't approach, so his brother walked up to him and stared at him without blinking and without moving.

"You nervous?" Kriminal asked.

"Huh? Nah. I'm good."

Pretty Boy looked away but again, there was no foolin' Kriminal. No bluffin' and no mock-bravin'.

"Hey. Look at me."

He looked back at Kriminal.

"It's good to be nervous," he said to Pretty Boy.

So confident, so carefree, so tough. So square, so built, so rough.

"Yeah," Pretty Boy.

His skin felt electric and his breaths kept forgetting to come and he just wanted to run somewhere far away from here.

The white van waits the white coffin wake the white mound base the white man takes.

His brother grabbed his arm, forcing him to focus and look and get right.

"This is our one move. We take Nefarius out, it's gonna be a whole new world, little brother. Everything changes for us. This is how we make do. How we take care of our own."

The torn-up worn-down chair seemed to wave at him with its flattened arms. G-Ma was in her La-Z-Boy already sleeping and missing the rest of the night. The living room was bare but messy, with crumpled up fast-food bags and empty jumbo cups. One of those ancient, square televisions that looked like a big block of metal on a flimsy table in the corner. A table full of trinkets G-Ma had assembled over the years.

He wanted out of this hole and this life. He wanted to move on, and maybe this was the only way. Gangster beginnings. Then he could get street cred and get his songs made and played.

He gave Kriminal a nod. Pretty Boy didn't want to think about Nefarius. He didn't want to go there and get nervous. He was still just the backup and playing the part of an accessory. Just like last night.

The onion on Kriminal's breath was a little too strong. His brother made him keep looking at him.

"Listen, Pretty Boy. It's gotta be done right. No hesitation. You with me?"

Of course, whatcha talking about?

"Yeah."

"You trust me?" Kriminal asked.

" 'Course."

"Live together, die together. Right?"

Heart beating and fears fading and head nodding. "Live together, die together."

"Now let's do this."

Kriminal picked up a flopping duffel bag and headed out the door. Pretty Boy followed him and watched him climbing behind the wheel of the van. He walked across the street and unlocked the black BMW. Kriminal's car. It was a rare thing for him to drive. But everything about this night was rare and Pretty Boy wanted it to stay that way.

Maybe nights like this would be over tomorrow.

ENGLEWOOD TURNED INTO no-man's-land after dark. They were surrounded by wastelands they couldn't see. Clusters on the corner, walking and blocking the lanes. Pretty Boy drove his car in front of the van, casually, trying to look like he belonged here. The music helped him try to not think of anything else. To anybody outside, Chiraq was a term but to them it was a shadow. A way of life wasn't the right expression because there was no life and no way. It was Chiraq, the murder capital where a gang member no longer gunned down another member. It was killin' kids and shootin' strangers and firing in the night to kill mothers and fathers and leavin' no one safe.

Faces watched, the closer he got to the house belonging to Nefarius. Suspicious faces even though they could see the driver. Some might recognize him, and others knew the car. He could see the lights of the van following. The modified van. The van fixed for action.

The street had its share of nondescript houses on it. The fourth one down didn't look any different on the outside, but Pretty Boy knew what was inside. The fading white two-story with closed-up windows and a scarred lawn. Inside, three, four, maybe more men waited, all carrying guns. All sitting around all day waiting for the customers. Black and white, male and female, young and old. Some soccer moms with no business at all around here came simply to buy a little white bag of heroin. Some hard-core junkies desperate to do *anything* just for another fix.

Guns to protect the money given for the drugs given by the gang.

The guns weren't the only problem. The front door was reinforced steel. They knew this because Little B had seen it himself. This was the problem they faced—that *Kriminal* faced—trying to get in.

Nobody got in unless Nefarius wanted you to get in.

Until today.

The BMW tore down the street and then turned and whipped into a U-turn only to head back toward the house. Pretty Boy could still see the glowing lights of the van approaching.

Then the hard right. The big white beast careened like some runaway fridge rolling down a hill toward the house. It pounded and bounced over the curb and across the dead grass of the lawn before it tore through the front of the house. There was a crashing sound accompanied by exploding glass and tearing metal.

A quarter of the house suddenly seemed gone. Pretty Boy saw the van engulfed, like a whale swallowing Jonah. The black sports car screeched to a halt and Pretty Boy focused on the hole in the wall where the van had been. The entire vehicle was now inside the house.

A flash. Another burst of flashes.

They're out.

He heard the shots. Automatic fire that could belong to Kriminal and Little B and 40 Ounce or could belong to the others.

Come on come on let's go.

For a moment, Pretty Boy stopped breathing. All he could do was watch and wait. His glance turned to behind his car, then all sides, then back over to house. All while more seconds ticked off.

He was ready to peel out and drive off, but right now all he could do was sit and wait. A voice inside told him to stay patient and focused.

More gunshots went off, and Pretty Boy almost jerked open the door handle. The figure emerging from the shadows of the house stopped him.

Come on, Kriminal.

But it wasn't him.

The weasel limping out of the house was Nefarius. Tall and lean and thinking he's the king of the world, only now this king was bleeding from the side of his head. Nefarius looked dazed and confused and weak, trying to escape the mayhem behind him. Just like any weasel would.

He staggered toward the BMW and then he passed out on a nearby lawn, crumpling only a few feet away on the driver's side. His face looked gone, defeated, but still defiant.

Do it, finish it off.

Pretty Boy just sat there. He had a piece on him but he wasn't getting out of the vehicle and he sure wasn't finishing *anybody* off. No way.

Pretty Boy had to look away.

He had to act like he hadn't seen Nefarius.

In the distance, sirens swirled all around. Then the sound of a chopper approaching.

He knew he should go. But he couldn't leave Kriminal.

On cue, his brother tore out of the cracked oval opening in the house, carrying the athletic bag, full and heavy and leaking cash. He kept looking back, carrying the gun in his hand, making sure nobody was following. Pretty Boy opened his door, and Kriminal crammed and crashed in.

"Did you see Nefarius?" his voice spilled out. "Did you see him?"

"No."

Obviously Kriminal hadn't seen him on the lawn on his side of the car.

"Where's 40 Ounce and Little B?"

"The price of doin' business, little brother."

Pretty Boy mashed the accelerator and felt pushed back in his seat as the car burned down the road, leaving the wreckage and death behind.

He wouldn't be able to leave it behind, however. Pretty Boy was certain of that.

*H*ere we go.

You know . . . professional athletes aren't the only ones who feel a burst of adrenaline before the race or game starts. Pastors can feel the same thing. This was what I was feeling before that Sunday evening service. My heart was full and I wanted to share some things. *A lot* of things.

That night, as people entered the church, I gave a gift to every single person who entered the sanctuary doors and sat down in a pew.

We had bought the church building after its founding congregation had dwindled down and then decided to change locations. They had gone to something more modern with a gym serving as the place of worship. We'd gotten lucky, to be honest. And we continued to be blessed by all those who came and sat in those traditional seats. Sometimes I wonder how many people under the age of twenty even know what the word *pew* means. At least a few, thanks to Good Shepherd Church.

I watched the congregation file in as always, greeting them in the foyer by the two doors that led into the sanctuary. The Newtons were among the first to arrive that evening. I had asked how they were doing, and especially how they were *feeling*. They were doing well. Yet as I glanced through the glass windows that looked into the sanctuary, I could see them sit down in the familiar row, and then noticed Teri putting the cross I'd handed her in the seat next to her.

Bobby and Elena Wilson arrived without their boys, telling me that Uncle Carlos was taking care of them. Bobby didn't appear to be so confident about that, but Elena had seemed excited for her brother to be back. I waited until it seemed like almost everybody was here. There might have been a hundred people total, and stragglers would arrive all throughout the service. Happened every time, and I always welcomed them.

The music team opened up with a few songs. There was a guitarist and a drummer and a couple of singers, and they poured their hearts into the contemporary songs they sung. We liked to switch things up, doing traditional one night and the opposite the next. I loved the variety. And some—most—of our members liked it, too.

I know you can't please everybody.

I know I was nervous singing and watching the band playing on the stage in front of the backdrop of the large wooden cross. Normally I'd follow up with a greeting and ask everybody to shake the hands of those nearby. But on this night, I decided to do something different.

I made my way up the steps and then walked over to the cross. On the floor next to it was a paint can. I picked up the large sponge and plunged it into the liquid, then I lifted it above my head onto one of the arms of the cross.

The red swath dripped as I brushed it into the place they would have nailed a prisoner's hand to the cross. I could hear the gasps and the hushed murmur behind me. I didn't look back, but instead dipped the sponge again and scraped the other side of the cross with a crimson stain.

I turned around and then walked to the front of the stage, the cordless microphone on my ear turned on. I looked at everybody not as members of a church but as friends and family that I desperately wanted to talk to on this night.

"Good evening. I'm glad to see all of you this evening."

I didn't spend long on the greeting. I didn't give any announcements. I didn't even mention the cross that each of them had been given. I would in due time.

"I'm going to ask you a question that was asked of me late last night," I began. "It's a simple question, but for some reason it affected me so deeply, so *profoundly,* I wanted to share it with you."

I paused for a moment, looking at different faces that all stared up at me. Young, vibrant faces; weathered souls; different colors and shapes and outlooks. Everybody so different, yet all wanting the same sort of thing in life.

Hope.

"The question I was asked was: 'Do you believe in the cross of Christ?' "

I waited to let them consider it. Then I casually gave them a shrug.

"That should be easy enough to answer, right? Of course I do. And yet, as I thought about this late last night, this question haunted me."

Turning and facing the cross again, I slathered more red paint at the top of the cross where the crown of thorns would have been. Then below, at the foot of the cross. Then I dipped the sponge and smeared the stain at the place where the spear would have pierced his side.

When I turned again, I could see Grace in the front row wondering what I was doing and where this was all headed.

Good. I've got their attention. Just like he had mine last night.

"What does it mean to believe?" I asked them. "I remember hearing once that true belief is an *action.* So if we believe that

Christ died for us, it should bring us not just to our knees, but to our feet."

Again I could see the big black guy coming in my direction carrying that big old cross. He was certainly using his feet and his arms and his muscles and getting out there.

I pointed at the cross behind me.

"The cross is a gift. The greatest gift of all. It's forgiveness, redemption, new life. And it was paid for with blood. Yet, when most of us look at the cross, we want the blood *gone*. We're ashamed of it. *The blood that my sins—and yours—required as the price of our ransom.*"

The sponge still in my hand, still dripping on the floor, I continued making sure they were all there with me. Watching and listening.

" 'But, Pastor,' you might say. 'Jesus is *risen*. The blood is *gone*. It's just a memory now.' But I tell you it's as real today as it was on that first Good Friday. It's as *real* as though it had just run, warm and red, from the veins of Your Savior, Jesus Christ."

My words were growing stronger, louder. I hadn't come there on this evening to condemn anybody. We were all condemned. But this symbol behind me and the color on it meant there was something beautiful we could do with that condemnation.

But we all needed to know. Needed to be reminded.

So I was there letting them know and trying to remind them.

Them and myself.

PRETTY BOY

———

The buildings passed in a blur. Driving one block, turn-ing and heading north, heading away, getting out of there. The BMW racing and forgetting about street signs and stoplights. Pretty Boy just made sure the speedometer kept going up.

The two cop cars just came out of nowhere. *Nowhere.* Like they knew somehow.

The chopper.

It had to be. Pretty Boy couldn't figure out how else. He jerked on the brakes and heard the tires howling on the pavement. Krim-inal cursed next to him as Pretty Boy looked in the mirror and saw more rollers ripping down the road toward them. At the last intersection they passed, another set of cops were coming in from both sides.

There was absolutely nowhere to go.

No jail, I'm not heading to jail no way.

Kriminal was next to him, taking a pair of Glocks out from the bag and getting ready for war. Pretty Boy had seen enough. He'd done enough.

Enough.

He almost broke the handle ripping open the door.

"P.B., the money! Don't forget the money!"

Kriminal didn't just scream. He practically roared. He stared at the bag between them and thought against it, knowing it wasn't a good thing and knowing that—

Pretty Boy took it.

His hand felt warm touching the bag but it didn't matter. He took it and took off running.

There was one thing he was good at besides rapping and it was running. He'd done a little sports when there was still a little room for that life and he could always outrun the other kids. Track and basketball and football. He could run, brother, and that was what he was doing now.

Every second he expected to hear the pops of Kriminal's handguns behind him. But none came. Maybe Kriminal decided there were too many. Maybe he was running, just like Pretty Boy.

The athletic bag was heavy but it didn't matter. The terror raced through every place his blood pumped. Pretty Boy was tearing down the street. He found an alley and darted down, then reached a fence, threw the bag over it, and climbed it in no time.

He ran.

Over a street and into a deserted junkyard. Away from the lights and the noise. Away from them.

Not turning behind and not stopping.

No jail no time no blood no crime.

He reached another set of houses. Pretty Boy had an idea of where he was at, but he didn't know exactly the neighborhood. Dark, mostly deserted, small houses, former homes, forgotten after the big housing bubble burst.

He reached an old body shop he somewhat recognized, then

crossed the street, slowing just a bit, breathing in and trying to figure out where to head.

A cop car was across the street, the officer snoozing, but he was suddenly awakened by his steps.

He cursed again.

Just his luck.

God's judgin' me and he's sendin' them after me, right, G-Ma?

A hundred steps led him to another dark alley and he didn't hesitate to go down it. The roller's lights were after him now. Then he heard a door open and footsteps and a flashlight trying to keep up with him.

The dead end was fifty yards ahead of him.

He didn't stop.

There was no stopping now.

His eyes scanned the back of the alley, barely lit by the lights from the apartment buildings on either side.

There.

On one side he could see the fire escape that led to the second story.

Just try nothin' to lose go.

Light bounced up and down as the steps behind him continued and the voice kept ordering him to stop.

A building and a wall and no escape. That's where this alley went.

Your pathetic life in a nutshell, P.B.

While still running, Pretty Boy heaved the bag of money up on the fire escape, then hurdled onto a garbage can and bounced up onto a dumpster. Thank God it was a rollaway with a top.

Still moving in a way that would make LeBron James proud, he launched himself toward the metal stairs above him.

His hands found the rusted-out railing and they clung and didn't let go. It took him a second to pull himself up.

The cop kept coming. That light still moving around. He scanned the stairs and already started to run up them, shifting the bag in his hand and heading up.

But he was like a wide receiver thinking downfield before catching the ball.

The duffel bag slipped out of his hand, falling down to the alley, landing with a thud behind the dumpster.

He cursed and stared at it in disbelief.

Go go go go go.

Sucking in breaths now, he thought about it, but he knew. There was no way. The cop coming . . .

He raced up the metal steps toward the rooftop. Then he tore across a flat space until he reached the other side of the building. Another fire escape waited for him.

Escaping the fire's right.

Now on the other side of the building and on another street he could hear the sound of the helicopter looking for him. Maybe looking for Kriminal. Maybe looking over Kriminal's body after a cop filled him with a six-pack of slugs.

Pretty Boy didn't even notice the sign he passed while he rushed into the parking lot until he reached the front doors and looked back.

First he could see a cop car passing the lot.

Then he saw the sign in bright and bold colors.

Good Shepherd Church

Good enough for me.

He opened the door and slipped inside the building.

As I was speaking, I saw Joe welcoming the stranger. I loved this about the big guy. That such an imposing figure could be such a kind soul to those stepping foot into the church for the first time.

Long ago Joe had been one of those. God had already saved him, but he was still searching for a home. For a safe place.

I'm glad he found it here.

And now the wiry young black man who looked almost as if he was sweating was talking to Joe while I continued to deliver my words in front of everybody. They spoke briefly and then the man walked down the center of the aisle toward a seat in the middle of a row.

The young man sat and looked around and then up at me. I smiled even through the words I was saying, hoping he felt welcomed.

I had some strong words that were for the weary of heart. But the heart needed to be opened to hear them.

Maybe this young man was one of those weary ones.

JOE

H e sees the trouble stepping through the door without having
to even see its face. Joe knows right away. Fear and desperation and haunting all cover this black kid. He's just a kid. A young
punk, obviously in trouble.

Hello, fellow failure. I'm here for you, brother.

Joe reaches out and extends a hand. The guy takes it and gives
him a strong, nervous shake.

"There's a seat for you up here," he tells him.

The black guy wipes his forehead and breathes heavily and
looks behind him at the front doors.

He's thinking about bailing. I can see it.

There's something else, however. Joe knows it.

What're you running from, son?

"I'm not staying," the newcomer says.

"I think you should," Joe tells him.

The windows of the lobby show enough of what's happening.
Joe can see the cop cars and has already heard the helicopter above.
He looks at the kid and tries to sum up whether he's a danger, but
Joe's confident he's not. He's just desperate and feeling alone.

Been there.

The guy looks at him with grit in his eyes. *"You don't know me."*

Joe doesn't blink or debate about responding. "Sure I do. I been where you're going—and believe me, the only way out you're *ever* going to find is right in here."

They're standing in the middle of the foyer for anybody and everybody to see. It's so obvious and the kid seems to know it, looking back at the front doors, knowing what waits behind them.

The kid nods and lets Joe scat him.

The pastor's got a fire lighting him up tonight and Joe knows it. Maybe 'cause God knew this kid was going to wander in here. Maybe because others needing a little firing up.

Starting with me.

He leads him to the middle of the sanctuary to a crowded spot. He'll be surrounded by others. It's a place he can be overlooked. Maybe.

If God wants him to be.

PRETTY BOY

———

Pretty Boy does a double take before sitting down. There's something on the seat in the pew. Something that reminds him of G-Ma and their place back home.

A cross.

He picks the small wooden cross up and then sits.

For a moment, he stares all around him. There are people looking and watching and wondering. Mostly white folks, mostly families, mostly wondering what in the world he is doing there.

I'm hidin', folks, so help me out a little won't you?

Then he stares at the pastor preachin'. He can't remember if he's ever sat in a church like this with a white pastor talking. The guy looks ordinary, a family man, a regular sort of dude. But he spots Pretty Boy and smiles at him. Pretty Boy can't help but look back down, then stares at the cross in his hand.

Look at me now, G-Ma.

"The Bible says in Romans 6:23 'for the wages of sin is death,' " the pastor says, holding a cross himself. "And because we are all sinful that's a death we deserve. But the cross promises us a way out. The *only* way out . . ."

The irony isn't lost on Pretty Boy.

The only way out. That's right, brother, preach it.

He wants to disregard the words and simply settle in and get by and stay unseen, but he can't help but listen.

He's afraid. Afraid like he's never been before.

Afraid of being found and put in jail and locked up for a while.

The faces of 40 Ounce and Little B appear as if they're sitting on a pew in front of him, looking back at him.

Where were you?

That's what they're asking.

Where were you, P.B.?

Somewhere their bodies are still bleeding, maybe still unfound. And like trash they're going to be eventually taken away and soon forgotten about.

The pastor keeps talking and Pretty Boy can't help but keep listening.

"When you come to the cross, you come by way of repentance. And 'repentance' means to *change* the way you live. To turn from your sins—and turn to Christ. The cross of Jesus Christ says, 'I will save you. I will forgive you. I will give you new life.' "

G-Ma's there right now. Right beside him. Holding his hand and nodding and saying, "Amen." He knows. Somehow, someway she's there.

It's the same thing she's been tellin' them her whole life. This Jesus. This cross. These sins. This forgiveness.

"Don't believe me?" the pastor asks. "Then believe God when He says through the apostle Paul in Romans 10:13, 'For everyone who calls upon the name of the Lord shall be saved. . . .' "

What would that be like? Pretty Boy wonders. To be safe and to not wake up feelin' like the worthless state he's livin' in. To actually not feel this lump of awful inside his heart. To not feel guilty.

You're a good boy.

G-Ma's words that he's never believed.

He sees something moving from behind him and he spots the cop. There's another coming in on the other side of the room.

Pretty Boy sinks down in the pew a bit.

They're taking me away right now. I'm done. I'm over.

The dreams of gettin' away and livin' a good life. His songs. His future.

Done.

Pretty Boy grabs the cross in both hands and then closes his eyes.

A last-minute prayer. A Hail Mary throw. A deathbed call.

The guilt wrapping around and closing in on his heart.

"Please Lord—save me."

It's a prayer for everything. For all of it. For this place and for his place back home and for his life and for everything and all that he has.

SAVE ME.

Clutching that cross, closed eyelids, open heart, open wounds.

He's not sure how long time passes. Maybe five seconds or a minute or more. But when he opens his eyes, the cops are gone.

Just like that.

"Thank you, Jesus," he whispers. "Thank you."

The pastor, as if on cue, takes the cross and holds it out in front of him for everybody to focus on.

"I challenge all of you tonight: carry this cross with you. Let it be a reminder of the gift Christ gave to us. Let it inspire you to live your life as Jesus lived."

The pastor raises the cross now above his head.

"This is not just a symbol, not just an idea. It's truth. And if you *believe* that truth, then let your actions show it."

The music begins to play and Pretty Boy breathes in and out in the pew.

He's not filled with disbelief or relief but instead he's filled with a strange thing he hasn't felt . . . well, maybe ever.

Hope . . .

ELENA

Well, that was heavy.

Elena climbed into the passenger seat of the SUV still holding the cross. It had been an unusual service, to say the least. Pastor Wesley had been more passionate than ever before, and the thing with the cross had been quite a performance.

Bobby shut his door and started up the vehicle.

"Maybe I'll hang it from my rearview mirror," she said to him while she examined the wooden piece.

"I don't think that's exactly what he had in mind," Bobby said. "The point was it's not just a decoration."

Ouch.

His tone was judgmental. The last thing Elena wanted was an argument, but she wasn't in the mood. He didn't have to be so gloomy.

"Well, I think it would look cool," she told him. "Now let's get something to eat. How about the Blue Fish?"

She knew Bobby hadn't exactly been thrilled to leave the kids with her brother. The kids loved Uncle Carlos and his sense of humor and his funny stories, but they didn't know the other parts of Carlos. The parts that Bobby was worried about.

"*Seriously?*" he said. "The Blue Fish?"

"Why not? My brother can handle the kids." She smiled. "Let's live a little."

Bobby didn't seem to believe her, however. For somebody who spoke about his faith so much, Bobby sure didn't seem to have much in others.

We just need some time for both of us.

And Elena believed that Carlos needed some time to get comfortable being around them. Spending time with the kids was a great start. To get used to having people he could rely on, people who could look out for him, people who loved him. She knew he was wary of anybody and anything. Maybe, just maybe, if they gave him time, he'd come around and become the brother she once knew.

"Interesting sermon, huh?" Bobby asked as he turned down a street, a signal that he'd given in to her request for dinner.

"Yes, very," Elena said.

"Pretty convicting stuff."

She nodded but didn't say anything more. Elena knew that Bobby was trying, that he was figuring out what this newfound faith he claimed to have meant. She didn't understand it. It wasn't like she didn't believe in it. But it didn't have to be so front and center in his life and *their* lives. It didn't have to go everywhere with them. It was fine to do the church thing—they'd always done that in bits and pieces their whole marriage. But now Bobby was talking about it all the time with her and the boys. He was doing things with the church and other ministries. Donating time he didn't have and money they didn't have.

She wanted to tell him to ease up on things, but how could

she do that without sounding awful? She really wanted to respect what he was going through.

The question she always came back to was, why? Why did he want to talk more about the sermon they just heard? Why feel the need to listen to the Christian radio station that was playing similar music to the kind they just came from?

Why, after entering the restaurant, did Bobby feel the need to take her hand and make a public display of praying for their meal? Out loud? For several minutes?

Elena didn't understand. Maybe, in time, she would, but now it was becoming a little too much.

She simply couldn't force herself to tell Bobby. At least not yet.

DR. FARELL

———

She hadn't seen him, and that was a fortunate thing. Thomas Farell had seen Elena and her husband, however. He couldn't remember her husband's name even after they'd met on numerous occasions. Rickie or Robbie or Bobby. A name that ended with an "ee" sound. The doctor was glad that the couple hadn't seen him. The last thing he wanted to do was strike up small talk with the nurse who annoyed him and her husband he didn't know. Especially since dinners with Andrea were still a fairly new thing.

Something new that was hopefully going to be a regular sort of thing.

Initially, Dr. Farell had been skeptical of anything to do with Andrea. She was a friend of a doctor working at the hospital. A lawyer. It had sounded like the start of a joke. *So a doctor and a lawyer agree to go out on a blind date . . .*

Actually, it hadn't been exactly a blind date. Dr. Kesey had shown him some pictures from her Facebook page. She was friends with Andrea, and it turned out this lawyer happened to be extremely attractive. "She's hot," had been his casual response to Dr. Kesey.

"She's very smart," the doctor had been quick to tell him. "And she's single."

"I like the single part," he had said back, half joking and half not.

The two of them had many things in common. Both had been in serious relationships before—he having been married and Andrea having been engaged—so they both had some war stories to share. They were successful in their fields and were happy to talk about that success. Thomas enjoyed people who owned up to life and actually took pride in their accomplishments. *Why shouldn't they?* In a day and age when everybody was so *nice* and inoffensive and worried about what others thought, he was always pleasantly surprised when he met people who freely spoke their minds. Especially when they were blond and shapely and available.

The food had just arrived and they were slowly starting on the meal. Andrea had ordered the blackened mahi-mahi while he had chosen the filet mignon. He took a sip of his wine and remembered a question he'd forgotten to ask.

"Are we still on for our little weekend getaway this weekend?"

She finished her bite. "As long as my deposition doesn't run late. No point in making the trip if we're not out of here by noon Friday."

He'd been thinking of the trip for a long time. It had been his escape, his fantasy during the day whenever he could take time off patients and work. Getting away with Andrea for the first time. They'd spent the night together, but this was different. This was Miami. This was a weekend. This was going to be Heaven.

Almost nothing could have ruined the warm space the doctor found himself in, glancing at her red lips and dark green eyes and her long hair falling down to one side. He was going to say something else but then something made him glance toward the table near the corner. The table the nurse and her husband were sitting at.

They held hands while they prayed.

Oh come on . . .

He didn't even realize he had sighed so loud until Andrea asked him what was wrong.

Dr. Farell nodded at the couple. Andrea turned just in time to see them finishing their prayer. Their *blessing.* Their *who's going to say grace tonight?*

"Can't someone go to dinner without being proselytized to?" he said while he took another bite of steak.

Andrea smiled and nodded in agreement. His eyes cut over to Elena, who didn't seem to be very engrossed in what her husband was saying.

"What's the point?" he continued on, feeling irritated and annoyed that his dinner had suddenly been ruined. "Jesus was a carpenter, not a chef. If they need to thank someone for their meal, shouldn't it be whoever's in the kitchen?"

He couldn't stop looking toward the couple. Dr. Farell shifted in his seat, loosening his tie.

"You know, I actually know that woman," he told Andrea. "She works at the hospital. I just don't know what she's doing here."

"Well, how about you don't let it ruin your dinner. Or mine."

She gave him a cute little knowing smile. He knew she wasn't interested in the woman at the table or even the silly little prayer they'd given. He also knew he should drop it, but he didn't want to.

"I'm just sick of it. *I* save their lives, and who do they wake up thanking? '*Thank you, Jesus. Thank you, Lord.*'"

Andrea laughed.

"Hey, no argument there. I grew up with those people." She rolled her eyes. "They're a bunch of hypocrites. But you know—I never realized you had such a God complex."

"It's not a complex," he said, completely serious. "I do his work. I should get the credit."

Andrea nodded and then took a sip of wine. "And I thought *lawyers* were full of themselves."

Her grin and her teasing lightened the mood. He loved that about her.

Dr. Farell didn't want to think about the nurse or about faith anymore. He just wanted to think about Andrea. And Miami. And leaving the hospital and the Windy City behind for a while.

It couldn't come soon enough.

PRETTY BOY

He wasn't sure how long he sat in that pew. But it was long enough that they turned the sanctuary lights off. Pretty Boy had been sitting there, looking up at the cross, wondering what had just happened, wondering about what he was supposed to do now.

Everything kept telling him the same thing.

Tell G-Ma. Ask G-Ma.

He needed to tell G-Ma about what happened. Not all the details about Kriminal and Nefarius and the robbery and cops, but just this bit about church and God and the cross of Christ. About his prayer. About his prayer being answered.

G-Ma's gonna ask what I was doin' here but that's okay.

Slipping out of the pew, he saw the big guy with the blockhead and short crew cut shutting off the lights. Slowly, knowing Pretty Boy was still in there. He walked toward him.

"Why'd you do it?" Pretty Boy asked him.

The man kept shutting off the lights. "Do what?"

"You know . . ." he said.

The big guy finished turning off all the lights and thought about his answer for a moment.

"The Holy Spirit put it in my heart that you were in trouble and asked me to help you."

Pretty Boy just laughed. "You expect me to *believe* that?"

The stranger just shrugged as they walked into the foyer of the church.

"Doesn't matter if you do or if you don't," he told Pretty Boy. "You're still here, aren't you? Speaking of which, I gotta close up."

Pretty Boy stood near the doorway, but before he left, he turned and looked at the unlit church. He didn't want to go. There was a restless longing that made him want to stay, at least for a little more time.

"You okay?" the big guy asked.

"Yeah, I'm just thinkin'."

He saw a small smile on the man's face, beneath his gray stubble.

"Tends to happen when the Spirit gets involved," he said.

Pretty Boy was going to ask him what he really meant, to ask him to elaborate and fill in some more details. This guy looked decent. He knew what was happening and he still helped Pretty Boy out. He actually saved him in a way. So Pretty Boy knew the guy was looking out for him.

His cell phone vibrated in his pocket. Before he even slid it out of his pants pocket, Pretty Boy knew who it was.

The name on the screen told him he was right.

The good news was that Kriminal was still alive. Unless, of course, someone else was using his cell, but that surely wasn't the case.

The bad news was that Kriminal probably wanted to know about the money. Yeah, sure, he was probably checking in on his little brother, but that money was what mattered.

The money I don't have.

Pretty Boy declined the call.

"Thank you," he told the big guy before opening the door. "Take care of yourself."

On the street again, no blinking lights or guys carrying guns could be seen. No cars were in the parking lot, making him wonder about the guy he'd just seen and where he might have parked.

He slid into the night still on a mission.

IT WAS STILL there.

The duffel bag lay upside down, still obviously full of something. They hadn't found it behind the dumpster. He assumed maybe they didn't think he'd be stupid enough to drop a big bag of cash on the side of the street.

Pretty Boy had run back to find it but deep down he had hoped it was gone. He had hoped he could tell Kriminal that the money wasn't there, that the cops or someone had found it. There was nothing they could do. It wasn't there anymore.

But it's right there.

His phone buzzed again. It was Kriminal calling, as if being able to read his mind. He sighed and then took the call this time.

"You okay?" Kriminal sounded out of breath, worried, talking fast.

"Yeah, I guess. But I keep thinking about Little B and 40 . . ."

"I know."

There was a pause.

The guys get shot dead and left behind and all his brother can say is "I know."

Would you say the same about me?

"You got the money?" Kriminal asked.

"No," Pretty Boy answered.

"You gotta find it, P.B. Nefarius made it out—you know he's gonna have his boys huntin' us down. We *need* that money."

"I hear you," Pretty Boy said.

Pretty Boy asked where his brother was at, then told him he needed to hide away for the night.

"Where're you gonna go?" Kriminal asked.

"I'll figure it out."

For a while after hanging up, Pretty Boy stared at the money. All this time, he'd believed that this was a way out, that this was their chance. The hope and the dream.

This bag is nothing but desolation and death.

He didn't want to pick it up.

The wages of sin is death.

The pastor's words stuck in his head.

We are all sinful. We deserve death.

He thought of the cross in the pocket of his leather coat.

The only way out . . .

He could feel his whole body shaking as he bent down and picked up the bag. Then Pretty Boy disappeared.

ELENA

The house slept again, just like the beating hearts inside it. Yet again Elena was coming home after hours. The only difference this time was that Bobby was right beside her. At least this felt right, the two of them pulling into the driveway and climbing out of the SUV. She wished they had more opportunities to go out like this.

Time and money.

The two things that often put a stranglehold on lives and families and marriages.

Bobby opened the front door and they slipped in, more quietly than usual, knowing Carlos was in the nearby living room. The lights were out and sure enough she could see the outline of the covers and the body on the couch. For a moment she considered turning on the light in the kitchen but then decided not to. She didn't want to wake her brother up.

As she put her purse in the kitchen, Elena noticed the empty pizza box on the counter, along with the cans of soda. She smiled, knowing the boys had gotten Uncle Carlos to order their favorite food. For a few moments she cleaned up the mess as she heard

Bobby heading up the steps to check on the boys and then call it a night.

Something fell in the living room. She stopped, shifting her head so she could hear in the room. Carlos was shifting on the couch and must have pushed something off the nearby table.

A mumble. Then a groan. Then she heard him saying something, mumbling.

Elena walked back into the room slowly, still listening, not breathing and trying not to make a sound. She didn't know if he was talking to her or having a dream.

She saw him turning again under the covers, hearing him talking fast but saying nothing but gibberish. His head bobbed around. He wasn't just dreaming, he was having a nightmare.

She walked over beside the couch and shook his shoulder gently.

"Carlos . . . Hermanito. Wake up."

He was still muttering words and didn't know she was there so she shook him a little harder.

His eyes snapped open, suddenly glaring and bulging at her. He bolted off the couch and grabbed Elena's neck in one fast swoop, taking her breath away. She felt herself almost lift off the ground as he drove her back against the wall with a hard thud. Everything in her body froze and she couldn't talk or breathe or even gasp. Elena pushed his arms as much as she could simply to scream out at him.

"Carlos . . . you're . . . choking me!"

She felt like gagging, her body stiff and her mind reeling. For a few seconds she tried to get him off her, to pry his hand free, to try to get him out of this rabid fever dream, but nothing worked.

A figure suddenly raced across the room and tackled Carlos,

and he let go of her neck. Bobby tried to pin him to the floor but Carlos fought for a few moments, wrestling him and turning him around and then locking an arm around his neck.

Then, as suddenly as it had happened, Carlos let go. He almost hurled himself back, away from Bobby.

He'd finally snapped out of it.

Elena coughed and grabbed at her numb neck while Bobby stood up and faced the attacker.

"What is *wrong* with you?" Bobby screamed as he flicked a light switch on.

Those dark eyes still looked wild and electric. They ignored Bobby and instead faced Elena. Carlos walked toward her with an open hand.

"I'm sorry, Elena. I'm so sorry." He was shaking his head, astonished and shocked, looking at her and watching her still cough and catch her breath. "You know I'd never hurt you. I—"

He stopped and looked away from Elena. She turned and saw the sleepy, surprised stare from Michael. His messy bedhead and his bright blue pajamas were all she saw at first. Then he seemed to realize the wrongness of this room, the strangeness happening right there. His face collapsed, and Michael began to cry before running back upstairs.

Her brother gave her a wounded, ashamed look.

"I can't stay here," he said, turning away from them and heading toward the corner of the room where his open Marine Corps duffel bag sat.

He grabbed a sweatshirt and stuffed it in the bag, then started to zip it up. Elena glanced at Bobby and then at Carlos. She didn't know what to do, what to say, what to even think.

"I knew this was a mistake," her brother said to himself as he slipped his boots on.

It hurt to swallow, but that was fine. She'd be fine. Her throat could get over that. She was worried about Carlos and his heart.

"Carlos, wait."

Bobby remained silent and still, his face still angry and his body still rigid and defensive. Carlos didn't look back at her while he slung the bag over his shoulder and headed out the door.

She had almost followed him out of the house when Bobby grabbed her arms and stopped her.

"Elena. Let him go."

"He's upset," she screamed back, yanking her arm away from his hold.

The door was open and Carlos could surely hear their words.

"It's making you *upset,*" Bobby said as he lowered his voice. "This is what happens. It's not good for you or the boys."

Outside in the faint light of the yard, she could hear her brother's tired voice. "He's right. It's better if I'm not here."

"That's not what I said, Carlos." Bobby took a step so that he could face Carlos.

"It's okay, man. I get it."

His boots hit the driveway and he began walking down it without hesitation. Elena couldn't take this. She darted into the house and raced to get her purse, then she jogged after her brother and stopped him right by their mailbox.

"You don't have money or anything," she said to him as she stood in front of him to block his way.

"I'll be fine. But not here."

"Carlos, please. Look at me. You can't just disappear again. I need to know where you'll be, that I can reach you . . . something."

"Don't worry so much, sis."

She knew him well enough to know Carlos wasn't sticking around. There was no persuading him. The kid she used to know could have been convinced to stay, but not anymore.

The war hadn't been good for his soul.

She opened her purse and dug in her wallet to grab whatever cash she had. The cross from the church service was still in there, right next to the leather wallet.

"Here," she said, giving him the money. "Take this."

"I can't take that. I *won't* take it."

Again, the voice and the look said, *Uh-uh. No way.*

He was a stubborn and troubled fool. But she had no idea *what* to do with him.

Elena put the money back into her purse, then pulled out the wooden cross.

"At least take this," she said to him.

He stared at the cross for a moment, then he gave her a nod and took it. She wasn't exactly sure why. He wouldn't stay and wouldn't take cash, but he was fine with this item she'd received from church? Why? Did he not want to get into some conversation about faith? Carlos knew that Elena wasn't sold on faith, that she had issues. She had admitted them before to him. And Bobby wasn't out there to give anybody a lecture.

Carlos walked past her, done.

"Promise me you'll call," she said to his back. "Let me know where you are. Please."

He glanced back and looked at her, but then turned and kept walking. Elena stayed there watching, seeing his tall figure get smaller and smaller until it was gone.

Carlos had arrived without even a breath of a warning. Now he was already gone.

If only that cross was like some kind of magical genie. Or like a winning lottery ticket. Maybe then Carlos would be safe, could recover. But Elena knew it was simply a piece of wood.

There wasn't any sort of magic for saving her brother. No doctor could write a prescription for his heartache. It was just going to take time to get things right.

Time . . . and maybe a miracle.

"**D**ear father, help my words and the words from your Holy Word make an impact on everybody who was there tonight. Have your Holy Spirit work in their lives. You know the hurts out there, Lord. You know what every soul is going through. Show them your face. Lord, show them what the cross really, *truly* means."

It was late Sunday night and I was praying in my office before bed. I wish I could say I did this every night in earnest. Sure, I prayed, but tonight I was making a conscious decision to pray for every single person who took one of those crosses. They were symbols, that was all. But I knew that the Spirit could do whatever He wanted. He could use words and symbols and even donkeys to speak to people.

I've always loved the story about Balaam's donkey. I've often compared myself to him.

"Whatever hardship or obstacle or spiritual attack or failure is troubling someone, take it away. Let them know you're there. Let them turn everything over to you. Let *me* know to continue to turn things over to you. Crush our egos. Erase our regrets. Let us ask for forgiveness and know that it's only through the cross and the blood of Jesus that we can even pray to you, that we can ask for mercy. Pour that mercy over us, Lord. Pour it over me."

So many names rushed by in my mind. Joe and J.D. and Teri

and Bobby and Elena and their boys and so many others. I could see faces, especially the young African-American boy sliding into the pew in the middle of the service. I had seen the police searching the aisles. I had wondered about him.

"Whatever his name is, and whatever is happening in his life, Lord, please bless him. Please shine your grace on his life. If he doesn't know you, Lord, please open up his heart. Move in his soul. Give him hope tonight. Give us all hope. I ask these things in the name of Your son Jesus. The only name that counts. Help me—help us—to remember that."

My mind wandered to those who hadn't been able to make it, people like Maggie and others I knew who had been invited but still remained away. I prayed for them, too, asking for the hope to go find them wherever they might be. To knock on their doors and to not stop pounding away.

Meanwhile, our house was still. Too still. Like a black fog sweeping over a town and forcing everybody inside. It was a quiet that carried a heavy weight.

LACEY

She turned off the television and sat back on the couch, her eyes looking at the ceiling before closing for a moment.

Everything—every glance, every swallow, every breath, every touch, every joint, every step—felt so *heavy*. Too heavy for someone so young, so light.

Lacey had tried calling her father back twice. Sure, he might be out and not checking his phone, or maybe he wanted to simply let a night pass to let things cool off, but still.

A part of her almost called Donny but she stopped herself. She knew she couldn't.

There was something about the shadows that arrived once the sun departed that felt so fearful, so final. She hated the darkness. The mixed bits of despair and anxiety that it brought with it.

I'm tired of all of this.

She thought of the smug doctor from this morning. He was so very *not* helpful. Imagine if someone like him actually sat down and talked to her, asked her what was really going on, wondered how he could help. Oh, she knew there were good people out there who actually did that, but they all lived in a place far, far away.

Maybe they just didn't like the cold Chicago winters. Maybe they were all living in California, where the sun never seemed to set.

Once she dreamt of going to a place like that. This happily-ever-after place. But then she realized dreaming was like watching the movie *Titanic*. It's so romantic and amazing but in the end you're left with credits on a screen and a sappy song. You're left in the dark watching all those names just roll past. *The end. Go and have a merry little life without Leo.*

Chicago was calling for her. Lacey couldn't be inside this apartment anymore. Everything was starting to smother her, to suffocate. In this place, the voices whispered.

You're an adult now, on your own . . .

She started to go.

Can't do this anymore. We can't keep up with your moods . . .

Whispers swirling at every side.

Not ready for this. Can't do this. I'm not equipped for you.

Her father. Her ex. Her mother.

All gone. Just like she planned to be. Tonight she would do it and nothing would stop her. Nobody would notice, and when they did they might feel bad, but they'd move on. They'd keep going just like everybody does. The rest of the world with its restless feet and fortunes moving on from failures.

She put on her slight coat and put her keys in her pocket, and then she slipped out of the apartment.

Those whispers followed, shadows in the spotlight, footprints in the snow. Impossible to escape, like a life she hadn't planned but inherited.

Lacey wanted—she *deserved* more. But more simply wouldn't silence those whispers and walk alongside her.

Nobody would have to worry anymore after tonight.

PRETTY BOY

———

The room at the Starlite Motel wasn't so bad, especially for seventy-nine bucks a night. He'd been in far worse. His own bedroom wasn't that much nicer than this square, clean room. He'd paid with money from the duffel bag.

Thank you, Nefarius.

Pretty Boy was pretty sure Nefarius wouldn't say that he was welcome.

He had walked in the room and locked the door, then waited at the doorway. Just to hear anything outside that sounded strange or suspicious. There were no sounds he could hear.

The bed beckoned. He flopped onto it and propped some pillows up and continued to sit there in silence, wondering what was going to happen. Wondering if he would ever see his own bedroom again, or G-Ma, or even Kriminal. The bag sat on the table.

A currency of hope lined by the currency of dope.

He wanted to find the remote to turn on the television that sat on a short shelf in front of the bed. It was one of those heavy, boxed thirty-six-inch televisions, the kind Kriminal and he used to steal when he was just a kid. These days everything was so light and so easy to haul off yourself.

The remote was nowhere to be found, but a Bible sat on the nightstand next to him. He took it and then opened it up to a random page.

G-Ma used to read through the Bible every year, before her eyesight got to the point where she couldn't read even with her glasses. She sometimes wanted Pretty Boy to read to her but he hated doing it. The words always made him feel guilty. Even though they were written years ago, they always seemed to be about stealing and lusting and lying and sinning in some way. It was like every single verse he ever read sounded like some judge reading the sentence against him.

He looked down and read a random passage.

But God showed his great love for us by sending Christ to die for us while we were still sinners.

There it was again. Christ. The cross. Dying. Sinners. Yet this verse didn't condemn at all. It said what was done for that condemnation.

He flipped back to find another verse. Maybe God was talking to him tonight. Maybe there would be something else he'd find. A way to escape from harm. An idea that would allow him to know what to do now.

> *I can never escape from your Spirit!*
> *I can never get away from your presence!*
> *If I go up to heaven, you are there;*
> *if I go down to the grave, you are there.*
> *If I ride the wings of the morning,*
> *if I dwell by the farthest oceans,*
> *even there your hand will guide me,*
> *and your strength will support me.*

Pretty Boy turned again and scanned the first thing he could see.

"Can anyone hide from me in a secret place?
  Am I not everywhere in all the heavens and earth?" says the
  Lord.

If these verses were true, then it meant God could see him there at this cheap little motel. In this room where the only thing he possessed was a bag of stolen money. But God would have seen the whole night unfold as well. He would have seen Pretty Boy escaping and fleeing and entering the church and praying.

He closed the Bible and then did the same with his eyes.

"Help me, God. Help me to know what to do. Help me to do the right thing. To get out of this. To live. To live and be able to leave."

For a long time he sat up in the bed, staring at the walls and the ceiling, wondering why God would be staring down at him. But maybe God was, for some reason. He had to try and believe. God had already rescued him once tonight. He wondered if he could be rescued again.

CARLOS

_____

He'd been here before.

Twenty-four hours ago—give or take some time, it didn't matter—Carlos stood at this exact railing overlooking the black river that seeped through the city toward the lake. He was no longer Corporal Carlos Delacerda of the United States Marine Corps. He hadn't been that in some time.

Carlos had disappeared over in Afghanistan and then Corporal Delacerda disappeared after he came back home.

He heard cars passing on the four lanes behind him, but it didn't matter. Nobody was stopping to get out and help him. Carlos knew that. This wasn't some little town. This was Chicago. This was the middle of the night in Chicago. And he looked a bit menacing with his crew cut and tall stature standing there peering over the railing.

Nobody's gonna care.

This had been a mistake. He knew it now. Going back to see Elena and the kids. He thought—a part of him actually _believed_—that it was going to be okay. That he could just stay for a while and figure things out. To just take some time and talk to someone who actually wanted to listen. Elena had always been there. It was just that the last year or two, he hadn't wanted to talk. Not to anybody. He'd just wanted to move on and escape the demons in whatever way he could.

Nothing had changed it, however. The drugs and the booze and the women and the parties and everything had only allowed him to sink just a bit lower. Further into debt. Further into despair.

I just tried to choke my sister. One of the few people who still love me.

Bobby's look had summed it all up.

What are you thinking, you monster?

He hadn't always been a fan of Bobby, but he agreed with his brother-in-law this time. Carlos had turned into a monster. It didn't matter that it was the war that had done it. There were too many to blame and that got tiring. He really only had himself to blame. People had tried. They had really tried to get him help and counseling and jobs and a life. But those people couldn't see the smiling demons on each shoulder, laughing at all the handouts that were going to amount to nothing.

There was just one thing he had to do.

He pulled out the items he'd stashed in his pocket and placed them carefully on the flat stone of the railing. Some guys he had known had spent lots of time trying to figure out what to do with things like this. They'd spent lots of money framing them and hanging them up or displaying them. Carlos had always carried them around with him. Not because he was worried about them being out of his possession. He just didn't know what to do with them. They were supposed to represent courage and valor and bravery and all of those other words he had heard time and time again. To Carlos they were pieces of the people he'd left behind. Because that's all those people were now. Pieces that could be stuffed in a pocket. Their lives were gone and only fragments of them lasted anymore.

The Afghanistan Campaign Medal went down first. Then the Purple Heart. Then a Bronze Star.

Courage and bravery.

Sometimes descriptions like that made him angry. People loved to heap them on his shoulders, the same way people used to tell him they were praying for him. He grew to believe those prayers weren't ever really prayed. And now he believed that people didn't really truly believe those words. They didn't understand what the words meant in the first place.

The wind whipped and slapped around him on all sides. Voices from the dead echoed in the wind, haunting him at every side.

He felt something else in his pocket get his attention. He knew there was no other medal in there, but his hand dug and found the cross his sister had given him.

For a moment, he stared at the cross under the light of a nearby streetlamp.

Carlos was fine believing in Jesus Christ. Sure. History made it clear this man existed. That he really preached and that he really died on a cross. But he died alone. They buried him and the story ended. There was no rising from the tomb. There was no Easter Sunday. That whole story was just like the Easter Bunny. Made up to make people feel better about themselves.

Jesus died alone and I will, too.

If only there was someone who could relate to the howling winds inside him. A kindred spirit to simply listen and smile and wait and sit alongside him. Those kindred spirits had been left for dead on the battlefield. The few that remained, the ones that came back and understood what he was going through, were the true walking dead. Some were violent, others crazy. All of them people Carlos didn't want to have anything to do with. It was bad enough to live with himself. He certainly didn't want to look into a mirror on a daily basis.

His eyes moved back to the railing, to the space in front of it, to the black syrup running below. Carlos began to move forward as he still held the cross in his hand—

The loud horn blaring jerked him around. He could see the Mercedes passing on the other side of the bridge, and barely had time to make out the couple sitting in the front seats. Of course they didn't stop. He had just been proven right. They did the good deed of honking and getting his attention and making sure he turned.

He noticed a woman on the other side of the street turning, too.

He squinted his eyes wondering if he was imagining something. A figure with curly long hair wearing a winter coat could be seen looking at him. It was a woman—a young woman— standing there. She didn't have any bags or possessions in hand, and seemed to have no reason to be standing in the middle of the bridge at this time of night.

Carlos knew right away. He wasn't the only one with this idea on this particular night.

For a moment, he almost laughed out loud. It was too coincidental, too unlikely, too unbelievable.

Maybe she was a ghost who just happened to be haunting him. Or maybe she was his guardian angel trying to get his attention in the most unlikely of ways.

Then again, maybe she was just another troubled soul. And maybe they were both the two luckiest human beings alive to meet each other like this.

LACEY

"Hey there!" the voice called out to her.

This was unbelievable.

For the second night in a row, some miraculous bit of bad luck had broadsided her. Last night her neighbor must have smelled the Chinese food and had a yearning for some sweet-and-sour chicken. Now some dangerous-looking guy she hadn't seen before across the street was calling out for her. But he didn't look like the type to try to rescue her.

What's he doing here?

She yelled back a "Hey."

What else could she say?

"You okay?" he called out.

Another car passed between them. The last one had been some fancy car with some idiot behind the wheel. Why wouldn't people let her die in peace? Why did they have to bother her when she *wanted* to be left alone? Most of her life that bit about being left alone hurt. But now she desperately wanted it. She needed it.

She didn't answer the guy's question at first. Then she mumbled an "umm" until telling him that she guessed she was fine.

"You?" she asked.

His eyes looked at her and didn't look away. They looked strong and tough, the kind that wouldn't back down at anything. But something in the way those eyes and that face changed after she asked "You?" made her feel a bit better.

The man looked amused. As if that was the lamest question he had ever been asked. And Lacey knew it was.

He was gonna do the same thing I was gonna do.

She wondered if he actually chuckled a bit.

"Somehow I was expecting a little more privacy," the guy said.

"Yeah, me, too."

This time she smiled. There was something about this man— something in the way he looked—that made her pause. It was a sadness on this stern man's face. And the softness that had suddenly washed over it.

More cars passed while they faced each other, not moving, not looking around.

"Did you change your mind?" he called out.

"I haven't had time to think about it."

Another car passed blowing its horn at them.

"Maybe I should come over there so we don't have to shout."

"Are you a crazy person?" she asked, half joking and half serious.

"I could ask you the same question," he said.

She laughed, knowing how true his statement was. They were both a bit crazy, probably.

And very lucky.

"Hey—look. You wanna get a cup of coffee?" the guy asked her.

The wind blew sideways and she felt her body shiver. This might be the second most ridiculous question of the night. But taking a look at both of them, one might say they were both a bit messed up in the head.

What's there to lose?

"Sure," Lacey said.

The river would have to wait. Maybe they would decide to jump in it together.

The man crossed the street and then greeted her with that same friendly smile.

"I'm not dangerous," he said right away. "Promise."

Lacey gave him a nod but didn't know what else to say. He told her there was a place not too far. They could get off this bridge and out of the cold.

They walked a couple of blocks in silence until they could see the sign for a twenty-four-hour coffee shop on the corner of an intersection. As they approached, the man who walked next to her seemed to be moving slower. He kept looking at the shop and then at her.

"Hey—you know—I didn't see much point in hitting an ATM on my way to the bridge," he told her.

She looked at his faded coat and his buzz cut and the bag he was carrying and then realized he was a soldier. Maybe Army or Marines. She wondered if he had an account to withdraw from.

She nodded to let him know it was okay. "I got this."

They paused near the shop, then as a couple exited and began walking toward them, Lacey stood right in front of them to stop them.

"Excuse me, have you got a fiver?" Lacey asked without any hint of shame. "We were over there at the bridge about to commit suicide, but we changed our minds. Right now what we *really* need is a cup of coffee."

The couple, a well-to-do couple in their forties, didn't say a word and appeared both shocked and embarrassed. The guy reached into his coat and pulled a twenty out of his wallet. The manner he did it in—so quickly, as if their lives depended on it—

almost made Lacey laugh. But her adrenaline was still coursing through her veins. She felt amazed that she was still alive. That she suddenly wasn't alone.

After grabbing a couple of hot drinks, they sat near the back of the coffee shop. The guy sipped his coffee right away as if it didn't scald his tongue. Maybe he just didn't care. They didn't speak for a few moments as they sat there, the background music playing some happy song for these two sad souls.

"I don't even know your name," she said. "I'm Lacey."

She offered her hand and he took it. His grip was strong, his skin coarse.

"Carlos."

In the light, Carlos was very handsome, with striking eyes and a square face like a model. He just looked so far away even though he was sitting right across from her.

"So, Carlos, why didn't you . . . you know? Do it?"

He nodded and smiled. "I met someone."

The words were spoken as if he had just come up to her at a bar. She would normally roll her eyes and act like it was such a lame line, but she kind of loved it. She grinned and nodded.

"How about you?" Carlos asked her.

She shrugged. "I don't know. Maybe I'm still in the beginning stages of feeling sorry for myself."

He was playing with something in his hands. It took her a moment to realize it was a small wooden cross.

"Are you some kinda religious nut?" she asked him.

"Hardly," he said, letting out a laugh. "I got it from my sister. Her husband got himself saved a couple years back. Elena? I guess she's about half saved."

Half saved?

"I'm not sure it works that way."

"It doesn't," he said with a nod. "Which is sorta the point. The funny thing? I think it's what kept me up on the bridge. I was just there holding it and thinking and then you appeared . . ."

The cross was still moving and spinning in his hands.

"You're not God, are you?" he asked with a smile.

"Me? No. But if I was, I would change a few things."

"Like what?" Carlos asked.

"Let's see. Flowers would last forever. Puppies would always stay as puppies. And fathers would never abandon their children . . ."

"You got my vote."

She watched him take another fast sip from his coffee.

"How about you?" she asked. "If you were God?"

His eyes looked down for a moment, then back at her. "Easy. No more war."

"Wow . . . Pretty heavy, Carlos."

She knew now without a question that he was some kind of soldier. She bet he had served over in Afghanistan or Iraq. She wanted to ask him but decided to wait. For now.

He glanced at her and then laughed.

"Yeah, well, so was your thing—about fathers leaving their kids or whatever."

There was this strange thing filling her face that had been absent for a while. It was infectious, too, because Carlos was grinning himself.

"Fair enough," she said. "We're even."

His eyes didn't look away from her, and that was a nice thing. They felt like a blanket covering her after being outside in the cold for so long. A favorite blanket that had been with her for a long time, that had comforted her on many long, dark nights.

What were the chances that Carlos would call out to her on that bridge? At that moment and time?

Something weird is going on.

He still played with the cross and she watched in a bit of wonder. Lacey didn't want to leave this place. Not for a very long time.

It was nice to have another voice to answer her. To have another voice around her. Especially one who knew without her having to even tell him.

It was more than most knew.

More . . .

For the first time in a long time, there was more.

woke up that next morning thinking about the crosses I handed out the day before, wondering whether my words had had any impact. This was part of being a pastor. The curiosity of how the words would stick. *Whether* the words worked. I had to trust the Holy Spirit, but at the same time, I needed to always show up and do my part. Just like professional athletes. Well, the Chicago Bears oftentimes didn't show up, nor did the Cubs, but they're not the best examples. I had been given the great opportunity to instruct and inspire the people at my church. Now I was curious whether I had done either.

The day ahead of me was a full one, but I made a mental note to check on the young girl again. I didn't want to bother her, but I also needed to figure out what was going to happen. She couldn't stay in that room forever. Obviously. But I needed to make some calls today at my office.

You also need to get Joe to call about the plumbing issue in the basement. And call back Richard about the upcoming missions trip. And to visit Rene in the hospital. And to have lunch with Pastor Frederick. And to—

The list was endless.

Grace told me all the time that I worked too hard. We'd been married for eleven years and she'd been telling me this even on our honeymoon. I sometimes wondered if this was just my lot in life. To wake up and go to bed with an endless amount of things that never get fully done. I'd spoken with plenty of pastors over the years who expressed the same feelings. Some got burnt-out and quit to go into something more stable like the financial markets or becoming a musician, I like to joke. But the truth was that some ended up simply being squeezed out like a wet rag and then tossed aside after years in the ministry.

That's not gonna happen, I told myself.

God willing, I quickly added.

I've learned that making declarations about things happening and not happening hasn't always been the best thing. God often has other plans. Even when we hope and believe that certain things should and could happen.

On my way downstairs to make coffee, I passed the guest bedroom that we had always thought would become our child's room.

It was like a road that I passed by on my way to work every day. An abandoned road that we had driven down for a while. A road that led to a dead end.

Sometimes I wished . . . I wondered maybe about turning and heading down it again. Just to see what it would be like. But I knew I couldn't go alone. Grace needed to be with me.

And I think the road was forever blocked for Grace. The thought of even bringing it up and reminding her was too much. I couldn't. Life had its share of reminders anyway. She didn't need me to hold up any more.

Instead I tried—I really tried—to hold *her* up. Yet it was hard when I often felt so unstable myself.

BOBBY

Seconds matter.

A millisecond is a thousandth of a second, so Bobby knew he was dealing with hundreds of thousandths of seconds trying to save the life that was quickly draining away.

Morning had hit like a meteorite striking the earth. Bobby had risen before the sun and driven slowly into work, while working on his coffee. Thoughts of the night before and everything that happened with Carlos still rumbled through his mind. They had gone to bed without talking about it. He knew that Elena would talk about it when she was ready. Bobby hadn't done anything wrong. He'd simply protected his wife like any husband would. He wanted to extend grace to Carlos but at the same time feared for Elena and the boys.

Bobby's team got the alert around midmorning over the PA system in the fire station. They needed to send the ambulance out to an accident in a nearby neighborhood.

When they got to the scene of the accident, it looked like any street might on a sunny Monday morning, except for the accident on the side of the street, and the dying man at the center of it.

Bobby and his partner Max had been the first responders on the scene. They had both been in a state of disbelief when they arrived. At first, Bobby thought the overturned vehicle on the side of the road near the rising driveway was a tractor, but then he saw the full view and realized it was a massive road roller used on road construction. Several crew members were hovered around the roller and one came up, immediately explaining the situation.

"We were startin' to grade out a footpath ready for the tarmac, and he'd just started to put the roller in reverse to go up the path slightly. But it pulled and he got it stuck and then the thing toppled over like that. Not really sure how but it did it and it landed right on him. He flipped out. There's no side protection on these things."

The man telling him the story was talking a mile a minute, obviously in shock himself.

Bobby and Max went through the usual routine, first making sure the scene was safe and taking all the universal precautions. Max parked the ambulance as close to the roller as he could while Bobby grabbed his jump bag and assessed the situation.

The road roller sat sideways on top of a man's lower body. Even before checking the breathing and pulse first, Bobby knew.

He's not making it. No way.

But Bobby also never gave up. His job was to be there and to help and take care of the patients.

In seconds, Bobby was on his knees hooking an IV to the man's arm and yelling back into his com link. The fire department needed to get down there with more men and tools, yet they weren't coming fast enough. They didn't know his only chance was if they got there right away. Even then, it was going to take a miracle. He wasn't in the miracle business. That was God. All he could do was be an instrument for Him.

"We don't have *thirty* minutes," he lashed out. "I need a specialty team here now."

As Bobby stabilized the man's neck with a brace and then put an oxygen mask over him, the man screamed and focused on him with a startling look of fear and pain.

"Understood, Eighty-One. But Air-Med One is en route to Kenosha, and Air Two is grounded with electrical problems. Stabilize in place and wait for Life Flight assist."

Electrical problems?

He wanted to let out a series of curses but he held back. It wouldn't do anybody any good anyway, even if he did still have a foul mouth.

"I don't wanna die," the middle-aged man said in a weak, out-of-breath way. "Help me . . ."

Bobby held the back of his head gently. "I'm trying. I'm doing everything I can. Can you tell me your name?"

He needed to try to make the guy stay with him, to wait until help came, until *real* help arrived. The firemen were beginning to cut into the road roller with metal saws.

"Steven."

Bobby checked the IV. Along with just being there and talking to Steven, there was nothing else he could do.

The second they got this beast of a machine off this man's lower extremities, he would almost certainly go into hypovolemic shock. With the loss of so much blood and bodily fluids, the heart would not be able to give the rest of the body enough blood. It would shut down.

"All right, just hang in there, Steven. We've got a lot of good people here."

But good people can't save you.

Why couldn't they get there sooner?

"Please . . . I'm scared," the voice barely said, his eyes wide open like twin spotlights. "I'm really scared."

Bobby tried not to show his fear or anger but instead stayed calm. He nodded and gave the man a smile.

"I know you are. But I'm right here with you, okay?"

Elena had always spoken about his *presence*. About his ability to be there in the moment and be calm and rational. Even last night, Bobby hadn't lost his cool. He had simply been protecting his wife and doing the best he could for his family. He had always been levelheaded. Emotions only made things worse when you needed to stay calm.

Tears of pain or fear or both filled Steven's eyes. "I can't feel anything. What's—what's going to happen to me?"

Bobby breathed in and swallowed. "Honestly, I don't know."

He didn't want to lie to the dying man. Bobby didn't know what was going to happen. They were trying to get him out from underneath the road roller. Several men were now trying to dig the ground around him.

What's going to happen to me?

Bobby blinked and saw himself asking that same question a year ago. He remembered sitting in the dark with tears in his eyes, wondering if he had lost it all. Wondering where to go. Wondering how in the world he was going to survive.

It was the question every single soul asks eventually: When will they die, and what will happen after their last breath?

For a second, Bobby thought about grabbing the shock pants from the ambulance. They were old school, the kind that every ambulance used to carry for situations like this to try to avoid a body going into complete shock.

Wait a minute.

He realized they didn't have them on the truck. It was on

another vehicle, the one from the other night that was being serviced.

Bobby shook his head, holding back his sigh, continuing to try to think of what to do.

He realized there was only one kind of hope that he could offer now.

He dug into his pocket and produced the wooden cross he'd brought to work. He had wanted to carry it on him as a reminder. Bobby had thought that maybe he could put it in the ambulance or possibly give it out to someone. He didn't think that someone would show up so soon.

"Here. Take this."

He pressed the cross into Steven's hand. The man didn't understand what he was holding or why he had been given it in the first place.

"What is it?"

Seconds, Bobby. Milliseconds.

Too often they're wasted. Too often someone's standing over a coffin wishing to have said more. To have done more. To have offered more.

"Do you believe in God, Steven?"

The face, drained of all color with sweat beads on his forehead and tears on his cheeks, looked surprised.

"No. I mean . . . I don't know."

Bobby thought of one of his favorite stories in the Bible. Suddenly, he wasn't some paramedic talking to a victim. He was a man talking to his brother. Talking to a friend. Talking to another person created in the image of God.

"Well, I can promise you this—Jesus wants to know you. He loves you and he suffered and died on the cross so we could be forgiven."

Suffering and dying next to two thieves on either side.

"Forgiven?" the man muttered out as if he was saying, *Wait, what?*

"Absolutely," Bobby said without thought or hesitation. "If you believe . . . and accept Jesus Christ as your Savior . . ."

The face looking at him winced and then appeared to be thinking, confused but wondering, blinking and trying to figure out what he was hearing. But before the man said another word, they heard the piercing gasp of a woman. Screaming about her husband, she rushed to get to them.

Bobby saw her being restrained by an officer.

"That's my husband! What happened to him?" she howled, flailing her arms and trying to move forward. "Let me go, that's my husband!"

The cop was telling her to stay there, that it wasn't safe, that they needed to do their job.

Bobby looked down at the man, who started to mouth words again. His voice wavered and shook as he spoke.

"Please, God, take care of my wife. My children."

More sirens could be heard. The sound of the cutting saw biting into the metal blasted at them. His wife behind them continued to scream. Doors opening and men calling out and voices speaking on their radios. Shovels scraping up the dirt around them.

Yet for a moment, Bobby heard nothing but Steven's words. He looked up at the EMT with that look Bobby knew well. The stinging look of defeat and hurt. Like a blank whiteboard with no words to fill it. Destitute and hungry and ashamed.

"Jesus, please forgive me," Steven said in a gasping tone. "I'm sorry. I'm so sorry."

"Then he said, 'Jesus, remember me when you come into your Kingdom.'"

The thief on the cross asking and begging for mercy in the last moments of his life.

Holding his hand, seeing that desperation, hearing those words . . . Bobby couldn't keep his guard up anymore. The tears began to block his view. Once again he did the only thing he *could* do for this man.

"Lord, hear Steven's prayer and bless him and his spirit. Have mercy on him and give him strength even in these moments . . ."

For a few moments, Bobby lifted Steven up in prayer, quoting from Psalms, asking for help, asking for anything. He then couldn't help but quote from the passage he had just remembered.

"Lord, help Steven to know, to be assured that on this very day he will be with you in paradise. Jesus, smile on his face. Please, Jesus."

Steven's grip loosened, like the boys' did as they fell asleep. The face below Bobby softened and shut down at the same time. He watched the man and then could hear the screaming right behind him.

Steven's wife was now on her knees next to her husband. Wailing, clawing at his lifeless body, begging for him to wake up.

Bobby stood up and waited for a moment, trying to console the hysterical woman. She was dangerous now, and she would fight him off. She called out Steven's name several times through the choking tears. Then she stopped for a moment as she held up the loose arm.

The cross fell out of Steven's hand and onto the ground.

"What is this?" the woman shouted at Bobby.

"Please, ma'am," Bobby said as he offered a hand to help her up.

"No," she said as she swatted him away. "Tell me what this is doing here. What's going on here?"

Frantic, desperate, the woman looked like a rabid animal.

Bobby had seen what grief and panic could do. He stayed strong and stoic, waiting to help her up, waiting to walk away from the scene with her.

He couldn't help Steven anymore. But he could help his wife.

I have to help his wife. Whatever she needs I need to be there.

J.D.

J.D. looked at the Victorian-style dollhouse he had built thirty-five years ago. Kathleen had loved it so much and had wanted to keep it in her room even as she got older. It was a reminder of her childhood, one Kathleen had cherished. It was a reminder that Daddy loved her enough to spend hours cutting and building and painting a house like this.

It was still a reminder. But it no longer filled the room with hope. Now it was a relic. An echo of a voice and a laugh and a name that no longer could be heard.

He knew it was finally time to silence all the echoes in this room.

The box he was filling stood in the middle of Kathleen's room. Around it were the snapshots of a life. A name on the wall. Pictures from the time of her birth until her last year. A newborn bundled in a towel, held by her mother. A toddler giggling. A father with his kindergartner on her first day of school. A smile, missing a tooth. A school picture. A gathering of girls for a birthday party.

Yet pictures weren't the only thing that filled this room. There were books they had read to her. There were diaries she had filled. There were her favorite CDs stacked together. A jewelry box stuffed full. Posters on the wall. Her favorite stuffed animals, still tucked away in the corner. A closet full of dresses and clothes. Trophies.

The picture J.D. held in his hand was one of their favorites. Kathleen was posing for her picture in her ballet outfit before her first big performance with the company in Chicago. It was during her junior year of high school.

His eyes started to mist over, of course. This hefty, loaded tug pulling at him again. It was familiar. But J.D. knew it was time to finally unload a bit and move on.

The thing that no picture or piece of video could re-create was Kathleen's laugh. It had torn through this house the first moment she had let it go as a baby. It grew into this magnetic, infectious, life-affirming blast of oxygen. He couldn't remember how many times it had revived him after coming home from a long day at work.

God, if only you could give us back a few more of those laughs.

He wiped his eyes and started to put the framed photograph in the box. And that was when he heard the footsteps and the memories stopped for a moment.

"What are you doing?"

Here we go.

J.D. had been ready for this. He looked up at Teri and just offered a calm, serene stare.

"Something we should have done a long time ago," he told his wife.

She stepped into the room for a moment, slowly, as if something might happen, looking all around to see the things he had already packed away.

"No, stop it!" she cried out at him. "What's the matter with you?"

It was worse than J.D. thought it would be. He stayed calm. He had to stay calm.

"Teri, Kathleen is gone. She's not away at college—or working in Minneapolis—she's not going to be back for Christmas."

"I know that, J.D. But this is her room. Now put it back!"

She ripped the frame from his hands. He put a hand on her arm, trying to calm her down, trying to reason with her for the first time in a very long time.

"Teri, just stop."

Her arm pulled away. She looked at him like he was a stranger breaking into their house. Those beautiful blue eyes turned into a tsunami of fury.

"No," she screamed. "How *dare* you. You have no right. This is my daughter's room. It's all I have left."

J.D. moved toward her and wrapped his arms around her. She moved and wiggled and wrestled away from him, moving her arms and then pushing and lashing out at him and even trying to punch him. But he just held on to her, taking the blows and making sure she knew he was there. J.D. was still there even though Kathleen wasn't. He was there and he wasn't letting go.

Soon Teri's entire body grew limp and she began to sob into his chest.

The dam's burst wide open.

It had been a long time since he'd seen such emotions from his wife. This anger—it surprised him. Scared him, actually. But these sobs and this childlike anguish—they had been there once, until they had been buried.

He let her cry into his arms. Soon as she started to calm down he spoke into her ear.

"This isn't a room, sweetheart. It's a museum. And we're not honoring her memory. We're living in the past."

She moved away to reveal swollen eyes, her mascara starting to run.

"What else are we supposed to do?" she asked.

She sounded lost now, unsure, more like she had years ago.

J.D. thought of the reason he had gone in there in the first place. It had been the words of their pastor and the gift they'd been given. It was still in his pocket and he found it to show to Teri.

She simply looked at the cross in his hand in disbelief and despair.

"What good can that do?" she asked. "I've carried my cross for *twenty* years."

"Teri, the world didn't end when she died."

"Ours did."

He shook his head, understanding and wanting to be comforting, but also wanting to *change*.

"No, it didn't. We wanted it to, but it didn't. And ever since, we've been selfish."

His hand grabbed the photograph from his wife, then he nodded at it.

"Without meaning to, we've turned our grief into our most prized possession. God doesn't want that."

The lost girl started to leave again as the bitter victim began to appear.

"Where was God the night we lost Kathleen?"

"I'll tell you where He was. He was asking Gordon Hewitt to not take another drink. He was begging the bartender not to serve it to him. He was hoping he'd call a cab or go home with a friend or do anything besides getting behind that wheel. And when it was all over, God cried. Just like we all did."

Like a balloon hovering overhead but starting to deflate, Teri shook her head and stared at the floor.

"Why are you doing this, J.D.?" she asked with slow, soft, weak words. "Why now?"

It was a fair question. He understood it and accepted it. But he also needed Teri to understand his heart. He had carefully considered what he was doing now, so he started to explain why.

"Remember how Matthew said belief is an action? Well, it's time for us to act. We need to get back up and start living again. I want to do more with the time we've got. There's a world full of people out there who need help, who have no place to stay. Every time it rains, they sleep wet. And every time it's cold, they sleep cold."

The sigh felt like a slap on his face. Teri looked up at him with cynical, cold eyes.

"You're telling me you're turning our whole life upside down because of a *sermon?*"

"No," he hurled back right away. "I've been thinking about it for a long time. But his sermon's given me the courage to actually do something about it."

Before he could say more and try to help Teri understand, she turned and walked out of the room. The steps heading downstairs were fast and full of spite.

This time J.D. was the one to let out a sigh. He turned and then saw five-year-old Kathleen looking at him with a big, overflowing smile.

It made him feel ashamed for a moment.

Sometimes he wondered if she could see the two of them from Heaven, if she could hear their conversations. He worried sometimes that she could. That Kathleen was trying to tell them it was okay, that she was fine, that she was loved and that she loved them.

J.D. didn't know, however. One day he would know. One day

he would know what Kathleen could or couldn't see. One day he would see that smile again, not frozen in a frame.

He didn't want to go to Heaven asking God why He took her life.

J.D. wanted to enter those gates thanking God for giving them Kathleen in the first place.

GRACE

The song blasted through the car and made her feel like a teenager again. She sometimes liked to do this when she was driving by herself. When she didn't have to use the time to connect with Matthew. When she didn't have to hear the same songs over again on Christian radio. When she didn't have to hear a story about someone at church. She liked not having to hear any of it.

Sometimes, like now, she just wanted to imagine. To hear the words about some silly, sophomoric love story. Once upon a time, Grace found herself in that story. But the songs always hinted at the happily-ever-after. They always left something in your imagination.

Grace no longer used her imagination. It was a dangerous thing to do.

The receipt she had found on their dresser earlier this morning had prompted her to do something. To get into her car and start it up and turn up the radio while she drove down the street. Maybe she was just trying to get into the right frame of mind. Teens— some of the students who went to their church—but she still didn't know what it was like to be a teen these days. Such a dark, scary world with so many potential pitfalls. Grace was reminded that she was grateful to have grown up in a better time. Still ripe for failing, but not as dangerous as these days.

The motel wasn't far away. Grace thought of this young girl staying there alone. A young *pregnant* girl all alone in some kind of solitary prison. She knew Matthew had done the right thing, but it was also such a guy thing to do.

Uh here let me get you a motel room.

She didn't blame her husband, however. She blamed herself. He had asked and she had refused. He had made the offer and she had taken it back. Yes, it had been late and she hated being woken up, and yes, Matthew did have a lot on his plate these days. Grace had just assumed that he would find a good place to bring her and be done with it.

Done with it.

Those three words filled her with shame. It was as if they were painted on a billboard she passed.

What if God did the same thing to you?

Another voice inside her wanted to sneak out a whisper that God had indeed done the same thing with her. With them. And that she had been wondering why for quite some time.

Don't go there, Grace.

She had spent too many hours in counseling and too many moments with friends to go back to that place of grief and anger. Sometimes God didn't answer prayers and we would never know the reason why. Period. Grace had accepted this even though there were days where the questions rolled in like some kind of thunderstorm. As always, she would have to wait out the weather.

The Starlite Motel sat there like some kind of dirty child on the side of the road waiting for his mother. There had been several times when her husband had helped someone out and gotten them to stay at this place. Yet those other times it had always been adults.

A man who had been kicked out of his house for his addiction to porn. A woman running away from her abusive husband and not sure where to go. Even the janitor in the church, a wonderful man named Joe, who had just been let out of prison and needed somewhere temporary to stay.

Matthew and she had talked about the church someday building or buying a house where people like this could come. A recovery home. They had a growing ministry called Celebrate Recovery that was already thriving within their small body. Maybe, possibly, the recovery home could be something done with this ministry.

For now, it seemed like the Starlite Motel was their go-to place of refuge for the broken and needy.

The woman behind the desk recognized her even though they didn't know each other's names. The woman was maybe fifteen years older than Grace but had a hard look stamped over her face. The serious look wasn't unfriendly. It was probably just that the muscles for smiling hadn't been used much over the years.

"My husband brought a young girl here the other night," Grace said. "A teenager. She's been here a couple of nights."

The woman didn't have to question whether it was okay to tell Grace which room she was in. This lady understood things. She knew Matthew and Grace were only there to help people out.

"Room 124," the raspy voice told Grace.

She thanked the woman and headed toward the girl. She knocked. When the door opened, the sound of the television blared behind the petite figure in the doorway.

"I'm Grace, Matthew's wife. The pastor's wife."

Right away she wanted to let this girl know who she was and why she was there.

"It's not right for you to have to stay here alone," she continued. "I'm the one who turned you away the other night. Please forgive me."

Wide eyes full of curiosity and surprise and even a hint of humor just stared at Grace.

"Okay . . ." The young voice trailed off.

Before she could say anything more, the door next to them opened. A tall African American in his twenties stepped out and walked past them, a friendly smile on his face. Grace first saw the duffel bag over his shoulder, but then saw the Bible in his hand. Even in his leather coat and with the stubble on his chin, he looked like a good guy. The eyes told the story. They were a window into a safe place.

Once he was past, Grace asked the first and most important question.

"What is your name?"

"Maggie."

The name seemed to fit this girl like some kind of handmade sweater. Grace gave her a nod and a smile.

"Maggie, I want you to come with me, okay? Our home is your home. Until we figure out a better place for you to be."

Her innocent face looked uncertain, as if Maggie was trying to figure out some way to say no. Her small figure seemed even more tiny because of the round belly that she held with one hand.

"I allowed myself to say no the other night. I apologize for that. So I'm not taking a no from you."

Maggie gave her a silent nod. It was a start.

They would figure things out together. In a much better and safer place.

"Let me help you with your stuff," Grace said.

"It's okay. I only have one bag."

THE LIGHT FELT like it had been red for about ten minutes. Grace watched and waited while the girl next to her did the same. For the first few moments in the car, they had driven in silence. No radio drowning the voices inside this time. Soon the car started to move again and Grace knew she had to ask.

"Have you had any prenatal care?"

The girl only shook her head and remained silent.

Grace was concerned about Maggie but even more concerned about the baby inside her. A teen living on the streets . . . Had she gotten any kind of treatment, any sort of professional care and advice?

She was walking around with a precious gift and she didn't even care about it. She had no idea how valuable that gift was.

Grace searched for the right question to ask next, or perhaps the right thing to say. There was nothing worse than saying some kind of trite thing, making some kind of glib response. She had genuine concern. And this girl was just a teenager. But she still deserved respect and care. Grace needed to be sensitive.

Just as she started to talk again, Maggie surprised her and began talking.

In a way, it seemed like she'd wanted to talk to someone for some time.

"My stepmom took me to what I *thought* was my first appointment. I didn't realize until I got there that they were looking to get rid of the baby."

Maggie wasn't even looking at Grace, but instead glancing out her window. Grace knew that some memories had to be buried just in order to keep on walking and breathing and living.

"I felt the baby kick for the first time on the way into the clinic, and I couldn't get the feeling out of my head. It was like the baby was telling me not to let them do it. Before that I'd felt these little movements, but this was totally different. This was a real kick. I realized everything they were telling me was wrong. And I just—I had to get out of there."

She glanced over to see the look on Grace's face. To see her reaction.

"It's why I ran away," Maggie told her as if she was still trying to defend herself.

The anger Grace had felt suddenly evaporated. She had judged the girl all wrong.

Maggie glanced back out the window, toward the city sidewalks they passed. She continued talking in a soft, faraway voice.

"When I'm alone . . . it's like there's this little voice inside of me that keeps whispering, keeps telling me the same thing. 'You can have your life back. There's still time. All you have to do is get rid of it. And that wouldn't be so bad. It's not even a person anyway.' I hear these whispers but I know they're a lie."

Maggie's head shifted down and her hands covered her face. Even her cry was soft and understated, a slow and deep whimper. Grace put a hand on the back of her curly hair.

"It's my baby," Maggie said.

Grace could feel the tears in her own eyes now. Not just because of the pain and the confusion filling this young girl's soul.

No.

She realized that Maggie knew full and well the gift she had been given. She had run away in order to protect that precious gift.

Maggie wasn't there because of some mistake or misfortune or foolish decision. She was trying to protect a life. She simply didn't know how to do it. Grace realized now that Matthew didn't randomly stumble upon her. God had brought Maggie to them.

Grace believed this. She also believed—she absolutely *knew*— that Maggie was in safe hands.

sat in my office chair in silence for a while. I'm not sure how
long. Just staring down at my desk and thinking of the phone
conversation I had just experienced. A family in our church just
received the news that their four-year-old son had leukemia. I
spoke to the father, who sounded stronger than I did. I offered
words that hopefully encouraged and offered support and prayer.
Yet as I sat there replaying the conversation over again, I wondered if I could have said more. Something different or better or
more pastor-like.

I wasn't sure.

This family—a family of four, a young family, with so much
to offer and such a joy to be around—didn't deserve this news.
Obviously things happened and you couldn't control them. Yet I
was asking the question the man had never brought up during our
conversation.

Why, God?

I glanced at the small item sitting on my desk right there in
front of me. I picked it up and studied it.

Why . . .

I believed in the cross and believed in the words I had spoken
yesterday. Yet time and time again, I didn't understand the *whys*
that wandered around in this world.

For a moment, I stared across the room to where a bookcase stood. On the side of the middle shelf sat a frame without a photo. It had been a gift from Grace that I still didn't have the heart to take down. She had given it to me at a time when we were trying and praying and hoping.

The top of the frame said four haunting words:

Look Who Loves Daddy

I swallowed and then thought of the Babiaks with their two boys. Why would God bless them with children and then suddenly allow this? I had the words a pastor could say to a parent and I had uttered them all, but I still didn't understand. I wanted God to show me why.

I had long ago come to the realization that the picture frame would never be filled, yet I still wondered why.

Verses from Job filled my head. I knew the Book of Job well. I certainly couldn't relate to this man who lost *everything.* Yet I still understood a little about loss.

"Who is this that questions my wisdom with such ignorant words? Brace yourself like a man because I have some questions for you, and you must answer them."

God answered Job's questions—much like the questions that often filled my heart like they did now—by asking Job a series of things nobody could answer.

In the end, Job was simply left to fall to his knees in forgiveness and shame.

"I was talking about things I knew nothing about, things far too wonderful for me."

I knew the Bible and I believed in the message and the hope inside it. I believed in the cross I was holding and what happened on it.

If you believe that truth, then let your actions show it.

I had been sitting there with questions, with hurt, with wonder. What I wasn't doing in my chair was praying and thanking God for His love and care over us. I wasn't giving this over to the Lord even though I had *just* tried to rally the troops with a message saying to do that very thing.

"Forgive me, Lord. Forgive my failures and my doubt. You oversee everything. Nothing happens without you allowing it. You know this young boy and you're watching over him and you know every single thing about him. Heal him, Jesus. Be with him. Be with his parents and his brother. Give them all unnatural strength. Bless him today, and bless the road ahead. I pray it's a long road, full of miracles and grace. I pray that the cross is present in their lives today and tomorrow. I pray that for myself, too."

These prayers were always and only prayed in Jesus Christ's name. He was the one who allowed them to be prayed, who took them and put them before his Heavenly father.

I couldn't question. I didn't have the right to. But I could ask for mercy and grace so I did. Yet again.

BOBBY

"Bobby—battalion commander is waiting for you in the captain's office."

He had only been back in the fire station for ten minutes before a new fireman named Dex who looked like he had just graduated from high school delivered the message. This wasn't a good thing to hear. The chief only made appearances when he was handing out some kind of medal or disciplining someone. He didn't think he was getting a medal.

As he walked to the office in the back of the station, he thought of the man who had died beside him that morning. This wasn't the first time something like this had happened. Those other faces and figures stayed with him, too. They would remain shadows for the rest of his life. That simply came with this road. He could handle the reminders.

Chief Russell didn't stand or even greet him, but rather seemed eager to get down to business. His weathered face showed lines from wear and tear, not of emotion.

Bobby sat in the chair facing the desk and the man behind it.

"The widow's looking to file a complaint against the department," the low growl of the chief said.

A complaint?

"It's the prelude to a suit against the city," the chief continued. "Typical shakedown. Probably looking to claim fifteen to twenty million. The charge will be 'proselytization under color of authority.'"

A suit? Fifteen to twenty million?

"What exactly does that mean?" Bobby asked. He was suddenly out of breath and felt like he was twirling around on some fast-moving roller coaster.

The thirty-year veteran always seemed like he had a droopy face, but Chief Russell gritted his teeth and gave him a cold stare.

"She'll claim you implicitly threatened to withhold necessary care from a dying man unless he accepted your religious beliefs. And that your inattention to duty contributed to his death."

He let out a *that's ridiculous* chuckle. He shook his head.

"I'd never do that. Besides, she wasn't even there."

Chief Russell nodded, obviously taking his side, obviously believing him.

"She'll claim the restraining officer was complicit in your actions. Look, we've gotta defuse this thing before it gains traction. So here's how it's gonna work: You're gonna craft a carefully worded apology, explaining how you made a mistake in the heat of the moment. A professional lapse. And it'll *never* happen again. I'll help you draft it. Then you'll read it on camera for one of the local news affiliates that gets it on the record."

It suddenly felt like Bobby was on a grill and tongs were grabbing him from both sides, squeezing.

"I can't do that," Bobby said.

This got a reaction from the chief. His thick eyebrows shifted down and his eyes thinned. The look on his face suddenly became cloudy, questioning.

"Why not?" Chief Russell asked in a low-rumbling roar.

Bobby moved to sit on the edge of his seat, trying to get closer to the chief to talk frankly with him.

"I'm not sorry for what I did. And if I ever wind up in the same situation, I'd do it again. It's part of my obligation as a Christian. But only after my professional duties as a first-response caregiver are complete."

Chief Russell gave him a look a father might give to a child who just fell off his bike trying to do a wheelie.

"Look, Bobby. You've got beliefs, and I respect that. But I've got a membership and a pension fund to protect. On behalf of your brother firefighters. Am I getting through here?"

Bobby's faith wasn't a brand-new thing. The guys knew about it for various reasons. For the times he had declined to go out with them, or the moments he had walked away from conversations. It wasn't that Bobby tried to preach to anybody or even talk about his faith. But it wasn't a secret.

"I'm not sure," Bobby said. "What exactly are you saying?"

"If you can't find your way to apologize, then the union is gonna have to distance itself from you. We're gonna have to admit that you acted *outside* your authority, and on your own behalf."

This was crazy. Bobby had only been trying to help the man *live*. Then he was simply offering the man *hope*. Now he was being sued and told to lie about things?

Glad I pay my union dues.

Chief Russell wasn't finished.

"Your legal defense—as well as any damages—are gonna have to come out of your own pocket. Plus I'll be forced to suspend you without pay until this thing is settled. Off the record: you're gonna lose *everything*. Is that what you want?"

"No," Bobby said.

"Good. So you'll read this statement."

The chief offered him a sheet of paper but Bobby shook his head and told him no.

"Chief, I won't apologize for sharing the Gospel with a dying man. And I can't promise that I'll never do it again."

Chief Russell now looked like a bulldog after a long walk. He was more tired than frustrated. Bobby knew this was one big inconvenience for the man.

"I hope you know what you're doing," the chief told him.

Bobby didn't move until being told what the next steps were going to be. But as he listened and waited to be excused, he couldn't help hearing the same voice over and over in his head.

What are you doing, Bobby?

He didn't know. But he did know this.

He was doing the right thing.

J.D.

There was believing, and then there was acting on it.

Sitting in the pew. That was fine. That was listening and understanding and believing. But the acting part . . . Well, that was something unfamiliar to J.D. But he was trying to act. And this felt like the right thing to do.

They stood in a packed gymnasium in the lunch line holding trays. It didn't feel much different than being back in school or maybe being at some kind of church function. Several people serving out food and greeting people wore red Salvation Army smocks. The room smelled like bacon.

J.D. glanced at Teri, who stood as straight as a ruler holding her purse with both hands against her chest. Her eyes wandered around with suspicion. He shook his head at her.

"I don't want to be here," she said in a hushed voice.

"Come on, relax. It's an adventure."

There was a mother and her young daughter a few steps behind them. They were talking and not paying attention to J.D. and Teri. He realized that's what happened when you got older.

People stopped paying attention to you. *They're just the older couple.* Nobody ever bothered to really notice you.

When they reached the food, J.D. took a moment to decide. There wasn't just soup even though he had told his wife this was a soup kitchen. There were sandwiches and soup and various kinds of casseroles. They looked pretty good, too.

"What can I get you?" a woman with a smile that smothered him with love asked.

"Hi. Can I have some of that chili-mac-and-cheese, please?"

It looked wonderfully unhealthy. It was something Teri would never make in a million years.

"Nothing for me," his wife said to the server.

He couldn't believe her. He wanted to tell her to just order something, to not act so insulting, but J.D. didn't want to bring any more attention on them.

"How come you don't wanna eat that?" a voice out of the blue asked. "Is it cuz of the carbs?"

They both looked back and saw the little girl looking at them with curiosity. She looked pale and thin but also quite feisty.

A smile covered his wife's face. It was nice to see.

"No, it's not that," Teri said. "I'm just—I'm not very hungry."

J.D. leaned toward the round cheeks and big eyes staring up at them. "You sure seem to know a lot about food."

"Yeah, I know a lot of stuff. I'm Lily."

It wasn't just a simple introduction. It sounded like some kind of declaration. Almost like *I'm Lily, haven't you heard of me?* A warning of sorts.

"Pleasure to meet you, Lily. I'm J.D." He gave the mother a friendly smile. "Mind if we sit with the two of you?"

Lily answered for both of them. "Sure. If it's okay with my mom. She gets a little weird about strangers. Especially big ones named Joe."

The mother simply shook her head in a combination of embarrassment and pride. The woman looked much like her daughter. The only thing missing was the fire that made the girl's face glow.

"It's fine," a subdued voice told them. "That would be lovely, thanks."

The long tables were full but J.D. and Teri found a section in the middle of one where they could sit and face the mother and daughter. A couple of grizzled men, bundled up even inside, sat on one side, devouring their food, while a couple of friendly faces sat on the other. J.D. decided to take the seat next to the men.

Without even thinking about it, he gave his usual thanks to God before eating.

"For what we are about to receive—and for the gift of our new friends, Samantha and Lily—may the Lord make us truly thankful. In Jesus' name, amen."

As he lifted his head and picked up his fork, he saw both of his new friends looking at him.

"Do you always pray before your food, Mr. J.D.?"

There was something about the unabashed honesty of children. The world quickly stomped it out, J.D. thought. Especially in today's politically correct, careful-not-to-offend, unobtrusive culture.

"Yes, I do," he said.

"Me too," Lily bounced back. "Even when they run out of beds, and we have to sleep outside in the parking lot. And all we eat is potato chips for *two whole days.*"

Maybe your mother doesn't love that honesty.

"Sleeping in the parking lot, huh?" J.D. said as if she were talking about a new toy she received for Christmas. "Sounds like fun. Sorta like camping. Right, hon'?"

Teri gave a nod and polite smile but remained silent.

Lily kept talking through a big mouthful of food. "It's not really camping. We have a car. Mom calls it the 'orange dorkmobile.' "

"I love the name," J.D. said.

He could tell Samantha appeared embarrassed and defeated, a one-two punch. A flood of questions filled him, yet he had to wade through them and try to figure out if any of them were appropriate to ask. He wanted to help, wanted to offer any sort of suggestions or aid. But he was brand-new to this and the last thing he wanted to do was to heighten that embarrassment or defeat.

"This is good," he said about his chili-mac-and-cheese.

Teri gave him a *you-are-so-lying* look.

"Seriously," he said. "Look. You can't ever go wrong with anything with chili *and* cheese."

He took a big bite and then nodded at Lily while raising his plastic spoon. She laughed and then did the same.

Samantha gave him a polite smile that looked like a painting in a museum. A portrait of someone with a thousand different stories to tell but unable to share a single one.

HALF AN HOUR later, while driving back home, J.D. kept trying to pull something out of his wife. She hadn't said much and had only answered his questions with simple one-word answers.

"That wasn't so bad, right?"

"Right."

"They were a cute family."

"Yes."

"Are you hungry?"

"No."

Teri never overdid anything, including talking. She liked to bury her thoughts and emotions. If they did actually bubble to the surface, they were still always carefully spoken and thought out. It made her impossible to see right through. Some people wore their hearts on their sleeves, as the saying went. Teri's heart was hidden behind a bulletproof vest.

So when she finally said something before arriving home, J.D. couldn't help but be surprised.

"I thought . . . they'd look a little different."

He chuckled. "You mean like orphans in a Dickens novel?"

She looked over and laughed. It was genuine. This was her way of admitting that it hadn't been so bad, that he had been right. She would probably never utter those very words, but J.D. knew she had been pleasantly surprised by their lunch.

He waited to see if she said anything else, especially about Samantha and Lily. But nothing came.

He'd wait. Perhaps that mind and heart of hers would start to stir. Perhaps she would eventually mention them, providing an oh-so-slightly opened door.

J.D. had already walked through it. He knew what he wanted to do. What needed to happen. His wife just needed to be convinced. And it usually worked best when it seemed like the idea was hers.

The evening was hours away. He had time to work on her.

DR. FARELL

The salad in front of him was half gone. Most of the important emails on his phone were read. Dr. Farell had managed to escape any random conversation and eat lunch in peace as he waited for Andrea. He hated being bothered by trivial conversations from colleagues, but he also hated when people were late. This wasn't a business meeting, but it was still a scheduled time to get together.

He spotted Andrea the moment she stepped out of the serving area and into the cafeteria full of tables and chairs. She was tall, and seemed even taller in high heels. She wore a dark blue business suit that was the perfect complement to her golden hair. Dr. Farell admired her as she approached even though he still gave her an annoyed look.

"You're late," he said as she placed her tray down and then sat across from him.

"New client," she said without an apology. "The wife of an accident victim."

"Ambulance chasing?" he joked. "That's not your style."

Andrea took out the plastic fork in the clear bag and then began to mix her salad. She looked wired today, her face focused and her actions busy.

"It is when the victim is forcibly converted to Christianity while he's trapped, *dying*, with his wife restrained out of earshot by the police."

She took a quick bite and nodded at his surprised reaction.

"Picture this: a Bible-thumping paramedic has poor Steven Carson as his captive audience, painting him pictures of hellfire and damnation in his final moments. Horrible, right? To say nothing of the psychological pain and suffering to Mrs. Carson. Her last memory of her husband forever tainted by the thought of him being strong-armed to renounce his own worldview."

Andrea looked like an animal eyeing its prey in the middle of the field, ready to devour. He liked that about her. On the outside, she looked so pristine and proper, but inside she was a predator. It was one big reason she was great in her job.

"Maybe he already believed and nobody knew," he said, playing devil's advocate.

Andrea shook her head and finished the bite of her salad. "Both were members of the American Humanist Association. Their motto is 'Good without a God.' "

She appeared amused by this, the sparks in her eyes.

"Still, won't it be her word against his?"

"That's the best part. These Christian types? You swear them in—have them put their hand on the Bible—and what do they do? They actually tell the truth. Plus the ACLU's already promising to draft an amicus brief. They see this as a watershed case for misuse of authority."

Dr. Farell was impressed. And this wasn't an easy thing to do.

"Sounds like fait accompli," he told her.

She agreed, her animated and sweet face looking in direct contrast to the snarl on her lips.

"Nothing wrong with a witch hunt," she said. "As long as you're after the right witch."

PRETTY BOY

The neighborhood looked different when you didn't want anybody to see you.

Pretty Boy checked his phone again but Kriminal had stopped calling. Their conversation earlier had been short before he hung up on his older brother. Kriminal had asked him about the money and Pretty Boy had told the truth. Yeah, he had it, but no, he couldn't bring it back to Kriminal. When asked why, he told him the truth.

The thing I should've said before this all went down.

"It's not right . . . what we did."

Kriminal had cursed and yelled and told him right had nothing to do with it. He told him—threatened him—to bring the money back to him. Pretty Boy had simply responded by hanging up and not taking any of the other calls that had come in.

Now, hours later, he sat in the back of a cab sitting on a ripped-up seat. Pretty Boy hoped this wasn't symbolic. He had waited long enough before heading home. He doubted Kriminal would be found there. His brother was in hiding, especially since he didn't have the money. Pretty Boy wanted to gather some of his belongings before taking off. For how long, he didn't know. Where to, he didn't know. But he had some things to get. And he had to tell G-Ma goodbye, at least in his own way.

Just as he had hoped and suspected, Kriminal wasn't anywhere to be found. His grandmother was on the couch listening to some program on the little radio next to her on a table. After walking through the house, Pretty Boy placed the duffel bag beside an armchair and then settled back on it. He didn't want to make G-Ma wonder what was wrong.

"Where's your brother?" she asked as she turned down the radio.

She knows somethin's up.

"Don't know."

The leathered face stared at him. "You boys fighting?"

He gave a casual shrug. "I guess so."

She kept looking at him, studying him, enough so that he had to look away.

"Come on over here," she told him.

Pretty Boy didn't want to. He didn't want to stay here for long. But this was his opportunity to listen to his grandmother and then tell her goodbye. He should've done this a long time ago.

Sitting next to her on the couch, he stared at a face as constant as the sky above. He wondered when he'd see it again.

If ever.

It was like she knew. G-Ma always seemed to know. Even when she was quiet. Even when she decided to not do anything. Somehow she always knew.

Her frail body leaned over, and then bony hands with skin dripping off them held each side of his face.

"My pretty boy," she said.

It had been G-Ma that gave him his name. The name that had stuck.

"Think back about all those nights when I'd sing you to sleep. Every night, the same song."

Her ragged, low voice began to sing and it took him back to being a boy. Still full of hope and dreams. Still growin' and still believin' and still not knowin' all the bad stuff beyond these walls. Just a boy looking up at his grandmother and listening to her sing "Seek Ye First."

The rumbling deep inside started to shake again. Pretty Boy felt his eyes gloss over with emotion. He remembered it well. He'd never forget that song and the voice that sung it even if he was miles away from both.

When she finished the song, she didn't pull away. Those wise eyes just locked on to him and didn't let go.

"I know it ain't easy for you out there," she said in a way that felt like some kind of parachute flapping behind him. "You got voices pulling you in all different directions. But there's only one voice that matters."

The hand that slightly shook against his cheek now moved to his chest. Right above his heart.

"You listen for that, and you follow it. And you'll be just fine."

It seemed like that one voice G-Ma spoke about had been following him around for some time. And it had finally caught up with him and sat him down last night. He had finally heard it in a way he hadn't heard it before his whole life. And this time Pretty Boy had spoken back, asking, *begging* for help.

And it answered.

He thought about maybe telling G-Ma, but he didn't. He couldn't. Not now.

The less she knew, the better.

"Are you gonna stay around for a while?" G-Ma asked.

Pretty Boy realized that he couldn't leave now. Not after this.

Not like this. He swallowed and looked out the front window he had stared out a million times before.

"Yeah. For a while."

Pretty Boy knew that he had waited long enough. Another few hours wouldn't hurt anything. But then he was going to be gone.

Maybe—no probably—gone for good.

Man, he'd miss this woman sitting next to him.

S he was gone.

The day had slipped away like so many of them did and by the time I could get over to the motel to check on Maggie, she was already gone. The guy at the front desk, a younger guy I had never seen before, hadn't seen anything and just gave me a blank stare with a not-so-helpful shrug. I thought of calling Grace, yet realized she didn't know that the teenager was still around. I planned on telling her eventually.

Guess it needs to happen tonight.

I thought of that young girl walking the streets again, perhaps going back home to some kind of nightmare she'd run away from. I wondered if I should have asked more, if I should have tried to get her some help.

I pictured her round belly on her petite frame. Then I pictured Grace, sitting beside me in this very car, weeping into my chest while I held her in a parking lot.

Life doesn't come in chapters. It doesn't have character arcs. It doesn't feature foreshadowing. It arrives, one day after another, with chances and choices and confusion.

The tests and the doctors and the second opinions all told us what we'd already figured out: Grace couldn't have children. There was lots of technical stuff we learned about. I honestly never want to hear the words "fallopian tubes" again in my life. I wish that it had been my fault that we couldn't have children. My issues. Maybe then things would have been different.

Maybe Grace wouldn't have worn the guilt like a straitjacket. Even when I spent months begging her to take it off.

My car seemed to sludge through the shadowy evening. This cloud still came every now and then, reminding me. Forcing me to look behind me and see the empty seats in the back of my car. No car seats, no spilled Cheerios, no remnants of saltine crackers, no fallen hair bows, no missing stuffed animals.

It had been five years ago that we gave up trying, but it felt like five minutes. Then as couple after couple we knew made announcements and sent celebration cards in the mail and showed off their smiling baby boys and girls, we had to watch. The worst thing for me was seeing Grace stand strong and smile and show love to each and every one of those couples. Our friends, some family members, even members in our church.

The dedications of those newborn babies were the toughest. Grace watched from the pew, tears in her eyes, knowing that this would never be us. The dimples and the fuzzy hair and chubby arms and legs could only be seen and appreciated for a few moments, then they were gone. And Grace's arms remained empty.

Talk of adoption had never gone anywhere. Grace always said she wanted to be there when our baby was born. I had tried—and failed—to pursue the issue. I knew I couldn't understand. I was the man. There were certain things and realities I knew I just couldn't fully fathom.

I arrived at our house, the porch light glowing, the light from inside leaking out the windows.

Be thankful for this day and for this life you've been given.

I paused for a moment after shutting off the car. Then I grabbed my computer bag and headed inside, expecting the familiar still that always greeted me.

Instead, I heard conversation. More lights than usual were lit. The smell of ground beef hung in the air.

Then I saw a face in the kitchen.

It was Maggie.

"Hi, honey," Grace said as she stood next to the young girl at the island.

I think I stood there speechless for a moment, both amused and surprised, wondering if I was really seeing this. Grace knew what I was thinking and directed her eyes toward the wall. The one where we'd put up the wooden cross.

"Can't just go giving these out and expect nothing to happen," she said while she began to start cutting vegetables on the chopping block.

I greeted Maggie and told her I was glad to see her, then I walked over and wrapped my arms around my wife. I kissed the nape of her neck. It was good to feel her and to reach out to hold her. There were few spontaneous moments in our marriage. Right or wrong it was just the way things were. But this felt necessary and felt *right*.

When I let go of her and then moved around the island in the kitchen, I noticed the tears in her eyes. She played it off with a casual and dismissive smile.

"These onions have really got me going," Grace said.

I looked down and could see what she was cutting with the knife.

"That's celery," I said.

She didn't say anything but kept working. I glanced over at Maggie, who was watching with animated, interested eyes.

"I'm glad you could join us for dinner," I told her, then quickly added, "Both of you."

LACEY

The buzzer first alarmed her, then made her curious, then inspired this tiny flicker of a spark of hope inside. They could be dangerous, those sparks. They could ignite hope into belief. Yet when she opened the door, she saw that sometimes hope was a beautiful thing.

It was Carlos standing there.

"Hi," she said in almost a gulp. "What are you *doing* here?"

He carried a brown shopping bag in his arm and had a Cheshire cat grin on his face. "I just wanted to make sure you were okay."

Carlos looked more handsome than she remembered, and she had certainly pictured his face plenty during the past day. They had talked through the night at the coffee shop. He had gotten the guy behind the counter to call a cab for her, then had asked if he could see her again. Lacey had given him her number and address.

She didn't think he'd show up so soon.

"Do you mind me stopping by?" he asked.

"No, not at all."

He still wore the faded leather jacket he had worn last night, but he had a buttoned-down shirt on underneath instead of the biker T-shirt. She could tell that Carlos had also shaved.

She smiled but didn't say anything.

"I don't want to invite myself in, but this bag is sorta heavy," Carlos said.

"I think you just did," she said. "I'm sorry. I'm just—surprised."

"Me too."

He followed her into the apartment as Lacey turned on some overhead lights and then told him to put the bag over on the kitchen counter.

"Sorry it's a bit messy," she said.

Carlos stood looking at the high ceilings and the living room and attached kitchen. "Looks pretty tidy to me."

"You're a guy."

"Nah. I've just seen far messier things in my life."

Lacey stood trying to figure out what to do. She realized her hair and makeup probably looked atrocious, that she was wearing black leggings and an oversized sweatshirt since she hadn't changed from working out earlier. She also realized this meant she probably smelled like sweat and body odor. Then she wondered if this was smart anyway, being around this guy she barely knew after everything that had happened.

He gave her an affirming *it's really okay* look just like he had last night in the coffee shop. For someone who was going to jump off a bridge the night before, Carlos sure looked content and comfortable in his own skin today.

"I don't have much to drink—I have some leftover beers I think from a party. Some wine."

"It's okay," he said. "I gave up drinking. I never figured out quite how to do it safely."

She smiled and understood. "I have Diet Coke."

"Great."

When she gave him the glass, he thanked her and then sat at a stool near the counter in a way that looked like he'd done it a hundred times. Moments ago she'd been restless thinking about him and about her father and about the past two nights and wondering what this night might bring. Little did she know it would bring him.

Carlos picked up the small framed photo on the counter.

"Nice picture," he said as he held it.

"My father and me."

"You guys close?"

She shook her head. Last night she hadn't said much about her father. She had simply told him that her mother was gone and she lived alone in the city.

"Fathers," Carlos said in a way that made it sound like the title of a long novel.

"Yeah."

They shared a look just like they had the first time they ever saw each other.

This is absolutely crazy.

It was. But in a really good sort of way.

"Am I the only one who sees the irony in this?" Lacey just had to say.

"Hey, that was last night," Carlos said, totally understanding what she was thinking. "Today is a whole new day. Besides—you gotta eat, right? I'm guessing people who jump off a bridge don't stock their refrigerator. So . . ."

She laughed. "You're right. But they do work out."

"In order to really make that last jump count, right?"

"Is it wrong to laugh about it?" she said, seriously wondering this.

"I've learned that it's the only thing you *can* do when you survive a near-death situation."

She knew he had to be talking about the war. Carlos had touched on it a little, but every question she had asked about it only got short, simple answers without explanation. That was fine.

She decided to empty the grocery bag. He had gotten all the basics: milk, bread, chips, ham and turkey, cheese, mayo, apples, and . . .

"Seriously?" Laccy asked.

She held up the greenest bananas she'd ever seen in her life. Carlos only laughed.

"Something to look forward to, right?"

It was one of the nicest things Lacey had heard in a long time.

J.D.

The spattering on the roof above filled him with guilt. Fifteen minutes ago the rain had started, and now it was just a steady sound of shame. In the dark of their bedroom, J.D. had waited long enough. He climbed out from under the warm covers and then reached for the pants on the nearby chair.

"What are you doing?" Teri's voice asked behind him.

So she's not sleeping, too.

"I'm gonna go get them."

He wondered if Teri had been thinking about the mother and daughter.

"Now?" she asked.

"Yes, now. While it's cold and wet and raining."

There was a pause. Then she asked the obvious.

"How are you going to find them?"

Buttoning up his shirt, J.D. realized he didn't quite know. "I'll figure it out."

"J.D. . . ."

His wife had been mostly silent since their argument earlier that day. He knew that Teri hadn't changed her mind at all, but was instead slowly starting to retreat. She knew he hated it when she did this. Turning inward, building and fortifying a wall that sometimes was impossible to get through. Sometimes—*many times*—J.D. had to just give up and wave the white flag. But in this case, he knew he wouldn't. He couldn't. It had been long enough.

He slipped into the bathroom for a moment, then started to make his way out of the bedroom.

"I'll be waiting," Teri said. "For all of you."

"Thanks."

Now he had to figure out where to even start to look.

On the drive toward the shelter where he had met the cute girl and her strained mother, J.D. prayed. He asked God to help him find them. He just wanted to help them in whatever way he could. Maybe he should have asked them earlier, but he didn't. Now, as the wipers tried to keep clearing away the rain so he could see, J.D. was reminded that you sometimes didn't get a second chance in life. To offer to help out a stranger. To ask forgiveness from someone you've hurt.

Or to say goodbye to a daughter you love.

Words came to mind. The young girl talking about their orange dorkmobile. Then something else.

The parking lot a block away.

Lily had said something about that in passing when talking about their car. He had simply forgotten about it. Well, *almost* forgotten about it.

He parked alongside the curb next to the lot. It was half full and had a fence around it. J.D. wondered if they had to pay to park in it overnight. Even if they did, it was still cheaper than a motel room.

Nobody needs to sleep in their car. Not these days.

Maybe they had gotten lucky and found space to sleep in the shelter. But something told him they hadn't. It had been a gentle nudge. Well, maybe not so gentle. Pulling him out of his bed. That's what it had been like. And maybe it had been the Holy Spirit getting his attention. J.D. wasn't sure.

He slipped the flashlight into his coat pocket, then realized he'd forgotten his umbrella. That was okay. Maybe the rain falling on his head would allow some of his hair to grow back. God could work miracles and maybe that'd be one of them.

He walked through the rows of cars, and it only took a few minutes to find the vehicle. It stood out like a toddler's drawing in an art museum. The flashlight pierced through the windows, and sure enough there was a head moving around in the driver's seat.

Hope I don't scare them . . .

It was definitely Samantha. J.D. could tell just by seeing the long hair. Her face turned, eyes squinting and shielding themselves with a hand.

"Samantha?" he called out to the closed window and door.

By now he was pretty much soaked, but that didn't matter. He didn't want to freak them out, but he also wanted them to know there was a better place for them to spend the night.

"What do you want?" the woman called out from behind the glass.

She sounded alarmed and defensive.

I don't blame her.

"Look—I'd like to offer you a place to stay—to get out of this weather."

"How'd you find us?"

The window hadn't moved an inch. Samantha was blocking any view to the other seat, but J.D. was pretty certain Lily was sitting right next to her.

"Your daughter mentioned you sometimes slept out here.

But—with the rain . . . I knew the shelter would be jammed. So I looked around for an 'orange dorkmobile.' And there you were."

"We're fine, really," Samantha said.

He could feel his arms start to shake. This coat wasn't helping much, either.

"I know. But you don't have to stay out here."

"Just because we're on the street doesn't mean I'm not a good mother."

"The thought never crossed my mind," J.D. said.

He knew she was wondering whether he was telling the truth. Maybe she was weighing their options, trying to decide if he could be trusted, wondering how safe it might be to go home with a stranger.

"Look, I don't mean to sound ungrateful, but I need to know what this is about," she said.

"Fair enough," J.D. stated.

He wiped rain off his face even though more simply filled its place.

Just tell her the truth.

"My wife and I? We had a daughter of our own once. But we lost her. And since then, we haven't felt anything but her loss."

The woman just looked at him, the fire in her eyes suddenly dimming. J.D. knew he was talking to a kindred spirit. This mother knew a little about loss.

"Truth be told," he continued, "I think we need this more than you do."

For a long moment J.D. stood there, soaked, silent, waiting for some kind of answer. But that's all anybody could do. Ask and then wait.

Just like they'd done for so many years with their Heavenly father. Asking for the ache to go away. Waiting for it to leave them. Yet they were still asking and still waiting.

The mother turned her head for a moment, saying something to her daughter, then she turned back at him.

Her answer was barely audible behind the window.

"Okay."

That was enough for J.D.

ELENA

This whole faith thing hadn't bothered Elena until now. Until she realized that it wasn't just changing her husband's temperament. It was also turning him into a bona fide moron.

"The union's gonna defend you, right?"

They had been talking in the living room for half an hour, long after putting the boys to bed. Bobby had come home late and he finally got around to telling her the news. About the fact that he had chosen to do something *stupid* and that he was on the verge of losing his job and being sued for money they didn't have. All because he'd been trying to stand up for some kind of silly thing.

"No," Bobby said, his face already showing defeat. "They say I acted outside my capacity. That I exceeded my care mandate. And if they're seen as backing my actions they'll become liable, too. So unless I apologize, they're cutting me loose."

Elena wanted to scream.

"So apologize."

"I can't. Not for bringing someone to Jesus. Especially since they're looking to turn this into some kind of example, where no first responder will ever bring up God again for fear of what might happen to them."

Bringing someone to Jesus.

It sounded so simple, so insane. This wasn't like stopping at a rest stop or going through the drive-thru at McDonald's. She didn't understand how Bobby could truly believe he'd brought anybody to Jesus when there was no person or face or voice or anything to bring the person to in the first place.

"So to prove a point, you're willing to risk *everything*?"

"I'm not trying to be prove a point," he said. "I'm trying to be faithful."

Bobby didn't look defensive at all, which made Elena even more frustrated.

"And you were. The guy's safe in Heaven now, right? Thanks to you and Jesus. End of story."

Dial up a prayer next time you're at church. Put the wooden cross by his gravestone. But leave this whole faith thing out of it. Keep it away from his family.

"For this man, yes, you're right," Bobby said. "But what about the next guy?"

Elena shook her head, staring down at the carpet, then over at the couch across the room. She had thought they already had enough to deal with after Carlos had come and gone in a blink. She still hadn't heard from him and she'd been worried all day. Now her husband was delivering shocking news in the most subdued manner he could.

She didn't know what to say. She truly didn't. She wanted to curse at him and leave the room, but that wasn't going to change anything. She could try to persuade him to change his mind, but she knew her husband. Nothing could change his mind after it had been made up.

"I spoke with Tom's friend Liam Katz. He's willing to represent me, but he's asking for a retainer of twenty thousand."

Well of course he did.

"Where are we supposed to get that kind of money, Bobby? We've got one's month's mortgage in our checking account, and all our cards are maxed out."

The face—blank, controlled, calm—didn't look away. Elena knew what was coming but didn't want to hear it, didn't want to even think about it—

"I don't know. But I trust God to provide a way."

Trust.

God.

Provide.

A way.

The Saturday morning cartoons were over. The comic book movie had ended. This wasn't some kind of fun little fantasy anymore. This was their *life*. And Elena knew she needed to gain some kind of control over it since Bobby had obviously lost his mind.

"Bobby, we're not in church. I need to know where we're gonna get the money. *Especially* since you insist on tithing on every nickel we make. Tell me—where is it gonna come from?"

He didn't say a word.

He didn't have an answer.

Of course, this man before her certainly had *all* the answers when it came to a man dying in his arms. He had all the words and the answers and he couldn't say enough. But now, sitting across from his wife, Bobby didn't have a single thing to say. Besides the whole *God's-gonna-take-care-of-it* sort of thing.

She stood up, done with this for now, knowing she was just going to say more angry and hurtful words that couldn't help.

"I can't go through this," she said as she headed toward the stairs.

"What do you want me to do?"

Elena stopped and turned around. Last night Bobby hadn't hesitated in protecting her. So why couldn't he do the same right now? Why couldn't he just protect her and their family in the most simple and basic way?

"Sign the statement. Apologize. Do *whatever* they want you to."

There was nothing more to do. That was the solution. The end.

He still sat, looking up at her, his face exhausted and searching.

"Or what?" Bobby asked her.

She had said enough. She answered by heading upstairs and ending this conversation.

There wasn't anything left to talk about. She wasn't a pastor or a shrink. She was a wife and a mother and a nurse and she lived in the real world dealing with real problems and solutions. Bobby would wise up. He had to wise up.

There was no other choice.

J.D.

Twenty-five hundred square feet for the two of them. That's how big their house was. It wasn't monstrous, of course, but it still was more than enough room for a couple. Of course, for a while there had been three of them. And of course, the spaces felt even bigger and more empty since she'd been gone.

J.D. had been trying to assure them that things were okay ever since he'd watched them climb into his car. Now he introduced them to Teri, who had been waiting in the kitchen. His wife looked dressed and ready for company, something that slightly amused him since it was past eleven. Lily already acted right at home, while her mother couldn't have looked and acted more awkward.

Teri had offered them something to drink, asked if they wanted something to eat, but Samantha had shook her head and said "no" over and over again. J.D. understood and told them he'd show them around the house. Then they could get to bed since it was late.

Samantha had made Lily take off her shoes before they headed up the carpeted stairs. J.D. showed them the guest bathroom.

"You make yourselves comfortable. Take a shower—use the kitchen—whatever you want."

"I appreciate you doing this," Samantha said.

He gave her a nod. "Don't you mention it. It's our pleasure—isn't it, hon?"

Teri stood at the top of the stairs and gave a nervous, uncertain smile. This was out of his wife's comfort zone. *Way* out of it. But then again, J.D. didn't have lots of experience inviting strangers into their home and telling them to feel free to do whatever they wanted.

The first bedroom in the hallway used to be a guest room, but they had converted it to an office. The only other bed in the house happened to be in Kathleen's bedroom. Both of them had known this, yet neither had said a word about the reality of the situation.

J.D. opened the door. Before they could enter, Lily gasped in joy behind him.

"Look, a dollhouse!"

He looked at Samantha and Lily while something fluttered around in his soul. Something he couldn't quite describe.

"This was our little girl's room."

At least they'll know now I wasn't lying back there in the parking lot.

Without asking, Lily darted into the room and knelt down in front of the dollhouse. She picked up a figure and moved it inside one of the rooms. The ground inside his soul shook as an ocean pounded against the stone walls more fortified than Normandy. There was something about this little girl kneeling down playing with her toys . . .

He felt Teri's hand clutch his arm behind him. When he looked around at her, he could see the tears in his wife's eyes. J.D. understood.

"I put fresh linens on the bed," Teri said to Samantha.

This surprised him.

He didn't even need to ask.

Teri moved away from them in a hurry. Probably to save face and try to control her emotions. J.D. just glanced at Samantha and smiled.

"It'll be okay," he said. "Make yourselves at home."

"We won't get in your way," the faint voice of the mother said to him. "And in the morning, we'll be quiet when we leave."

"Well, if it's all the same with you, we'd like you to stay. That is—if you like it here."

Tomorrow's a long ways off. Just be okay with today.

He'd heard that once and rather liked the simplicity of that statement.

"We'll see," Samantha said.

"Good. Fine by us. Good night."

IT TOOK HIM a few minutes to find Teri. She wasn't in her bedroom or the kitchen. For some reason she was standing in the unlit stillness of the dining room. When he got close enough J.D. could tell she was crying. They were silent tears, the kind she'd been good at keeping secret over the years.

Keeping secret from everybody except me.

He took her hand and studied the outline of her face. The world and the passage of time brought age and wrinkles and weight to the face in the mirror, but nothing could destroy love and connection.

J.D. didn't want Teri to hurt anymore. Yet the truth was obvious.

"This is the right thing to do, Teri."

She took her hand away and wiped her cheeks. She exhaled and he could hear the quiver in her voice.

"I don't want to do the right thing. I just want—"

Her voice faltered and more tears came. Those tender eyes were still there, the same ones he fell in love with on their first date in high school. The kind that looked up at him and asked him to come alongside and love her. The innocent kind that didn't know the dark world out there and needed someone to help guide her through it.

He wasn't sure he'd done a good job of that.

He tried to pull her close but she only shoved him away.

"I understand," he said in a gentle voice. "But that's never gonna happen. She's gone. And, sweetheart—wouldn't Kathleen have done this for them? For that little girl?"

There wasn't a hint of anger or patronizing in his voice. He sincerely meant what he had said.

Teri didn't respond but rather moved around him to head back out of the dining room. He knew that he had to give it time. That's what their counselor had said years ago. To give it time. So he marked the calendar in his soul with a red marker. Maybe in this lifetime they would find some kind of peace about Kathleen. It hadn't come yet. But J.D. wasn't giving up. Not yet.

MOMENTS LATER, AFTER shutting off most of the lights downstairs and double-checking to make sure all the doors were locked (something he hadn't found himself doing for a long time), J.D. ascended the steps the same way he used to when Kathleen was a newborn. Their house had been so silent then, with Teri almost obsessed with never waking up the baby. He still knew every crack in the floors of their house.

The door to Kathleen's room was ajar and he could hear voices talking as he passed. He didn't want to snoop, but he couldn't help stopping by past the doorway when he heard Lily's voice.

To hear a girl in their house again. It was like a man who'd been stuck in the city finally taking off his shoes and breathing in ocean air.

"Can I call them grandma and grandpa?" her sweet little voice said.

J.D. couldn't help but smile.

"Not yet, baby. We have to see if this works out first."

"But they like us, don't they? I mean, isn't that why they brought us home?"

"Well, they were gonna bring somebody home," Samantha said. "And it happened to be us. But—this is still new for them."

He wanted to say she was wrong, that it wasn't like they simply needed *anybody* to come into their home off the street.

You're our somebodies.

And he really believed God had allowed them to meet.

"I think we should thank Jesus anyway," Lily said.

There was a pause and for a moment, J.D. thought of leaving the hallway and heading to their bedroom. Yet he kept listening, waiting.

"C'mon, Mommy. I like being able to sleep in a bed and not be afraid to go to the bathroom."

"You're right, Lily-pad."

"Thank you, Jesus, for being so good to us. For watching over us. And for always taking care of us."

There was a shuffling. It sounded as if Samantha was giving her daughter a hug and a kiss. And if she hadn't, J.D. was going to go in there and give her one.

"What do *you* want to thank Jesus for, Mommy? You have to tell him."

"For you, baby. For *you*."

A river full of memories filled J.D. as he walked back to his room with a smile on his face and tears on his cheeks. He felt like the weight that had been holding him on the ground had finally given way, that now he was suddenly flying like a helium balloon let free. He wasn't staring down at the earth anymore. He faced the horizon wondering where the wind would take him.

Somewhere good, he hoped and prayed.

JOE

———

The burden wasn't there this morning, and that was good. Maybe that meant his faith was growing. Joe often would meet people at church or on the street and he'd get to know them and then they would leave. The burden would stay with him, which meant he needed to remember them and pray for them. He knew he shouldn't worry. That the Bible told him to give all his worries and cares to God because God cared for him.

He cares for Lily and Samantha, too. Wherever they might be.

It gave him comfort that God knew exactly where the mother and daughter were. Maybe Joe would never see them again. Waking up this morning and feeling the way he did . . . well, that was a possibility that might really come true. But it was okay. He had to trust God that His will would be done.

Now Joe had to make sure he finished the floor he was cleaning in the meeting area attached to the kitchen. The big beast of a machine he was working with—a floor-buffing machine that seriously seemed to be the same age as him—was unruly and feeling more and more heavy in his hands. It used to be that he could bench press more than anybody around him. People would be struggling to lift something and Joe would come by and swiftly pick up whatever they had. But those were the ole days.

The not-so-good ole days when I believed I was Samson without all the hair.

He was staring at the floor when a figure entered the room. Joe recognized the guy immediately. It was the black kid from the other night. He was carrying a duffel bag over his shoulder and a Bible in his hand.

The loud bellow of the machine's engine shut off.

"Back again, huh?" Joe asked with a welcoming smile.

The guy looked around the room. "I'm looking for the guy who runs this place."

"Well, He's in Heaven. But I think you mean Pastor Matt. C'mon, I'll take you to him."

Nothing had changed in the kid's demeanor. He still looked anxious and fidgety, like someone was going to grab him at any moment. As Joe led him through a back hallway and toward the offices behind the sanctuary of the church, he wondered if there would be any more visits from the cops, and if so, what he would do then.

He knocked on the pastor's door and then entered, seeing Pastor Matt at his desk. Joe liked the fact that the pastor had an open-door policy. People could come in when they wanted. They didn't need some kind of scheduled meeting or an appointment made by a secretary. If and when people needed the pastor—and people *always* had a need eventually in their life—there would be someone waiting and available.

"Pastor?" Joe asked. "I got somebody here to see you."

The kid slowly stepped in the office and glanced around. The walls were lined with books. There was a cross on one wall, larger than the wooden crosses Pastor Matt had handed out the other evening. The pastor stood up behind the large computer monitor he'd been working behind.

Joe started to leave the two of them, hoping the kid would find what he was looking for.

"No, please," the guy called out after him. "I want you to stay."

Joe shrugged and looked at Pastor Matt. He knew it was okay with the pastor, but he was curious what the guy wanted. Why he wanted Joe to stay.

The kid shifted the bag to his hands, then stood so he could see both of them.

"Listen, last night, this guy saved me," the kid said, nodding at Joe. "I mean, *Jesus* saved me, but this guy was definitely part of His plan. Same as you. And when I heard you talk, I knew you were talkin' to me even though you didn't know you were talkin' to me. What I'm tryin' to say is—I asked the Lord to save me, and He did. Which means this—this bag here—it ain't mine no more. I wanna do good with it, 'cause up until now? It's done only bad. I want this bag to help people. To change them like it changed me, if you know what I mean."

The kid's words were spilling out so fast with this nervous energy that Joe had a hard time taking it all in. He could tell the pastor was trying to process what was being said as well. Before either of them could respond, the guy took the bag and dropped it onto the pastor's desk. Then he unzipped it to show the contents inside.

It made Joe's wish jar look like a child's piggybank.

Pastor Matt just stood there looking at more cash than Joe had seen in his life. And in typical pastor fashion, he glanced back at the kid with his calm and friendly face.

"I can't take this," the pastor said.

"Don't ask me to bring it back," the black guy said. "It was already dirty when I stole it."

Pastor Matt gave a quick glance to Joe. "I still can't take it."

"Why not? Last night I read how Jesus got killed, that Judas guy gave the Temple back their money. They couldn't keep it, so they did something else with it."

Pastor Matt gave a *yeah-but* sort of nod with his hands starting to open, but the kid kept talking fast and furious.

"The way I figure, it's like this: The money's like sin. And sin is *death*. So me keepin' the money would be like *askin'* for death. But not just dyin'. More like hell and damnation."

Taking his time, the pastor gave him a nod and let a moment pass before talking. Joe liked this about the guy. Careful to talk, always trying to think before saying something.

"You've been reading," the pastor told the kid.

The kid held up the Bible in his hand and then gave an embarrassed smile. "I kinda stole it from my motel room."

Another pause. Joe stood listening, waiting for the pastor to speak. He wasn't about to say anything. He loved hearing about what had happened in this young man's life, but he didn't know what to do with all that cash.

I'd go bring it to the shelter and hand it out to all those in need.

He wouldn't think twice about doing that. But then again, Joe was no pastor.

"Would that I were Solomon," Pastor Matt said as if he were talking to the bag-o'-money.

"Who?" the young guy asked.

"The wisest of all men, who always knew how to solve difficult problems."

"Well, it seems to me—if he was so smart—he'd take the money."

The pastor gave him a nod, then looked again at Joe. "I

think you're right. He would take it . . . and then he'd give it away."

You're reading my mind, Pastor Matt.

Joe glanced again at the duffel bag stuffed full. He thought again of his wish jar.

This gave him an idea.

GRACE

Grace stood at the edge of the room at the pregnancy counseling center she'd brought Maggie to. The teenager had asked to go that morning. It wasn't something that Grace tried to force upon her.

Earlier that morning, after they had breakfast with Matthew and just before he left for work, Grace had managed to find something she'd been thinking about the night before. Sleep hadn't really come last night. She had been worried and wondering how Maggie was doing. She couldn't stop thinking.

This morning she had given Maggie the item she'd been looking for, an adorable pink outfit she'd spotted at the baby store one day, the kind children wore when being baptized or taking their first studio photo.

"I've had this for a while, but it doesn't look like I'll be needing it," she told Maggie as she gave it to her. "I want you to have it. I figure there's a fifty-fifty chance it's the right color."

Maggie, so cute and also so clueless, so like any teenager, just took the outfit and offered a smile.

"It's so cute. Thank you. Pink is perfect."

She paused and then looked down at her belly. "I really think it's a girl."

That was when Grace told her they could easily find out. And Maggie had almost literally jumped at the chance. She'd slid off her chair at the kitchen island with wide eyes. "Where could I find out?"

Now, with Maggie resting back on an examination table with her belly exposed and covered with that blue goo, Grace watched as the ultrasound technician started working.

"Are you ready to see your baby?" the woman asked Maggie.

Maggie gave an anxious nod. Grace responded with an affirming, *it's-okay* smile.

Grace had imagined this moment many times. The wand moving over her abdomen. The pulsing lights and lines on the flat screen on the wall right in front of them. The sound of the heart beating.

It took just a few moments, then the nurse stopped moving the wand.

"See it?" she said to Maggie.

Because the young girl was so far along in her pregnancy, the image on the screen was easy to see. The baby was sleeping, the round head and the sharp prick of a nose. The legs were balled up and a hand moved close to its face.

Maggie smiled, laughed, shook her head, marveling at the image that moves and shifts slightly.

"You were right," the technician said to Maggie. "That's your little girl."

The young girl absorbed the image and information. Then she looked over at Grace.

"She's beautiful," Maggie said.

Your life is never going to be the same, Grace thought.

There was something so pure in this room and this picture.

Grace didn't feel a bit of envy or jealousy and she wasn't even sure why.

She felt her heart full and beating, just like the little tiny life inside of Maggie.

A sweet little baby girl whose grandparents didn't want it. But whose mother wanted it. And needed it.

I need this, too, Grace realized. *This girl and her girl are two gifts God brought.*

Grace closed her eyes, already tear-filled, and said a quick and silent prayer to bless these girls in magnificent and amazing ways.

J.D.

The regular morning routine had been altered dramatically, which was fine to J.D. Teri cleaned dishes while he finished the coffee in the pot. They had made a large breakfast of eggs, bacon, waffles, fruit, and even donuts. J.D. had made an early run to the store to make sure they had enough choices. Samantha and Lily didn't eat much, but he was glad that they were still there.

The water running upstairs told him that Samantha was taking a shower. Another good sign.

He glanced at the pictures on the wall in the living room. Lily had asked about them this morning and he had told her the skinny guy in the camo gear was him. Then he told her about the Marine Corps and the Vietnam War and how he had earned those souvenirs now framed next to the photographs. Teri had been surprised that he shared as much as he did. He usually didn't say much about Vietnam. But Lily wanted to know, so he wanted to tell her.

The sound of a giggle upstairs made J.D. and Teri glance at each other. He loved hearing it.

"Now *there's* a sound we haven't heard in a while," he told his wife.

She dried her hands and then walked over to the stairs to investigate. J.D. sipped his coffee and waited for a moment, then he quietly followed.

Lily was twirling down the hallway in a series of pirouettes. Well, with attempts at pirouettes. But she looked adorable trying, her hands raised high, her legs twisting and bending. He noticed that she was holding a Ballerina Barbie in her hand.

She's seen the pictures on the wall.

Last night after they had arrived, the hallway had been too dark to see any of the portraits on the wall. But now they were evident, since the walls were covered.

Pictures of their little ballerina.

Some of the photos showed Kathleen around the same age as Lily.

Lily kept twirling and spinning until she ran into Teri, who reached out with both arms so the girl didn't fall.

J.D. stood at the top of the stairs, staring at the two of them down the hallway. Lily's eyes focused on the pictures she had just bounced by.

"She's so pretty," the innocent and honest voice said to Teri.

"Yes," Teri said. "She was."

Suddenly the bright and bold on the girl's face dimmed and diminished. She realized even at her young age the truth. These were pictures of their daughter, who was now gone. Lily looked like she thought she might be in trouble.

"I'll try not to remind you of her," Lily told Teri.

And then it came.

The moment.

The open door and the chance.

J.D. could only see the young girl's face, not Teri's. But he thought and expected and assumed what his wife might be feeling and thinking.

Then—

His wife bent down and sank to her knees, then took the girl into her arms.

"Don't you worry about that, sweetheart," Teri said. "You just be yourself, and everything'll be fine."

Teri clutched the girl in her arms, not letting go. Lily's face looked surprised and joyful. He assumed there were tears on Teri's face, yet he also thought that something was different.

Something had changed. In a good way.

Maybe there was only one person to help Teri move on. And it wasn't going to be J.D.

Maybe those pirouettes of hope would grace their house—and their hearts—once again.

Maybe they already had.

ELENA

She couldn't remember the last time she'd seen Bobby in his blue dress uniform. Even though she was still mad at him, Elena couldn't help thinking how handsome he looked standing in front of the mirror in their bedroom. A part of her didn't even *want* to know what was going on, but she'd just gotten home after a shift and she needed to ask.

"Where are you going?"

Bobby continued staring into the mirror while he twisted the tie in the most perfect knot he could. This seemed ironic, given Bobby's natural perfectionistic nature. It seemed at odds with his very *imperfect* actions.

"Preliminary hearing," he said. "The union wants to hear 'my side' of the story."

She stood, still facing him in the mirror, wanting him to look at her for a moment. He still didn't seem to *get* the gravity of all of this.

"Have you decided what that's gonna be?" Elena asked.

His eyes landed on hers. "The truth."

"Which truth? The one that keeps you working, or the one that gets you fired?"

He flattened down the tie, satisfied with the job he'd done, then turned to face her. Sunlight from the window behind him made his profile almost glow like some kind of angel.

He needs to take off the halo and come back down to earth.

Elena breathed in, calming herself, trying desperately to get him to just listen.

"Querido, I'm asking you one last time. *Please* don't do this."

The square, solid, strong face didn't change.

"I have no choice."

"Oh, you're making a choice, Bobby. You've been making a lot of choices lately."

"I've been what?"

This got his attention.

Good.

"*You* decided to start going to church without ever asking how I felt about it. You risk your life for strangers every day, but what about us? What about me?

"Do you have any idea how alone I feel? Do you even care? My own brother doesn't feel welcome in my house anymore. And now this. You're just gonna throw everything away. But hey—you have no choice."

Her words echoed off the walls in their bedroom. It was unfortunate that so many of their arguments—*too* many in fact—came in this place that should have been a sanctuary and a refuge.

"Elena, I'm trying to do the right thing. Don't you see that?"

She could only see a stubborn, foolish grown-up man acting like a child. He'd been acting like one for the last two years.

"Think about the boys. Will you at least do that?"

Elena knew there was absolutely nothing that Bobby wouldn't

do for those two boys. The only times he gave in to something or went against his wishes, it happened to do with Michael and Rafael. She knew this, and was now using it against him.

"I am thinking of them. I'm setting an example for how I hope they'll behave when they're men."

The words coming out of his mouth . . . So foolish, yet he believed every single one. With an earnestness that he had on their wedding day.

"Don't you understand," Bobby said, pleading with her. "The easiest thing I could have done on that day of the accident—and the easiest thing I can do now—is to not say a word and just walk away. But I can't. I won't."

She bit her lip and shook her head, exhaling and trying to control her emotions.

"It sounds like you've made up your mind then," she said. She might as well have been talking to some automated customer service line on the phone. "Hope it all works out, Bobby."

Something about the way she said his name sounded almost like a curse. Elena left Bobby and his decision and the fate of their family in the room behind her. She had tried and failed. There was nothing more she could do.

Bobby was her husband, not her patient. She simply wished he'd act like it.

LACEY

His laugh. Somehow it just seemed to fill in some of the cracks inside of her. There were so many but it felt good for once to not feel like she was apart.

"Nice view, huh?" she asked Carlos as they walked along the bike path close to Fullerton Avenue.

He nodded and then looked toward the city skyline. "I don't think I've ever been here before."

On their left, Lake Michigan looked calm and endless. Soon enough the water would be starting to freeze or possibly even covered with ice and snow.

"You should see this place in the summer," Lacey said. "It's where all the beautiful people come to ride their bikes and jog and show off their tanned, lean bodies."

"So does that include you?" he said with a smile.

"I'm the one who usually is not paying attention and almost gets hit by a pack of bikers. They can be pretty dangerous."

"Are we talking about the bikers who wear leather jackets or the ones wearing those little tight shorts?"

She couldn't help laughing, herself. It was another thing that had been missing for quite some time. Something that she hadn't even realized was gone until the sound of it reminded her.

"Are you going to go back to see your sister?" Lacey asked him.

He had already told her about the incident the other night. She had yet to tell him about the incident with the Chinese food. Lacey didn't want him to think she was really crazy. Only slightly would do for now.

"I can just see my sister asking, 'So how'd you meet her?' Trying to be all sweet and friendly. I'd be like 'Oh, we were both thinking about jumping off the same bridge. But you know, Lacey's totally great.' "

"Sounds like a match made in Heaven to me."

A blast of wind made her tuck her hands into her long coat. Carlos walked close to her, occasionally bumping into her arm. She liked the slight connection, the reminder that someone was so close to her, interested in her and listening to every word she said.

"Mind me asking why you became a Marine?"

Carlos shook his head. "The billboard."

For a second she thought he was joking again.

"No, I'm serious," Carlos said. "When I was a kid, I saw the billboard. You know, the uniform, the sword. If I could've signed up then, I would have been the first eight-year-old Marine. I loved being a Marine."

"So what changed?"

His face stared out toward the skyline again.

"Me," Carlos said.

"Got tired of being a hero?" she teased.

He chuckled and shook his head, his face still lost; he seemed to be searching for something in the distance.

"Funny thing about war. It shows you who you *are*, not who you wanna be."

They walked for a few silent moments until reaching a stone

bench that looked out over the water. Carlos sat down as if he might have been by himself, wanting a moment to just reflect and remember. Lacey felt awkward but sat down beside him, wondering where he had suddenly gone.

His body looked tight and rigid as he seemed to study the lake in front of them. Lacey noticed his hands grabbing his knees, then prying at them as if he were trying to screw them off. His fingers curled, the knuckles white, hands shaking even as he just stared off into space and didn't say a word.

The demons that liked to knock at her door late at night surely did the same to Carlos.

"You okay?" she asked.

"Not really."

A pause.

"Bad memory?"

He gave her a nod, still not looking at her, still not smiling. "Something like that."

"I'm a good listener."

The words hovered above them for a moment. Lacey didn't know what else to say.

You've said that to guys before.

The silence followed those times, too.

He'll talk when he's ready. He might just need time. Give him time.

They still had time. They still had today, tomorrow as well. The other night, tomorrow had started to slip away and become an impossibility.

He gave me back tomorrow, so I can give him as much time as he needs.

Lacey started to say that it was okay, that she didn't need to know, but Carlos spoke before she could.

"Early one morning, near a place called Sarbesha, we were

stuck on a mountainside at about eleven thousand feet, about to get overrun. Then—out of nowhere—comes this chopper, cutting its way across the valley, chain gun blazing. Looking to pull us out. The pilot was a friend of mine. Big Korean guy named Sam. I can still see his face. He was calm and collected and just smiled at me."

Carlos was looking at her now as he told the story, the intensity still on his face and in his eyes.

"But just shy of our perimeter, an RPG found him. Blew off his tail and took him down. I remember this huge fireball. Intense heat. Hot enough to melt the sidewalls of the fuselage. The crew chief and copilot were already gone, but up front, Sam was trapped in the cockpit. He was less than a hundred feet away. I wanted to save him. He came to save me. But I couldn't. I just stood there. Watching. I was too scared."

He let out a deep breath and then clenched his jaw. Lacey knew without even having to be told.

"He died."

His eyes searched the sky, the background, the city skyline all while Lacey stared and wondered what she could possibly say. There was nothing to say. Not now. She might be able to understand his pain but not these memories. She just needed to listen, to sit alongside him and wait for him to continue.

"Now I see it—over and over and over again," Carlos said. "It's my punishment."

She wanted to take off this coat of guilt Carlos wore the same way she always wished someone could do the same for her. It was like some thick, ugly, bulky coat that simply needed to be tossed. Yet as hard as one might try, you couldn't take it off.

The wind made her shiver, then pull her arms close to her sides. The lake looked so wide and so empty.

Talk to him. Say something. Tell him what you're thinking.

So she did.

"I don't know what you did or didn't do over there," Lacey said. "What I do know is this: you saved me."

She slipped her hand over his. Carlos didn't react. He simply kept looking out over the water, the hurt inside as clear as the city beside them.

There were so many things she could have said. So many things she *wanted* to tell Carlos. But Lacey simply leaned her head against his shoulder and stayed there. Maybe—hopefully—those words would eventually come.

JOE

For a second, while he sat on the exam room bed being checked by a nurse, Joe remembered that first night in prison.

Soaked in terror sweat, eyes awake, body numb from the hard slab bed, head hearing and seeing things that weren't there.

Everything in him back then and every aspect of his life could be summed up in one word:

Rage.

This was what made him kill a man with his bare hands. This was what sent him to Stateville, where more than half the inmates were convicted murderers. This was what kept him safe and alive those early days behind bars. This was even what finally brought him to his knees.

A raging fire finally being quenched and put out.

That man was long gone, and the fire that used to be there had been replaced by another fire out of his control. The kind that brought him back to the hospital, back to being prodded and picked over.

Joe had tried to joke with the nurse, but she didn't feel like laughing. Or talking. Or even really looking at him. So he'd shut himself up and let her do her job in peace.

"Sorry I'm a bit soaked," he told her.

His T-shirt looked the way it might have if he'd been working out on the beach in the middle of a hot Chicago day. He'd been sweating ever since leaving the church around lunchtime.

The doctor who eventually showed up didn't seem to be too friendly, either. He gave Joe a firm handshake and introduced himself as Dr. Farell. The nurse took out the digital thermometer that had been in his ear to give him the news.

"Fever's one-oh-four point six," she told the doctor. "He's burning up."

Don't think you need to be a doctor to see that.

Dr. Farell looked at the iPad that the nurse had been working on. "Any conditions I should know about?"

"T-cell prolymphocytic leukemia. Stage four."

Now *this* certainly got their attention. Both of them gave him that look, the one Joe knew well by now. The kind that people gave him even when they didn't know what the T-cell thing meant or how to even pronounce *prolymphocytic.* The look was like a death sentence, like someone about to watch a hanging. Most people don't know that this is one of the most rare kinds of leukemia, but he was betting the handsome young doc here knew it.

"There's also severe anemia," Joe continued. "Spleen and liver badly enlarged."

"Name of your oncologist?" Dr. Farell asked.

Joe liked this guy. He liked the fact that there was no trace of false hope or sympathy. This doctor wanted the facts and those were the facts, and okay then what's next?

"Dr. Emil Baranek. Stateville Correctional Center."

The nurse left them behind, having heard enough. *Dead man*

walking, gotta get to my other patients. The doctor simply gave a nod at the name.

"I assume you're out on compassionate leave?"

"Yeah," Joe said.

There was something so neat and orderly about the man standing in front of him. Joe would bet that this guy used one of those hair trimmers for his nose and ears. Probably got his hair cut every couple of weeks. Worked out regularly, got his clothes dry-cleaned, drove a luxury car, had a trophy wife or girlfriend.

But is your soul as orderly as everything else?

The messy, broken souls were the ones easiest to save. The ones Joe had met who lived safe, comfortable lives were often the most difficult to get on their knees.

Eventually, we'll all go on our knees, either in this life or the next.

"What about care since your release?" Dr. Farell asked.

Joe offered a sad sort of chuckle. "Well, mostly I just pray. I came in here the other night, but I never got treated. Ended up sleeping outdoors."

The doctor squinted his eyebrows and gave him a look of disbelief. "So—you're living on borrowed time, with a highly compromised immune system, and you decided to spend the night *outside?*"

"It's complicated," Joe said.

He didn't assume the doctor would want to hear the whole story, nor would he appreciate it in the least.

"There's an infection roaring through your system," Dr. Farell reminded him. "And it's highly unlikely I can stop it. I'll admit you. We can make you comfortable, but that's about it."

Joe thought about the other night, the chance meeting of Lily and Samantha. He couldn't help a smile starting to sneak out over his face thinking of the pair.

"Offhand, I'd say your little 'urban camping' adventure shaved your time down from weeks to a matter of days, if not less."

Joe gave Dr. No-Nonsense a nod. The guy wouldn't and couldn't understand and Joe didn't even want to try.

"Yeah, well—it was worth it."

J.D.

———

They could hear the knock on the front door. Whoever was there didn't ring the doorbell for some reason but rather pounded on the door. J.D. and Teri had been in the kitchen talking with Samantha while Lily played upstairs. The noise interrupted their conversation about Chicago winters.

It's gotta be something to do with the guests.

J.D. knew they never got unexpected visitors. Teri just wasn't the sort to tell friends and family to come by whenever. And by now, friends and family knew well enough to either schedule a visit or at least call ahead. So he opened the door, expecting someone looking for the mother and daughter, hoping that it wasn't some angry ex-husband or ex-boyfriend.

A man in a baseball cap and coat, probably in his mid-thirties, stood at the doorway holding a jar with money in it. J.D. was going to be polite and tell him "no thanks" but then noticed the taxicab still running in their driveway. Nobody was behind the wheel.

"Is Samantha there?" the guy with the thick Chicago accent and round, scruffy face asked.

J.D. turned around to call out for Samantha but she had walked to the entryway with Teri.

"You Samantha?" the cabdriver asked her.

"Yes," she said in an uncertain tone.

"This here's for you and your little girl."

Samantha moved closer to the doorway so she could see what was in the man's hands. She didn't take it right away, but rather stood carefully behind J.D., disbelief on her face.

"How did he know where to find us?"

J.D. didn't know who this "he" happened to be but he could imagine.

"He didn't," the cabdriver said. "He asked me to check the shelters near UC Medical, looking for a mother and daughter named Sam and Lily. Eventually I got to the one on Dillon Street. Apparently you slipped a note through the door, asking them not to tow your car and letting them know where you were going."

Samantha looked at J.D. with a tinge of guilt, but he admired her thinking. If he had turned out to be some kind of crazy person who kidnapped mothers and daughters and imprisoned them in the basement, someone would eventually come around looking for them.

The driver stepped in and gave the glass jar of money to Samantha. There was a note attached to its side.

"Do people usually trust you to go driving around delivering jars of money?" Samantha asked.

The man chuckled. "I *owe* him. Joe helped me out of a rough spot. There aren't many people willing to do that kinda thing these days."

"Yeah, he helped us, too," Samantha said.

"Make sure you read the note," the cabdriver said as he started to head back to the vehicle.

J.D. took the money jar from her so she could open up the folded letter.

"Dear Sam," she read out loud. "It looks like I'm gonna have to leave, and I don't think I'll be back this way. The 'wish jar' is for you and Lily. Turns out my wish is for both of you to have all your wishes come true. God bless. Your friend, Joe."

Samantha glanced at them with those dark, heavy rings under her eyes and a look of bewilderment, the same kind she had when J.D. brought them to the house. Then she stepped out the doorway quickly.

"Did he say where he was going?" she called out.

The driver paused by his taxi. "Joe's dying. I dropped him off at the hospital this morning."

Samantha turned to them, the note still in her hand. "I've gotta go see him."

J.D. understood. Whoever this Joe guy was, he was a kindred spirit helping these two out.

Samantha opened the jar and grabbed a wad of bills.

"Can you take me there?" she called out to the driver, who was still standing there as if he knew she was going to ask him for a ride.

"Sure."

For a moment, Samantha stood there, her glance moving to the stairs and the second floor.

"You go ahead," J.D. said. "She'll be fine. Teri and I will give her lunch and take her to the park for a couple of hours."

"Thank you. For everything."

He watched her rush down the sidewalk and climb into the cab. J.D. looked back at Teri, the glass jar still in his hands.

"Want to see what Lily wants for lunch?" he asked.

"What are you going to do?"

"I'm going to count and see how much the girls have."

had spent the last hour reading God's word and meditating on it. I know that those might be terms that seem natural coming out of a pastor's mouth, but they were *necessities* for any believer in Christ. They were necessary to grow, to be a child of God, to know what He wants in your life. I told people often that if the only time you spend with God during the day was during that fifteen-minute devotional, then your priorities were definitely out of whack.

The time I spent didn't mean all my questions were answered, however. It didn't mean that suddenly all of life's problems could be fixed. I still had this feeling inside me that something was happening, that the Spirit was moving. I still didn't know fully how.

But life and death don't wait for anybody. God controls those two things, and they were about to become front and center in my life on that quiet afternoon.

It started with a call from my wife. She didn't even greet me before launching into the news.

"Maggie's water broke," Grace's frantic voice said. "She's early—and she's already having contractions."

I instantly wondered if it had something to do with the ultrasound that morning. I didn't know much about childbirth. I did have an idea what contractions meant.

"Doesn't that mean—"

"Yes, that's *exactly* what it means. You need to get home and get us to the hospital."

"Why can't you take her?"

"She's in a lot of pain. I need you to drive so I can help her."

"Okay, just calm down," I said to my wife. "Everything's going to be okay."

And that was the precise moment I saw the revolver pointed directly at my head.

The kid with the money.

It wasn't him, but I instantly knew it had something to do with him. The guy holding the gun had snuck into my office somehow. I didn't think anybody else was at the church. Joe had said good-bye earlier in the day. My door might have been opened a bit—I wasn't sure. But now a broad-shouldered African-American man with a fearless glance aimed a gun at me.

Slow down. Slowly.

"I have to go," I told my wife. "I'll be there as soon as I can."

I carefully placed the phone down and then held up my hands.

"Listen," I said slowly. "There's a young girl who's having a baby right now, and I need to get her to the hospital."

"You should be worryin' about your future, not hers. My money?"

No surprise there. I nodded.

"It's right here. I haven't touched it."

I grabbed the duffel bag I had placed under my desk. Somehow I had known this bag would only bring trouble.

The guy walked over and took the bag, then stepped back. The gun didn't waver a bit. It'd be easy to say he was from a gang somewhere nearby, but that was too simple an answer. Who knew what this young man's story was? I'd heard enough of them and even been fortunate to have a few visiting the church, like the kid who stumbled into the church while I was preaching.

The stranger cursed as if he was spitting on the ground.

"What do you think Jesus would say about your taking my money?" he asked. My heartbeat was slowing down, but I still couldn't move in my seat and could barely breathe. My hands were still held out, and every single action I made was in slow motion.

"I think He'd know I didn't want it in the first place," I said.

"So you believe in Jesus?"

I had been asked that question twice lately, first by a man carrying a cross and then by a guy with a gun in his hands.

God's trying to show me something here.

"I do," I said with full confidence.

I was even more confident than I had been when I was asked last time.

"And you believe if I pull this trigger, you gonna *see* Him?"

I gave him a nod. "Yes. I believe we all will, sooner or later."

He let out a laugh, which released a bit of the tension in my back and sides. I could tell my comment cracked him up.

"Well, I'm sure you'll understand me hoping you're wrong."

I'll understand anything if you just get out of here.

I didn't move, the alarm in my head still going off about Maggie going into labor.

"I don't want to see you following me out, you got that?" the guy told me as he stepped back to the door. "And I don't want to hear you calling the police."

I gave him a nod. I wasn't about to tell him it made no sense calling the cops about a bag of stolen money that I was keeping under my desk. I didn't think they'd buy my story in the first place.

He stood in the doorway, still pointing the gun at me, the seconds dropping like dominoes. Then, thankfully, the stranger and the money were gone.

Frozen and silent, I waited, listening and watching for anything. And while I waited, I gave thanks for God sparing my life. Then I prayed for God to do the same for Maggie and her baby.

JOE

In his dreams, Joe saw a beautiful young woman coming to his side and smiling at him and holding his hand. *His* hand. Compassionate brown eyes looking at him not as if he was sitting behind bars, but rather as if he meant something to her. As if she needed to be there. As if time didn't matter, but waiting for him did.

It would have been a nice dream to have. But Joe realized when he opened his eyes that Samantha really and truly was by his side, looking at him and holding his hand.

"Well, hey there," he said in a weak voice that even surprised himself.

"Hi, Joe. I'm so sorry."

She sounded as if she had known him for years. It was a good thing to hear.

"I had no idea you were—"

"Everyone's dying," he said with a smile, trying to make her feel at ease. "I'm just at the head of the line."

She looked a little more comfortable, which Joe was glad to see.

"Thanks for coming."

"Isn't there anyone else you want to be here? Friends?"

"Don't really have any. Unless you count my pastor—he gave me a job, even let me serve as an usher. Knowing everything about me. *Everything*. But I figure he's already done enough."

"Family?" she asked him.

Joe figured it was about time he told her the truth. Not the horror stories, but the beautiful and awful truth he hated to relive. Like the ink on his body, this was a part of his life and legacy. He could never *not* see it.

Yet the light inside me blinds out the darkness of those past deeds.

"I don't have family anymore," he said. "A long time ago, I had a little girl about Lily's age. My little angel. I loved her, and she thought the world of me. I can still feel her wrapping herself around me to give me a hug and shout 'Daddy' in my ear. But I went and got myself into trouble. *Real* trouble, the kind you don't always come back from. By the time I got back? She was a fully grown woman with a life of her own. And no desire to get to know a dying ex-con. She didn't need a daddy anymore."

There was a pain that crept into Samantha's glance. Joe knew it well.

"I understood, especially since I hadn't been much of a father anyway. I guess that's why I was so fond of you and Lily. I was selfish, I suppose."

"Not selfish," Samantha said. "Just human."

Joe gave her a nod. He could only imagine being able to talk to his daughter now and to remind her again of his regrets and his hurt. To tell her he loved her and to ask for her forgiveness.

God didn't answer that door. Another one opened up.

The little girl drawing in her notebook that night at the hospital. Joe could still picture Lily next to him.

"Are you scared?" Samantha asked.

"No. Jesus has always had a soft spot for sinners, so I figure I'm all set."

That scared look crept back onto Samantha's face even though she was smiling. Joe understood. Man, if he could only explain how well he understood that uncertainty in the eyes, the heaviness wrapped around the face.

I've seen it for so long on so many.

"He loves you, Samantha. You'll see that. And somehow, someway, when you least expect it, you'll know. You'll *absolutely* know."

She tightened her shoulders and moved her hand to rub the back of her neck. "What makes you so sure?" she asked.

"Because He's God."

BOBBY

Sitting at the courthouse on the bench outside the pair of wooden doors, Bobby thought of the time in ninth grade he'd been sent to the principal's office. It had been his first and only time, and the only reason he was there was that he had been sticking up for a fellow freshman being picked on by some upperclassmen. He learned that day that there were far better ways to go about a situation than punching a kid in the face. That might have been one of the first times he realized he wanted to help people in whatever way he could.

Telling them about eternity. What *better* thing could Bobby possibly do? If this world and this life really, truly was just a blink in an endless series of blinks for the rest of time, why shouldn't he at least tell others about it?

The sound of heels walking down the hallway made him glance toward the approaching blond woman. She carried a briefcase and a bit of an air as well. A woman sure of herself—her looks, her job, her confidence, everything. The kind that would eat people up in the courtroom.

Bobby wasn't surprised when she sat down next to him.

"Bobby Wilson, right?"

A tough voice, too.

"Yeah. Can I help you?"

"You might not want to," she said like a cop might. "I'm the attorney for Lauren Carson, the widow of Steven Carson."

"Oh," was all he could muster up.

I bet you have some great news for me today, right?

"Mind if I ask you a question?" she said.

"Is there any way I can stop you?"

He was trying to be funny but that word probably didn't even exist in this woman's world.

"In a few minutes, you're gonna go in there, and the union, the department, the city, *and* the county are gonna look to hang you. To *hang* you. And you're gonna let them do it. Have I got that right?"

"That's about the size of it," Bobby said.

"And after that I'm going to take you for everything you own. Yet you're still going to go through with it?"

Tell me how you really feel.

"Yes."

He had already made his decision. It wasn't a decision anyway. There had been a choice and a decision made years ago. Around two thousand years. And it had been a lot tougher than the one he was making now.

The woman shook her head in complete bafflement.

"Why?"

Her tone suddenly felt a little off. It sounded as if this was her true self, that she'd taken off the business attorney outfit and was simply talking, one human being to another.

This was another opportunity, just like the one he'd been given with Steven Carson.

"I was once asked, 'If you were accused of the crime of being a

Christian, would there be enough evidence to convict you?' From everything you're saying, it looks like the answer might be 'yes.' If what I did has suddenly become a crime—well, then I'm proud to plead 'guilty.' "

The smooth, flawless face just hung there like some detached painting on the wall. She still didn't understand or even *get* it.

There's a place out there, and I was given the coordinates for it and I need to tell others about it.

"I shared my faith with a dying man. It's something I've done many times these last couple of years. I talked about God to others even when I didn't have a personal relationship. No one ever cared about it—only now they do."

She shook her head, dismissing his words. "Times change. People who are smart change with them."

Bobby did the same thing she had done, refusing to believe her words.

"I didn't fail your client's husband. Medically speaking. I did *everything* I could."

The woman glanced around them for a moment, then talked in a more subdued tone.

"Off the record? I don't really care."

"Then why—"

"For my client? It's about punishing you. You need to know that. And for all of us—including the city—it's about finally stopping people like you from pushing your beliefs on others. I don't expect you to understand that. But it's one thing you should understand if you don't already."

She reached into her briefcase and pulled out something familiar.

The wooden cross he'd given to Steven before the man died.

"This cross is gonna cost you."

The doors beside them opened and a county sheriff's deputy stepped out.

"They're ready for you."

At least the deputy seemed to sound like he had a little compassion for the situation.

They stood and Bobby straightened his uniform. The woman simply looked at him without any empathy or understanding.

It was the same kind of look that changed the fate of mankind two thousand years ago.

He walked into the courtroom, knowing God walked with him.

LACEY

I t was like a switch turning everything off.

They had been walking down the dimly lit sidewalk after a cab dropped them off near Lacey's apartment. Ever since Carlos had shared his story, a silence had draped over them. She had changed the subject and spoken about other things, had tried to joke around, had even allowed the silence to last for much longer than she would have liked. But nothing was working.

He's shutting down and I can't do anything about it.

There was a part of her screaming inside the closer they got to the door of her apartment building. She didn't want to arrive because she knew what he was going to say.

The same thing they always said.

Lacey tried to tell herself this was different, that Carlos wasn't like that, that this was a totally different situation. Yet that deep insecurity that blew around her like the Chicago winds whispered that maybe it was something to do with her. Maybe when people got to know her, they weren't very impressed. They saw what she was like and they felt a big, fat "meh" so they moved on.

Stop it, Lacey. Don't.

She could see his face under the glow of the streetlamp above them. It had turned dark quickly, yet they hadn't even talked about dinner. Lunch had been so easy and so enjoyable. But that had been before the past was brought up. Before the hurt was unburied and exposed.

"Do you want to stay for dinner?" she asked her silent friend. "I make a mean PB and J."

She wanted to keep things light and not go back there, even though everything inside her wanted to tell Carlos she understood. She *got* it. She hadn't served in Afghanistan and she hadn't seen people killed in front of her, but Lacey still knew about war and grieving. You didn't have to go overseas to see horrors in your life. You didn't have to see blood in order to grieve the loss of a loved one.

"It's better that I don't," he said in a muted tone.

"Why not? Tell me—what's wrong?"

"Nothing. It's not you. It's just—I can't remember what it's like to feel anything but shame."

She moved closer so he could see her face looking up at him with earnest eyes.

"Carlos, you can get past this. I can help you—"

"That's just it. Nobody can help."

Not so long ago, Lacey had said that about herself. She had believed it, too. But she had been alone and hadn't seen the remarkable power of coincidence.

Which I don't believe in.

"Us meeting each other wasn't a mistake," she said.

"No. But sooner or later, it will be."

She took his hands and kept trying to pull it out of him, this fear and this shame and this dark everything.

"You don't know that," she pleaded. "Please. All my life, anyone I cared about has left me. Don't you do it, too."

"Lacey, I care about you—I really do. Which is why I've gotta do this. You deserve someone better. And me right now? I'm just too broken."

He didn't wait to see or hear her response but simply pulled her toward him and swallowed her in an embrace. Everything about him felt so hard, so rigid. She felt like she fit in those arms, her soft sweater and even softer heart maybe being a good thing for him. Lacey could chip at the hard places. She knew there was a kind and gentle soul deep inside. She had already seen it.

Carlos held her for a long time, and for a moment, Lacey thought he might have changed his mind. Yet he finally moved away and glanced down at her with that look.

That's a goodbye glance.

She knew it well. She had seen it plenty of times in her life.

"I'm sorry," he said as he turned to walk away.

Stop him. Grab him. Bring him back.

"We're all broken, you know," she called out to the figure disappearing in the dark.

Soon he was gone, unable to see her face buried in her hands, unwilling to stay there with his arms around her.

Leaving her, like they all did eventually.

JOE

The light had faded already, leaving the cold glow of the hospital lights above them, yet that was fine with Joe. There was plenty enough light in this room. He just wasn't sure how long it'd last.

"Are you sure you don't have to get back to Lily?"

Samantha shook her head. "I called the Newtons while the nurse was checking in on you. They said Lily's doing more than fine. They said it would probably take a three-alarm fire to distract her from the dollhouse she's been playing with."

Joe chuckled. He could see her just kneeling, playing with the imaginary house and the imaginary people. That was the beauty of being a child. You still dreamt of having the perfect home with the perfect family. The only thing that ever broke in dollhouses were the toys inside them. Lily didn't know that part of growing older was having your heart broken.

"Do you have any regrets, Joe?"

Samantha might have detected some melancholy on his face. He gave her a nod.

"Nothing but regrets. But no complaints."

The coughing came and grabbed him for a while, shaking him and causing him to close his eyes with the rattling. When he opened his eyes, Samantha just sat there with an affirming and sympathetic look.

"Those regrets put me on my knees," he said. "And with that I got forgiveness. But you know—I really would've liked to ask you out on a date."

A shade of color drifted over her kind face as she gave him a shy smile. It was such a sweet thing to see. So different from the terror that had filled her face the first time he met her in the hospital.

"So you think I would've said yes?" Samantha asked.

He laughed at the comment. In another world, they might have met and been sitting somewhere else having the same conversation. She might not have been homeless and he might not have been near death's door.

But we would've never met then.

She moved closer to the bed.

"Joe. We haven't known you very long, but no man has ever treated us better. So consider my answer a definite 'yes.' Effective as of this moment."

"So *this* is our first date?"

She gave him a charming nod.

"Okay," he said. "But only if you let me pick up the tab."

He expected to get another chuckle out of her, but this seemed to make her want to cry.

"Hey, I'm sorry. I don't mean to joke. I just—sometimes it's easier."

Samantha nodded and understood. "I just wish . . . I wish there was something I could do."

She still has no idea.

"There is," Joe said.

"What's that?"

"Could I see Lily one last time? I'll understand if the answer is no."

He didn't have to wait for her to say something. The answer was in her eyes.

That look . . . It was one of the best ones. The kind you remember the rest of your life. The kind you carry to your grave.

PRETTY BOY

———

Avoice told him to run. To get out of there. He'd said good-bye to G-Ma. That was enough. There was nothing left for him around this place.

My brother.

He felt something in his pocket. Something that he'd been given and something that had changed his life. A small gift, a symbol of a much larger gift. The wooden cross urged him to ignore the fear inside him and to do what he needed to do.

That was to see Kriminal one last time, even if he knew it was dangerous.

Pretty Boy knew his brother would be hiding in the chop shop. Nefarius and his men surely didn't know about the place. Not yet. But they would soon enough.

One chance.

That's what Pretty Boy told himself. All he could do was tell his brother the truth as he knew it now.

The lights in the garage were on but it was quiet. He could only see one car. Pretty Boy wondered if Kriminal had taken off in one of the others, splitting town to save his life. Yet he knew deep down that his brother wouldn't do that. It wasn't just the money that would make him stay. This was his place, his neighborhood, his life. Nothing was going to force Kriminal to leave. Nothing but a bullet.

"Lookit who it is—the prodigal son," the voice called out from a side door of the garage. "You got my money?"

"No," Pretty Boy told his brother.

Kriminal looked like he hadn't slept since everything happened. He wore the same clothes as the other night, with dark stubble covering his face and bags under his eyes. He looked like an animal ready to attack.

"Trick question, P.B. I went and got it myself."

He pulled the bag out from underneath a table and then he unzipped it, showing Pretty Boy all the money that was still there.

The pastor . . .

"Is he— Did you—"

His brother gave him a demonic grin. "Too late now if I did."

For a brief moment, Pretty Boy felt his heart fall and shatter on the ground. But then Kriminal just laughed it off.

"Nah, he's still vertical."

"How did you know?" Pretty Boy asked him.

"Skeezer and Lester. They spotted you going into the church while I was looking for you. Looking for my own brother who was hidin' from me. Skeezer called me."

"They're just teens."

"Don't matter. They're smart."

"Like 40 Ounce and Little B?"

Kriminal ignored the comment. "Know what I told Skeezer? I told him about our aunt. Remember—the one that got saved by that TV preacher? Remember the first thing she did? She went and gave that man every dime she had. I told them sheep follow the shepherd. So I bet the shepherd got my money. And you know what? I was right."

The words echoed in the large open space. Pretty Boy didn't say anything as his brother walked up to him, his anger clear.

"What's the matter with you?" he shouted at Pretty Boy and added some curses. "Everything we've been through. What I've done for you. Live together, die together."

Pretty Boy wanted to never hear that stupid saying again for the rest of his life.

Kriminal shoved him back and then slammed him against the wall, cursing at him again. Pretty Boy could smell liquor on his brother's breath. That wasn't the reason for his fury. That came whether the whiskey was there or not.

"So after everything, what do you do?" Kriminal shouted, his hand against Pretty Boy's chest. "You go and *steal* from me? In front of everyone?"

"It's not like that."

More curses and a harder pressure against his chest. "Then what is it? You found Jesus and suddenly you think you're better than all this?"

"No."

"Is Jesus gonna pay the bills, buy you a car, get you outta this hood?"

He could if he wanted to.

"Listen to me," Pretty Boy said, moving and getting out of his brother's grip. "I see things now I didn't see before and I want to share that with you."

Kriminal laughed, his curses becoming more colorful, his anger more cynical and dangerous. "Oh, so you're tryin' to save me."

But God showed His great love for us by sending Christ to die for us while we were still sinners.

"We all need to be saved," Pretty Boy said.

"And your Jesus is gonna do that?"

"Yeah. He died for us all. So that we *could* be saved."

His brother just shook his head in disgust and disbelief. "Yeah, well I wouldn't dic for Him."

Kriminal walked back over to where the bag sat on the ground. He looked around, staring at the ground, thinking things over.

"Why'd you come back here?" Kriminal finally asked. "You know what I gotta do now. Or did you think I was just gonna forgive you?"

Pretty Boy stared at him for a moment. He pictured his brother only ten years old, passing him the basketball while they played on a court outside. Back before life handed them a sentence with guns and gangs and godlessness. Back when there was no GPS to take them out of this hellhole.

No way you can do it. No way.

He believed that. But even more than that, Pretty Boy believed in the truth. That truth G-Ma had spent their whole lives telling them about.

"I'm already forgiven," Pretty Boy said. "But not by you, K. You wanna forgive me so I can go back to doing what we did. Jesus forgave me so I don't have to. And neither do you. That's what I came here to tell you. We don't have to be who we are."

Kriminal's curse bounced around the walls and the ceiling around them. He spit his words at Pretty Boy.

"Shut up about Jesus, P.B. I mean it."

"I can't and I won't. He loves you. In a way no other person on this earth can love you."

The words had been too much for Kriminal. He cursed while

he rushed over and grabbed Pretty Boy's arms with both hands, shoving him back against the wall. His arm bolted up and his fingers clenched while Kriminal contemplated lashing out and doing what he did best.

A blast of ripping metal and the door slamming against the wall came from behind Kriminal. His brother turned around while Pretty Boy could already see the face coming through the door, like a wolf slipping out of the night.

"Remember me?" Nefarius asked them.

He held a SIG 9mm in his hand and looked a lot more conscious and alive than he looked when Pretty Boy last saw him.

Kriminal stood there, both hands empty, his body looking uncertain about what to do. Pretty Boy stepped away from the wall and behind his brother by a couple of steps.

Nefarius moved closer to them, the gun aimed at their heads.

"You thought you could steal my money? You thought wrong."

Nefarius smiled and then Pretty Boy moved. His arm clawed at Kriminal's side. He rushed in front of him just as the sound of the handgun went off and kept going off, ripping through the shop.

But God showed His great love . . .

The great seeping pain stole Pretty Boy's breath as the bullets tore into his back. Two of them. Everything went numb as he fell into his brother's arms.

The gunfire stopped as Kriminal's eyes widened and his arms held him for a brief moment. While Pretty Boy crumpled to the cement floor, he could hear his brother's footsteps. Then he heard shuffling and metal—probably the gun—clacking to the ground. More shuffling and then footsteps. All while the world leaked out like oil draining from an engine.

Half his body felt gone. Just gone. The pain took so much of him that he couldn't even try to fathom it. And meanwhile his head kept replaying the Bible verse over and over, as if the words were alive and mysterious and wrapping him up like a bandage.

Kriminal was hovering over him suddenly, cradling him for a moment, tears in his eyes. Disbelief covered his face, but not the angry kind of disbelief from before. This was the shocked and surprised and overwhelmed kind.

God showed His great love and I can do the same.

"P.B. you hold on, you hear me?" Kriminal screamed.

Pretty Boy's mouth felt numb, his muscles bending out of his skin, his breaths twisting together. Yet he forced his hand toward the pocket of his jeans.

Christ dyin' for us on the cross. Dyin' for us sinners.

Kriminal cursed again while Pretty Boy grabbed the wooden cross and then moved to stick it into his brother's hands.

"No no no no, P.B., no—"

"Believe," Pretty Boy said.

He saw Kriminal's wide eyes and shaking head and opened mouth and tried his hardest to smile at them before the world turned to black.

Then he saw another image of Kriminal. This time smiling. This time looking humble and heartbroken. This time looking like the brother he always knew he had.

Live together. Die together.

Pretty Boy was taking with him the dyin' part.

God, let him take home the livin' part. Please, God.

Eternity finally grabbed his hand and pulled him forward.

A pastor prays.

The streets blur by. Matthew drives the small car down the long streets while Grace sits in the backseat with Maggie. He can hear the grunts of pain and wishes he could do something.

Lord help her, be with her. Keep her safe, please God.

"Something's wrong," the young girl cries out.

He glances back and sees Grace panicking, her arm around Maggie and her eyes on him.

"Can't we go any faster?" she asks in an order.

"Not safely."

"Do it anyway. She's in trouble."

He speeds up. The hospital is not far, just beyond the bridge, just a little farther away.

The prayers don't stop, just like the car and just like the buildings and lamps they pass.

A soldier surrenders.

Deciding to leave the first and last glimmer of hope he found behind. Deciding to climb into the first vehicle that would pick up a hitchhiker at this time of night. Deciding to get into the long-nose Kenworth truck and tell the driver to take him anywhere.

Just far away from this place.

Carlos knows he needs to move to escape this cloud, this black covering, this cracked pavement in his soul.

Deep down as the truck moves along the streets toward the freeway and out of state, Carlos knows that he'll never be free and never be out of this state.

The shackles of yesterday will remain. But at least nobody else will have to know. At least he can try to keep them hidden again.

The war was won the moment he decided to not do a thing. He waved a white flag that would forever color the rest of his life. Whatever life that might be.

A criminal flees.

Leaving his brother's body on the cold floor of the shop along with his heart, Kriminal starts to bolt the garage. Yet someone else is waiting for him.

Another magazine of bullets tears through the space. Kriminal doesn't hesitate but sprints toward the emergency exit and out of the building, and then, knowing he hasn't been shot, he keeps running.

Down the street toward something he knows won't ever be okay.

Away from the only thing he ever wanted to protect in his life and that suddenly dripped out through his hands.

Gasping and running, Kriminal has nothing to lose and plans to do everything and anything to get out of this.

A woman prays.

Alone now, again, in an empty apartment, in an empty room, with an empty heart, Lacey hears the sudden downpour outside. She shivers on her couch, pulling her arms around her legs, then shoving her hands into the pockets of her sweater, trying to simply cover every part of her skin. Trying to simply hide every part of herself that she can.

Then she feels something with her hand.

She grabs it and takes it out and then looks at it. And she realizes that he put this in her pocket. That he wanted her to have this for some reason.

Why, Carlos?

The dim light still shows the outline of the wooden cross in her hand. This tiny lightweight piece she holds. She stares at it, studying it, feeling scolded by it.

Faith. Belief. God and Jesus and Heaven and hope and all that good great wonderful sort of stuff that people tweet and post about on Facebook. So sweet until life sucks everything from you and then you're left with what? With *what?*

She doesn't understand this cross and the man who gave it to her.

Why?

Her body trembles, so she decides to try. To not ask but to dare. To demand.

She stares up past the ceiling and past the stormy clouds toward somewhere she can't begin to fathom or even start to believe in. But why not? Why not?

"They say you're a God," she cries out, gripping the cross. "So show me. Show me."

The rain falls and the storm continues and she waits with drops of doubt and despair.

A medic doubts.

Bobby drives slowly, not eager to head home, taking the longer route to get onto the interstate. He thinks about the hearing, where nothing seemed to go right. Where the faces just watched him, wondering how he could be such a fool. Outside in the parking lot, the lawyer he'd met named Andrea pulled up beside him in a shiny black BMW and rolled down the window. And all she could say were two parting words.

"Told ya."

Just like his wife had told him. Just like others in the department had warned him. To just let this pass. To just keep his mouth quiet. To not make it a big deal. To just forget the whole thing and move on.

Yet this whole thing is about not hiding, about not keeping quiet, about not covering up.

"And then he told them, 'Go into all the world and preach the Good News to everyone.' "

He knows he's a paramedic and a husband and a father. But more than that, he's a believer. Armed and equipped to tell people about the Good News.

Yet the rain suddenly falling and night suddenly darkening bring question marks, as rapidly as the street signs he's passing. Bobby knows that he'll need to tell Elena everything. And she's not going to be happy.

A mother winces.

Afraid, knowing that something is wrong, that her baby is in danger.

Maggie doesn't feel how fast they're going and doesn't see the streets they're passing. She can barely hear or feel Grace beside her trying to comfort and soothe her pain.

All she can feel is the searing pain ripping through her belly and her bottom and every inch of her.

"You're gonna be okay. It's gonna be okay."

She barely can hear the voice next to her as she opens and shuts her eyes, simply thinking about seeing her sweet little baby girl. Maggie holds her belly, hoping and crying out and afraid that she's waited too long.

Afraid that this is all her fault.

This is her fault and her judgment and God's finally getting His due.

A grandfather navigates.

The storm suddenly stalls their drive to the hospital. J.D.

doesn't like driving at night, but at least he still can, unlike Teri. They are taking Lily to the hospital at the request of a dying man named Joe.

Only two nights ago they had been driven to this very same hospital after a heart attack scare. Now they're heading back, feeling like the whole world has changed.

J.D. looks in the back to see Lily's smile, her sunshine on this dark night. It's a glorious thing to witness.

"I can't wait till you meet Joe," she tells them. "He's special. You'll see."

Teri turns around in the passenger seat. "You do understand he's very sick, right, sweetheart?"

"Yeah. That's the sad part. But don't worry. I've been praying for him."

That sincerity is the kind that can win a war and cause a revival and birth a miracle. That simple, pure faith of a child. The kind Jesus talked about.

Turn from your sins and become like a child.

Blameless and full of faith and eager to run toward God.

J.D. wants to meet this Joe. He wants to pray for him, too.

KRIMINAL

———

Pounding pavement. Huffing and panting. Legs burning and lungs gasping. Kriminal ran in the rain. Unable to process everything fully. He just knew he had to keep running and to stay alive.

If he stopped he would be dead. Nefarius was following him and probably the only reason he hadn't caught up to Kriminal was the fact that the guy was still carrying the duffel bag. Plus he still carried some of the wounds from the other night.

Hate'll give you fuel you never thought you had.

There was a stretch of deserted buildings he ran toward, then another street he crossed without bothering to check for oncoming traffic. Kriminal saw the arches of the bridge on the horizon like some kind of dark halo. He knew that if he could get to the High Bridge crossing over the south part of the Chicago River he'd be okay. On the other side was a newer development with some wealthy areas where people like Kriminal and Nefarius and their kind didn't go into. Cops would see them sticking out like bloody thumbs. Nefarius would finally stop following him.

It felt so far away. Just like Pretty Boy. And G-Ma. And

40 Ounce. And Little B. And everyone else he knew. The life he once had. The boy he once was.

Pretty Boy hadn't realized he'd been doing all this for his brother. To help him—to help *them*—get out of this hellhole. To try to start another life. At least for P.B. To jumpstart the music thing. To get him going and to get him out of there. It was for him, and he had the right motives even if he wasn't on the right side of anything good.

"Believe . . ."

His brother's word kept up with him just like the footsteps following him.

He was going to be dead by the end of this night. That's what Kriminal believed. The money was gone. P.B. was gone. And Kriminal was going to be gone, too.

He crossed another street, hurdled over the curb to make sure he didn't trip, then he continued sprinting up the ramp, hugging the northbound lane of the bridge. They were running against the traffic, the cars flying by on his right as he ran.

Believe, just believe, brother.

Kriminal couldn't help slowing down a bit. Every muscle inside him hurt and he knew the sleepless nights and the bruises from the other night weren't helping. He was strong but he wasn't fit. That suddenly was very apparent as the steep incline forced him to falter.

He turned for a moment.

Nefarius was even closer.

The lights bearing down on them like spotlights from all sides.

He knew that his enemy wasn't going to stop. That he wasn't about to let him go regardless of where Kriminal was heading.

Nothing to believe in.

Nothing but himself.

Kriminal saw an opening, so he took it, jumping out into the two lanes of the traffic and trying to tear across it.

He heard the rip of brakes, and a skidding car suddenly jolted and blared its horn. Kriminal stopped near the middle of the four lanes, then heard the shout behind him.

"Time to burn!" someone called out.

It was like a ghost following him and warning him of what was to come.

Then the gunshots blasted through the night. Kriminal started to run but felt a slug tear through his arm. He fell down to his knees, more lights coming, more cars slamming on their brakes.

It's comin' it's too close it's gonna—

The vehicle squealed and lurched over to the other side of the bridge, over toward Nefarius, striking the guy and catapulting him into the side of the bridge railing. The duffel bag exploded, sending cash floating down all around them.

Kriminal still knelt, seeing more cars coming, turning, crashing.

A silver BMW veered off sideways and crashed into a stopped car, sending it into the other lane. A small Prius approaching in the other direction barely missed the oncoming vehicle, then turned sharply with brakes howling and flipped, the car turning upside down.

An oncoming truck tried to stop, its brakes screeching, but it clipped the overturned Prius and sent it spiraling across the bridge.

Kriminal watched all this, seeing the hand of God somehow protecting him while Satan himself moved the rest of the pieces, to devastating effect.

Amazing how a group of lives suddenly intersected on that bridge late at night under God's watchful eye.

All connected by one thing.

Two lines. Horizontal and vertical. The most simple design in the world becoming the most profound.

The cross connecting and combining and closing in and ultimately caring.

The figure on the cross knowing.

The man the God the Son fastened to those two lines all for them.

Begging to be there for them and take the fear and grief and the anger and the worry and the regret.

Dying for those things, for them, for all these broken pieces that can never be made whole without him.

Two lines.

The dying figure nailed to them.

Jesus.

Name above all names.

The abyss and the ascent.

The hand in the wound.

All of us can know and are allowed to know. The only question is, will we?

Will we allow those broken pieces to not be glued back together but instead to be overlooked?

These fears and these questions and these pieces were all about to be brought together in one singular event . . .

J.D.

J.D. still grips the handle of the steering wheel, staring forward for a moment at the scattered vehicles on the bridge, exhaling and then looking at Teri.

"That was close," he says.

They both turn to make sure Lily is okay. Her seat belt was on and she sits in the back on a car seat, a look of surprise on her face, her bear clutched in her arms.

He sees something else in the rear window.

A car. Not stopping. Headlights approaching.

Before he can say or do anything, a shrill noise splits the air.

His body tightens.

Metal on metal, mashing and moving the car. They're suddenly in the air, until another booming thud thrusts, then yanks them.

Then J.D. can feel it and he knows.

They're no longer entirely on the bridge.

The car has torn through one of the guardrails, and it's now starting to dangle.

Just like all of their lives.

CARLOS

The semi slows down and the driver points toward the bridge in the distance. Carlos can see the flames lighting up the carnage.

"Stop the truck," he yells at the driver.

"What?"

"Stop the truck!"

He rips open the door and doesn't wait for the truck to stop. Carlos had seen an overturned car, another vehicle hanging over the side on a broken guardrail, another one in flames. Figures moving around like the walking dead.

There's no sort of epiphany inside of him to act. No sort of *this-is-your-moment-Carlos* sort of thing. No triumphant music and no second-guessing. He begins sprinting toward the bridge and is halfway there when he realizes this is the High Bridge over the river. The same one he'd found himself going to. The same one he'd been hanging over.

The same place he'd met the angel named Lacey.

J.D.

Even though J.D. is still as a rock, his body still in shock over being pulled and then slammed against the side of the bridge, he can feel the car moving. The air bag has exploded and he can't see forward. Yet he can feel them swaying forward, the back side tilting up like some kind of teeter-totter.

His arm reaches over to Teri to make sure she is okay. She coughs, the air bag in front of her as well.

"Are you hurt?"

She gasps a no through her coughing. Then the crying begins

in the backseat. He turns and sees Lily still there, hair wild now and eyes swollen. She calls out for her mommy.

"It's okay, sweetheart."

J.D. is calm and speaks slowly. He knows this is a bad place to get emotional. They have to get out of the vehicle, starting with the girl. A searing pain races through his right leg. He knows that's not a good thing, but he's not going to say a word about it.

"Listen to me," J.D. says, glancing back at her. "Can you open your door and climb out? Carefully."

Lily tries but can't move the door.

"It's stuck!" she screams.

Lily unbuckles her seat belt and then scrambles toward the front of the car with them. The car starts swaying forward more.

"No, Lily, stay back there," Teri orders, holding her back with her hand. "Try not to move, okay?"

J.D. can see now in front of them. The dark night and the reflection of the water below them.

Far below.

He glances over at Teri, who gives him the same grave look.

They don't have much time left. But they can't move—not anymore.

GRACE

Maggie's head rests on Grace's lap in the backseat of the damaged Prius. The girl is still breathing heavily and crying, her face grimacing in pain. Outside the opened door, Matthew kneels, trying to help, but looking unsure.

Grace can see Maggie writhing in pain but she can't stop it.

"Matt, there's too much blood," she chokes out. "She's hemorrhaging."

"I know, I know."

His voice is as helpless as their situation. The smell of gas and smoke wraps around them. People around them are crying and screaming and hurling out names.

Maggie's knees buckle and she cries out as Grace helps move her dress up. This isn't a time for modesty. They have to do something. Anything.

"We have to get to the hospital," Grace says.

"We're out of time. There's just—the baby's coming—I can see her head."

"I can't do this," the young girl howls out.

Grace grabs her hand and grips it as hard as she can.

"You *have* to, Maggie," she orders with her lips talking against the girl's ear. "Your little girl wants to see her mommy."

Maggie keeps crying between the gasps of air and the deep exhales. Grace looks at her husband, who appears both ready and helpless at the same time.

The gas and the smoke seem to be getting worse.

God help us, please, God.

CARLOS

"Help me please help me help me!"

An endless burst of terror from some unseen voice shouting on the bridge. Carlos runs toward it until he reaches the fire. The flames seem to encircle the car.

"Get away, it's gonna blow," someone shouts at him while they pass running the other way.

The seconds flick out like a set of rounds lighting up the night sky.

Carlos bends over and can see through the orange and red

blaze. A head. Someone inside the car trapped. Glass broken next to them. They're still crying out for help.

He doesn't hesitate.

He's spent enough time of his life hesitating. Enough moments regretting that hesitation. And he's not going to wait for anything anymore.

Leaving the fear behind, Carlos darts and jumps through the flames while he heads toward the car, opening the door to free the man trapped inside.

BOBBY

The car skids to a stop right at the base of the bridge. Bobby hadn't been called here. He'd been trying to figure out what to say when he got home and had been driving slowly and carefully only to arrive at this carnage and mayhem. Everything suddenly sped up, and the medic in him rushed to action, peeling out of the car and then sprinting up the bridge.

He scans the scene and sees a black guy kneeling in the middle of the road, trying to move, but holding his side, obviously wounded somehow.

A car is halfway off the bridge, just hanging there somehow, stuck, but not for long. Another car is overturned. There are flames around a vehicle. Then he sees the silver BMW.

Andrea. The lawyer.

He runs even faster now, heading to the flames, trying to go to the most dangerous area to try to help. To try to save lives and get people out of here.

J.D.

"Teri, listen to me."

J.D.'s voice is almost as quiet as a whisper. It's as if he fears speaking louder will cause the car to move again.

"We need to get Lily out of the car. Now. And I can't move. My seat belt's stuck."

Teri nods. They're both trying to stay calm, especially for the girl who hasn't stopped crying but is not keeping still.

"Go. It's okay. Slowly."

Teri moves between the seats as carefully as she can. The movement sends the car forward again.

She stops and waits.

BOBBY

Bobby sees the dazed, bloodied face staring right at him but not seeing a thing. It's the lawyer, the one who looked so polished and so pompous back at the courthouse. Now she looked like a disheveled and wounded animal.

Someone from behind is rushing toward them, screaming to stay back. Andrea doesn't seem to hear or see or even notice.

"Andrea," Bobby calls out to try to get her attention, to try to get her to move.

He keeps running toward her, then reaches her and wraps his body around her, grabbing her and pulling her over to a nearby SUV. A fireball blasts out of the car and shakes the ground.

Bobby is shielding Andrea now, looking around him and trying to figure out a plan of what to do next.

The scared, messy face stares up at him. The woman is still in shock.

"Are you okay?" Bobby asks her.

Andrea can only nod. That's enough for him. He bolts up and then heads toward the swaying car that seems to be moving again, sliding farther down.

J.D.

J.D. can feel it. He knows what's going to happen as he braces one hand on the steering wheel. With the other hand, he takes Teri's hand. He looks at her with a glance that tells her it's okay and that he loves her.

The car begins to dip even farther, slipping down more, slowly, but not stopping.

Lily cries and calls out for her mother and Teri is gasping.

Then the thud on the back of the car stops the motion.

J.D. looks and can see someone on the trunk of the Hyundai, his arms and chest hanging over it, then his whole body starting to climb it. J.D. sees the head for a brief moment, the skinhead that makes him think of the military. Then the figure is hanging over the back window.

The motion has stopped. For a second or two. Then the car shudders and keeps slipping forward.

BOBBY

Bobby is almost there when he sees the tall, lean figure in the leather coat jump onto the back of the tilting car like some kind of superhero. Yet this isn't Batman or Superman, but rather his brother-in-law.

What in the—

"Hang on, Carlos!" he shouts, not trying to make sense of the situation, only thinking about the heads he can see inside the car.

He hurls his body and slams into the backside of the Hyundai next to Carlos. Bobby is now standing on the trunk, moving his whole body and trying to force the car back onto the bridge.

The sound of screaming comes from inside the car. It's a little girl in the backseat.

Bobby tries to jump up and then smack the car down again. But the two of them still aren't doing much good.

Another figure suddenly appears next to him. Another is behind him, another man launching himself against the side of the trunk.

There're more. They're helping.

With the car now being held down by maybe half a dozen people, Bobby hears his brother-in-law tell them to look out. Then he begins to kick the back window, trying to shatter the glass.

More screams as the glass finally gives way.

Bobby looks up and can only see Carlos staring down at the half-collapsed windshield.

"It's okay," Carlos tells the screaming voice in the back. "Give me your hand."

There are grunts and voices around them. The car is still pinned but continues to move a bit.

"I'm scared. I don't want to."

A voice in the front seat says something that Bobby can't hear. Then a small hand reaches out from the backseat. Carlos pulls her up and then passes her on to Bobby. He doesn't move off the back of the car but gently gives her over to another man waiting to take her.

Carlos kneels and looks into the car.

"You're next," he tells the woman in the front seat.

J.D.

Teri looks at J.D. and shakes her head. "No, I can't. I'm not leaving you, J.D. I won't."

J.D. still holds her hand and he grips it. Hard.

"I'm not asking you to," he tells his wife. "Now you get on. I'll be right behind you."

Fear is keeping her stuck in this front seat alongside him. Teri is shaking her head, tears in her eyes, a lifetime of regret and despair in this car, unable to climb out.

She doesn't believe him. She's never believed him, and that's been part of the problem.

She's never believed me because I haven't believed myself.

Calm, controlled, all there with her, J.D. simply says, "Darling, in thirty-six years, have I ever lied to you?"

Teri keeps looking, still so uncertain, still afraid to make one single move.

The car lurches forward again.

"We can't hold her, she's slipping," a voice from the back calls out.

The man standing in the backseat, the one who pulled Lily out, yells at them.

"If this is gonna happen it's gotta be now!"

J.D. is desperate. "Please, Teri."

He kisses her.

She sighs, still crying, still in terror.

"I love you, old man," Teri says.

They both know it's probably the last words that will ever be spoken between them.

Teri is pulled up and then lifted out of the Hyundai. The guy helping her now leans over through the seats so he can see J.D.

"You're finished here, son," J.D. tells the stranger with the short crew cut. "My seat belt's stuck. And my leg's broken."

The man reaches over J.D. and tries to get the seat belt loose. He pulls it and yanks it but it doesn't budge.

"He's stuck," the man shouts out to the back of the vehicle. "The belt's jammed."

BOBBY

Still adding weight to the back of the car, Bobby hears Carlos give them the verdict on the driver. He quickly scans the area, looking at the people around him.

"We need a knife. Has anybody got a knife?"

Nobody comes forward, so he gets on a knee and then climbs in the back of the car. A shard of glass skins his leg but he ignores it as he keeps going.

He reaches over the seat and tries to unjam the belt buckle with Carlos. Neither of them can get it loose.

Motion.

The car . . .

"The two of you need to get out of here. Now."

The man behind the wheel is an older guy, probably in his late sixties or early seventies. Bobby is impressed that he's so calm in the midst of this storm.

He has another idea. Bobby slides behind the driver's seat and then squeezes against the crushed door.

"One trick left," he grunts out. "If I can make it work. C'mon, baby—"

Where's the lever? Where is it?

He finds it and pulls, the lever reclining the driver seat back. The older man cries out in pain as the seat straightens out. Bobby climbs over toward the backseat and looks over the man, who is sweating and breathing heavily.

"His leg is broken," Carlos reminds Bobby.

"Then this is gonna hurt," Bobby says. "Start pulling him back. We gotta slide him *under* his harness."

Both men pull at the trapped body, grabbing under his arm and yanking.

For a moment it doesn't look like it's going to work.

Then he suddenly starts to move. And while they pry him free, the driver simply grimaces and keeps his mouth shut, still sweating and wincing but never crying out.

Soon the body is being lifted out of the back window by other helpers.

The car . . .

I'm not gonna get out of here.

Bobby is in the backseat, Carlos starting to head out the back window, when the car jerks again.

It all happens at once.

Elena.

Carlos is above him, standing, reaching out to him, then grabbing his hand and pulling and yanking.

He's scampering out of the car until he can't feel anything and he's in the air and then Bobby knows he's falling to his death over the bridge . . .

Until he slams down on the hard surface of the bridge, breathing and looking up to see the car now gone.

Bobby then looks at his side and sees Carlos on his back.

Out of breath and still reeling to take it all in, he can only think of one word to say to the man who saved his life.

"Thanks."

It's so insufficient but it's something. Carlos just shakes his head, his breathing still fast and quivering.

"Don't mention it," Carlos says.

f I could tell Maggie's daughter what happened that night, I would tell her this.

I would say that all her mother ever wanted was for her to live. To breathe. To have a life. To know a life that was better than her own.

Maggie was brave in those final moments. Braver than I would have been. Actually braver than I was just being there, trying my best to help her to push, to endure the pain, to make it through.

My wife was the one who really was her champion and cheerleader. I think the guy in me was simply too shocked and scared to know what to do.

The crying and the breathing and the sweating and the bleeding and then suddenly, I had the great honor to hold this sweet, precious life in my hands. They were shaking, but at the same time I wasn't about to let her go.

Neither was Maggie.

The first thing out of her lips was asking if her baby was okay. She asked how she looked, then wanted to see her.

Maggie's own life was fading. Yet she suddenly didn't seemed interested at all or worried about herself. She only wanted to see her baby girl and hold her . . .

The young mother's life—the tiny blink of a life she unfortunately had—suddenly seemed worth it when she held her daughter. The decision she had made in the first place had been validated. She was there. She was real. And her cry—that was very real and very loud.

The baby had survived the crash in some miraculous way.

In those first few moments, when Maggie looked at her baby with a look that seemed to know the gift that she'd been given, that *all* of us had been given, she told us her name.

Faith.

Even while Grace and I tried to tend to her, tried to figure out a way to get her to the hospital, still hoping and waiting for an ambulance to come, Maggie could only talk about her baby.

She said this to Grace.

She reminded Grace how she had wanted to be there when her child was born. Then she told Grace that she just had been.

Maggie wanted to know about the assurance of Heaven as she held her tiny Faith. She asked me whether or not it was a lie. She wanted to know that if she was going to see Jesus on that day.

"I've accepted Him in my heart. Promise me He'll accept me."

The last words I told Maggie were the following:

"With all my heart, with all my soul, I *promise* you. He will."

If I could tell Maggie's girl anything, I would tell her how her mother died holding her in her arms, watching over her. She didn't close her eyes while the light inside of them faded. My hands eventually took you and scooped you up into arms that weren't going to let go.

Two women were given gifts that night. So was a man.

Maybe, hopefully, when Faith is older, we'll be able to tell her the whole story. We'll be able to tell her how we stumbled upon her birth mother in the most miraculous fashion. How God truly gave us this gift in the darkest of nights.

I still can only imagine what Maggie saw after leaving her baby behind. I know she wasn't sad anymore. She wasn't frightened. She's wasn't young and alone.

One day I'm sure we're going to look at Faith and see that beautiful young woman named Maggie inside of her.

JOE

There were worse places—and times—to die. Joe knew this, and he found himself grateful.

The white, hollow glow of the lights above them didn't matter, nor did the beeps from the machines attached to and surrounding him. What mattered was that even though pain seemed to be swallowing him whole, someone still stood by his side.

"Lily's on the way, Joe."

He looked at Samantha from his bed, his back resting on it and his head propped on the pillow. This wasn't the way to talk to a lady. He wished he could simply sit across from her the way normal people did. To talk and get to know her and Lily and to be able to laugh and look forward to tomorrow. Yet that was for another person in another story.

A nurse named Elena had been coming into the room more frequently than the other nurses had, checking to see if either of them wanted anything, wondering if there was anything else she could do. She looked like a kind spirit, this nurse. Just like Samantha.

He could tell that Samantha wasn't taking this lightly. Sadness seemed to drip off her face like some kind of soaked rag being squeezed out.

"It's okay, you know," he said. "I'm not afraid. I know where I'm going."

She nodded but didn't seem to be cheered up in the least. Samantha seemed to be fighting the tears back, and the only way she could do that was by being silent.

Joe saw snapshots in his mind suddenly. His daughter when she was young. The curls in her hair. A woman named Naomi he once loved dearly. The face of the man he killed—not the face he saw that night, but the one the family made sure to show him at the court hearing when he was sentenced.

The small square confines of his cell. The way those uniforms never stopped smelling even after being washed. The hate tattoos he could remember getting. The preacher who never stopped talking to him. The feel of bare knees on the concrete floor of that cell the early morning when he finally surrendered it all and was unbelievably given *everything*.

He regretted those decisions yet still felt humbled to know they all led to that one great decision. And that led to many other bright things and moments of hope.

Even this moment.

Joe looked over at Samantha and smiled.

"You know, my whole life, I was only scared of one thing. It was dying alone."

With all the strength he had, which wasn't much right now, Joe reached over and took her hand.

"Thank you . . . for being here."

Samantha started to cry, her free hand reaching over to wipe off her cheeks.

For a moment, his eyes closed. It was difficult to push them back up. Joe knew. He just knew.

"Tell Lily I'm sorry," he slowly mouthed out. "Tell her I couldn't wait."

And with that he closed his eyes and took his final breath. This hard-fought scar-filled life was finally over, a painful blink leading to an eternity of eyes wide open to awe and glory.

ELENA

The woman's cries had turned into whimpering after ten minutes. Elena had tried to comfort her but she also knew it was best to let her grieve in her own way. Death worked itself into hearts in various ways. There was never an antidote or a prescription or a suggestion that anybody could offer. Time was the only thing that worked.

She had never gotten to know Joe, even though she had seen him at church whenever she went. He had seemed like a nice enough man, but Elena also knew the pastor loved taking in troubled souls. Little did she think she'd witness him passing away in front of her.

The door opened and the doctor stepped into the room carrying a clipboard. He stared at the EKG monitor. Elena watched Dr. Farell to see his reaction, but there was nothing. No alarm or surprise at the silent machine, no disappointment at the flat white line, no sympathy for the woman hovering over the bed trying to control her emotions.

"How long since the code?" Dr. Farell asked her.

"Twelve minutes."

He checked his watch. "Let's call it twenty-one thirty-five."

The doctor did his duty, recording the time on Joe's death certificate. Elena felt so helpless, but there was nothing she could do.

"Cause of death: unidentified staphylococcus septicemia," the doctor said out loud as he wrote onto the form. "Contributing causes: stage four prolymphocytic leukemia."

Elena could hear the pen scribble the doctor's signature. He then passed the clipboard to Elena and casually glanced over the still body on the bed. She could see Dr. Farell's eyes land on the nightstand next to the bed and stare at it for a moment in disbelief.

She hadn't noticed it before. There it was.

The wooden cross.

The doctor could only shake his head, then departed without another word.

The cross . . .

It felt like this thing had been following her around ever since they'd been given out. Following her either like some kind of stray puppy, or like some kind of storm clouds resting over her soul.

Just leave this woman to grieve.

She moved away from the bed and started to leave, yet something pulled her back in. Elena thought of Carlos for some reason. Seeing him walk away into the darkness, not turning around, refusing to stay.

She moved back toward the bottom of the bed so she could see the woman. Bloodshot and swollen eyes looked up at Elena.

"Is there anything I can do for you?" she began to ask, but then she was cut off.

Cut off by the EKG machine.

No.

The sudden beeps made them look at Joe, and then the machine, and then back at each other.

That's not right.

The woman looked at her with disbelief, with wonder at what was happening. But Elena didn't know.

The machine went flat again.

Did we just see that?

They were both silent, looking at the massive, still body on the bed, white and gray stubble on his face, eyes closed. He looked content.

Then suddenly his lips moved.

No, no, what am I seeing?

A whisper in the deathly quiet room.

"For thou art the Christ, the Son of the living God."

Elena couldn't breathe. Her body shook, her eyes unable to blink, her mouth suddenly half open.

Then the heart monitor spoke for them, with steady and suddenly loud beeps that kept coming and didn't stop. One after another after another.

The woman kept looking at Elena, wanting and begging to know what was happening. She was speechless, her eyes filling up again. The color was gone from the woman's face and Elena knew she probably looked the same.

All the signs. Every vital. Everything is just . . .

"Normal," Elena said out loud to make sure she wasn't dreaming.

She swallowed and her mouth felt dry. Elena suddenly felt afraid. She couldn't move and didn't know *what* to do.

Joe's pulse—it was steady. It was somehow strong.

There's no way.

Then he opened his eyes. Joe opened his eyes. A dead man suddenly looking up at them.

Move—get the doctor. Do something before you lose him again.

But Elena just couldn't for a second. She just—this wasn't happening. She wasn't witnessing this. Things like this *did not happen today.*

Joe just stared at them with a look of wonder and uncertainty. But he was indeed looking at them, his strong eyes moving from the nurse to his bedside friend.

"What—just—happened?" the woman asked both of them.

"Something pretty amazing," Joe whispered.

This was enough to get Elena moving, shuffling out of the room and then tearing down the hallway to get the doctor.

She went to the nurse's desk and told them to page Dr. Farell and asked where he might be and then she sprinted toward the stairs, knowing an elevator would take too long. She almost hit a patient slowly walking down the hallway and she apologized but didn't stop.

Her skin felt alive and she still felt like she couldn't breathe. A part of her almost seemed to fly down those steps as she turned the corner to take more of them.

What did I just see back there?

And the images filled her mind—the man talking, and the woman looking at Elena in awe, and then the wooden cross on the nightstand.

Could it be?

She hurled open the door and then saw the doctor near the elevator doors.

"Doctor, there's something you need to see."

Breathing heavily and finally stopping by him, she could see his annoyed, curious look.

"It's Joe Philips."

He gave her a nod. "The one whose death certificate I just signed?"

Elena had regained her composure. She stood upright and

then gave him a very Dr. Farell nod, a *yes of course and I know something you don't* sort of nod.

"Why?" the doctor asked. "Did I miss something?"

She laughed.

I think we both did. I think we've missed something for a long time.

"You could say that," she said to him.

She knew there was only one way she could tell the doctor what was happening. She had to show him. Men like him wouldn't believe otherwise.

People like *them* needed to be shown instead of believing.

I need to see Bobby. I have to talk to Bobby.

"Please—come with me," she told the doctor.

BOBBY

The first figure he'd seen in this whole mess—the black guy crawling around in the center of the street around all the carnage—was somehow still alive. Bobby had entered paramedic mode since several of his co-workers had arrived on the scene. Now he was looking over the unconscious man in the gurney and holding an IV of saline over him. They were loading him into the ambulance.

Two bullet holes and he's still breathing.

Whoever the guy was and whatever the story was, he was going to wake up and feel very, very lucky. Though Bobby knew luck had nothing to do with it.

Once the man was safely in the ambulance, Bobby went back to see who else needed help. Various people were attending to the injured. As he scanned the bridge, the blue and red lights of the siren moving around like some kind of dance hall, he took notice of several things.

Near the fire engine, a woman sat on a rear diamond-plate apron holding a baby. A paramedic—a man named James whom he knew and respected—was looking over the baby. Bobby knew that the woman and the baby—maybe *her* baby—were in good hands with James.

Close by, a man was standing near a gurney with closed eyes. *He's praying.*

The body on the gurney had a blanket over it, and Bobby knew what that meant.

He sighed.

Rest in peace.

Then he looked to see a group of cops surrounding a scary-looking guy in cuffs being led to a squad car. The world was not fair, and stuff like this constantly reminded Bobby. Whoever was on that gurney probably didn't deserve to be there. This man in cuffs surely was the one who deserved to be.

Then again, all of us deserve those cuffs. All of us deserve death.

He couldn't judge because he didn't know the stories. He had to just pray for all of them and give thanks for those who survived. Like that precious baby.

Bobby started to walk toward James and the woman with the baby but was stopped by a figure in a yellow EMS blanket sitting on the curb.

"Hey," a weak voice called out to him.

He glanced toward the voice and then saw the lawyer. The blond locks were flat, her makeup mostly gone, a look of shock on her face. As he walked up to her, she gave him a look of confusion.

"You . . . you saved my life," she said. "Why?"

A part of him wanted to say the obvious, that it was his job. But there were many people to try to help and rescue on this bridge. And the truth was right there in front of him. This was another one of those divine moments and he had to say exactly what his heart wanted to.

"Matthew 5:44."

Andrea still looked confused, eyes searching to understand. Bobby continued.

"Let me save you the trouble," he said with a smile. " 'Love your enemies and pray for those who persecute you.' "

He thought of the hearing, how he had asked them for a favor before he left, how he had taken back what he had been given. Bobby reached into his jacket and pulled out the wooden cross, then gave it to her. She took it without hesitation, still astonished and suddenly speechless.

"I'll be praying for you, Andrea."

His voice, his look, his everything told her that this was sincere, that this wasn't some pious sort of high-and-mighty looking-down-on-you thing he said. And Bobby believed that she knew that. He'd just helped her—maybe truly saved her life—so she knew how he felt.

He'd saved her temporary life here in this place full of death and darkness. What he hoped is that somehow, in some way, this would be an opportunity to lead her to another place of salvation. The place so many rolled their eyes at and mocked and simply disbelieved. A place too good to be true. And yet it was.

Maybe she'd know one day. Bobby knew this evening was a reminder to him. A confirmation that he had done the right thing with the dying man days ago. That he was doing the right thing now.

J.D.

"Are you okay?"

A voice so innocent didn't seem to fit in this scene of destruction and death and despair. It reminded J.D. that God was still with them, that He was watching over them and loved them.

Sometimes He speaks through the voices of little ones.

"I've been through lots worse," J.D. told Lily as he was secured to his gurney by a woman from one of the fleet of ambulances on the bridge.

Teri and Lily were standing next to him. They looked fine and J.D. couldn't be more grateful. To think that they had been driving with the girl and that it had been *their* car to almost kill all of them—it felt like too much. The accident hadn't been their fault, but to think of having to tell a mother . . .

Thank you, Lord. Thank you.

He glanced down the hill and could see the young man who'd rescued him getting a duffel bag from another man. All he'd been able to ask the man was whether he was military. The man replied that he was a corporal. J.D. had replied that he had been in Vietnam.

J.D. called out to the man to get his attention. The soldier walked toward them.

"That was mighty heroic back there, Corporal. Who were you with?"

"First Battalion, Sixth Marine Regiment."

The man said it with pride.

No wonder we're still alive. Thank God for the Marines.

"What's your name?" J.D. asked.

"Carlos, sir. You part of the 'Green Machine,' sir?"

He's smart, too. Knows his history as he should.

"Zero-Three for a while in a garden spot known as the A Shau Valley. Coulda used you there."

Carlos laughed. "No offense, sir. But I'm glad I missed that one."

"Wise choice, son. Still—I'm not sure I can convey how grateful I am."

J.D. reached out his hand and the Marine shook it.

"We don't leave our own behind, do we, sir?"

He sounds . . . relieved.

"Speaking of which, there's someone I gotta go see," Carlos said.

J.D. gave him a confirming *you go do that, son* sort of nod.

As they loaded J.D. into the ambulance, Lily asked what they were going to do.

"How about you let them take you to the hospital?" he asked the girl. "Ever been in an ambulance before?"

She shook her head.

"Well, climb on in so you'll never have to be in one again. Sound good?"

JOE

He didn't know what to tell Samantha when she kept asking him how and what happened and where he went. He simply smiled and then told her what he could.

"I'm here," Joe said.

He didn't know what to say because he was still processing everything. There hadn't been some sort of guiding light summoning him. He didn't see anybody flying around, no flapping wings, no golden gates. He didn't hear the voice of Morgan Freeman.

What he did feel now, and what he thought he had just felt, was this overwhelming sense of awe. A soul-crushing, knee-scraping, out-of-breath and blinding sort of awe. A fear, yes, but a glorious kind of fear. The kind that scared you until you felt that hand on your shoulder asking you to look up, telling you that things were going to be okay. The kind a child might feel when they were lost in a crowd, and then suddenly and inexplicably found their father standing on the curb *waiting*. The feeling of what it would be like to be wrapped into his arms, safe again, secure and absolutely *loved*.

The door opened and the nurse walked in followed by the doctor.

Ah, Dr. Farell. Now this is gonna be good.

The doctor had a different look now, one Joe had never seen. It was complete and utter amazement.

He's putting the dumb in the word dumbfounded.

"Impossible," the doctor said looking directly at Joe. "You were dead. *Dead.* For over twelve minutes."

Samantha didn't move or even look at the doctor. The nurse only watched and waited for Dr. Farell to do something. The doctor rushed over to check the machines. He fiddled with their settings, convinced they were broken. But he only grew more confused and bewildered at the realization that it wasn't the monitors that seemed off.

For a moment, the doctor didn't look so doctorly. He looked like a normal guy, suddenly scared and unsure of anything.

"I want a full blood panel immediately," the doctor suddenly ordered, finally regaining himself. "White and red cell counts. Hematocrit. Hemoglobin and mean platelet volume. Liver function ALT and AST. And a definite identification of the infection."

Elena began to get some of the tools for testing the blood. Joe simply smiled and looked up at the doctor.

"They're not gonna find anything, Doc."

"It's a miracle," Elena said, her expression of astonishment still very much there.

The doctor looked at the nurse with his usual arrogance. "There's no such thing as miracles."

The nurse stopped and simply looked at Dr. Farell. "Do you have a better theory . . . *Doctor?*"

Joe noticed something he had never seen before, something that probably rarely happened in this educated and assertive man.

Dr. Farell remained silent, not sure of an answer, unable to say *anything*.

Joe decided to fill the silence.

"For having eyes, they will not see. And having ears, they will not hear."

The doctor looked irritated, angry now. "Don't speak to me like I'm an idiot."

"Okay, Doc," Joe said with a simple grin he couldn't help. "But the man whose death certificate you signed is sitting here talking to you. And you don't believe in miracles? I'm just saying—you might wanna reconsider."

Joe reached over to the nightstand and picked up the wooden cross. Then he looked at the doctor and offered it to him.

Joe wasn't trying to be a know-it-all. Really, he didn't know anything. He just knew what it was liked to be saved.

Make that saved and then saved again.

The doctor looked at the cross then simply looked away. As easy as that.

LACEY

It was late now, but Lacey didn't want to go to her empty bedroom and climb into the cold bed. Her mind would race just like it was doing now. She might as well simply sit in the dark of this family room. Waiting, like she had for her whole life.

Drifting, eyes closed, wondering, so curious, so doubtful.

So doubtful that when she heard the knock on the door, she didn't believe it.

Until she heard the knock again. Then Lacey's eyes opened and she realized it was real. It was real and it wasn't going away.

Am I dreaming?

She knew she wasn't. The chill in the air, the gloom in the apartment, the grip in her stomach. Maybe it was her neighbor Pam checking up on her.

Sorry, no Szechuan pork being eaten here tonight.

She opened the door and saw him.

Carlos.

A grin on his face, the duffel bag over his arm. He looked like the man she'd met that first night.

"Wanna get some coffee?" Carlos asked in a casual manner. "My treat this time."

Things like this didn't happen to her.

Is this really happening?

She responded by wrapping her arms around him, shielding her face from tears that suddenly swelled over them.

"You came back," she said. "I can't believe it. He brought you back. No one ever comes back."

Lacey thought of the cross that Carlos had left for her. She thought of her prayer. Then she thought of her father. Her Heavenly father.

"Thank you, Lord."

ELENA

In the small hospital chapel, with a few chairs facing a cross on the wall, Elena sat with her eyes closed, praying. At least trying to pray. Trying to know how to speak words to the maker of them. Trying to understand how someone like her could be heard, especially after ignoring God for a lifetime.

How can someone who just did that—how can God actually want me to come to Him—how can He begin to care?

There was no medical explanation *whatsoever* for what had happened. And even though so many miracles had been documented in the Bible, Elena had never seen one in her life. She didn't think they actually happened. Maybe she had doubted miracles in the first place, just like doubting that Jesus had come down to die on the cross for her.

I don't want to doubt anymore.

She thought of the story of doubting Thomas. Elena had been around church long enough to know the story. The disciple who refused to believe Jesus had risen from the tomb, that needed to see Him in order to know. When Jesus had finally shown up, He said, "Blessed are those who believe without seeing me."

I want to believe. I want to be blessed. I want to know without a shred of doubt that I'm beloved, that I belong. That I can help make this world a little better by showing that.

Like Bobby . . .

The door behind her opened, and an unspoken prayer suddenly got answered. Her husband stood at the entrance to the chapel, his dress uniform looking stained and torn, his face cut and dirty.

"What happened to you?" she asked.

"It's a long story. What are you doing in here?"

"Praying."

He walked toward her and then sat beside her. "Oh?"

"Well, not praying, exactly. More like apologizing."

Simply saying that last word to her husband did something. It was like rattling a cage hard enough to fling the door open.

"Tonight, I saw a miracle," Elena said. "A real-life, in-the-flesh miracle. And it made me realize how I've been acting. Like the God who did that somehow wouldn't be there for us."

He simply looked at her, loving her, listening.

"I felt ashamed," Elena continued. "And then I realized—I don't wanna live like this anymore. I wanna give Jesus my whole life. All of it. No more holding back."

Bobby embraced her. She could smell smoke on him, and wondered what had happened. When he faced her again, he looked full of regret.

"I'm the one who should be apologizing," he told her. "I've been so busy sharing my faith with everyone else—I somehow lost sight of you. Please, Elena. Forgive me."

"Sure," she said with a shrug. She didn't agree, but she didn't mind this apology. It felt good to simply understand each other and to be a team again.

Bobby leaned over and kissed her. The kind of kiss that wasn't soaked in romance, but rather reconciliation. The kind of kiss that couples that made it eventually give. A kiss that reminded her that Bobby was there, that he loved her, that they were truly one.

"Will you pray with me?" Bobby eventually asked her.

"Gladly."

They knelt down together and bowed their heads. Then Bobby nudged her to get her attention.

"Oh—I ran into your brother," he said.

This was probably the *last* thing Elena expected to hear from Bobby.

The smoke. The tattered uniform. Now Carlos.

There had to be a connection.

"Really? Is he—how is he—"

Bobby simply gave her a confident nod and a smile. "Good. He's really good."

She felt him take her hand, then closed her eyes and heard his words as he prayed.

This felt unfamiliar. Yet it also felt right.

Like the man named Joe who had died and then come back to life, Elena found herself humbled and grateful and alive. Very much alive.

ANDREA

The nurse had told Andrea that she was fine, that the routine checkup following the crash had been necessary. No fractures or concussion, just some cuts and bruises and bumps. She was free to leave the hospital examination room, but Andrea asked to see the doctor. Surely Dr. Farell was busy, but not too busy to see her.

The nurse was wrong, however. Andrea wasn't fine. She hadn't been fine in a long time.

Her mind went back to the bridge and to everything that had happened. How quickly she'd been driving after the court hearing that night. How it just happened that her car ended up crossing over the bridge, a route she didn't usually take back home to her condo. How she almost died in the crash, then how she managed to find herself wandering and dazed before someone ran to her rescue.

Someone who happened to be the *least* likely candidate for being her Superman.

This guy—this paramedic who supposedly was great at his job—a husband and a father of two boys—had put his entire career on the line, for what? For this little trinket she now held in her hand. A tiny wooden cross.

For some reason, it felt very, very heavy in her hand.

Andrea had brushed off Bobby's faith in a way she had brushed off everything in her life. Her parents had given her everything she wanted and then more. Things in life had come so easily for her. Doors had always opened. She'd just kept walking and rushing and running as she got older, believing that at some point, she'd have enough success and respect and money and relationships to then maybe figure out the whole marriage and family and happily-ever-after thing.

I'm rushing to nowhere, hurting people along the way, ignoring so much of life while I go.

There was no way Andrea would have *ever* stopped to help someone trying to ruin her life. If she had been Bobby, she would have simply kept going the other way. Someone like Dr. Farell would have done the same thing. It's hard enough to help those who help you, but for those people who don't?

This cross is gonna cost you.

Andrea had spoken those words, but now they suddenly resounded in her heart.

She pulled out her iPhone from her purse and Googled the following words: **the cross of Jesus**

One of the first websites led her to a series of Bible verses. She clicked on a familiar passage and read it again.

"For God so loved the world, that He gave His only begotten son, that whoever believes in Him shall not perish, but have eternal life."

Andrea knew of John 3:16, of the way it had almost turned into a slogan, just like Nike's "Just Do It" tagline. She'd heard it so many times, and yet . . . Tonight, it seemed to be jostling her out of a long sleep.

She reread the whole passage in different versions, which was easy to do online. A version called the Message put it into different words.

"Anyone who trusts in him is acquitted; anyone who refuses to trust him has long since been under the death sentence without knowing it. And why? Because of that person's failure to believe in the one-of-a-kind Son of God when introduced to him."

Acquitted. Death sentence.

It was from John 3:18, a verse she didn't think she had ever read.

These were words in her universe, ones she understood.

A death sentence . . .

The curtain near the table she sat on whisked open. Dr. Farell appeared, a look of concern on his face.

"Are you okay?" he asked, coming to her side.

She could tell he'd been running around, surely dealing with people from the accident along with the other patients he was caring for. Though the term *caring* might be stretching it a bit far.

"Actually, no," she said, surprising even herself. "I'm not."

His eyes thinned, staring down at her. "What is it? Are you hurt?"

He began to put a hand up to her head to examine it, but she jerked it away.

"Tell me something. What kind of person would risk his life for someone who just finished ruining him?"

The doctor looked at her, then glanced off to the side while sighing.

"Andrea—look, it's been a long night. For everybody. Why don't I take you home?"

As usual, he hadn't heard a word she said. He was too used to instructing and prescribing instead of actually listening.

"No," she told him, knowing this wasn't a word he heard many times. "I think I've been wrong, Thomas. And I think you have, too."

Cold, calculating eyes didn't offer any sympathy or empathy, but they almost seemed to harbor on pity.

"Honestly, Andrea. What is wrong with you?"

"I don't know," she said as she stood. "Maybe I'm the one with the God complex."

She left Dr. Farell alone in the room. As she walked through the white hallways of the hospital, it felt like two roads stood in front of her as clear as day.

One leading to death. The other leading to an acquittal.

Maybe there was someone she could reach out to in order to help. Maybe even someone who had *already* helped her.

Maybe he'd be willing . . .

No.

She knew Bobby would be willing. His job was help sustain lives in emergency conditions.

This fit that description.

Maybe, hopefully, she'd figure out what a real acquittal looked like.

JOE

*S*o *what now?*

      But his question suddenly was answered by the high, piercing sound of Lily rushing into the room shouting for her mommy.

Joe watched as Samantha literally leaped up and grabbed Lily. The mother was crying, yet again. They had received the news about the crash. That everybody was fine *but* . . .

But things might've not been so fine.

Samantha had suddenly looked guilty and worried even though they were assuring her that things were fine, that Lily was okay.

First I die, then her daughter almost dies.

It was a night that would send a weaker woman to her grave. But Joe knew Samantha was strong. She was very strong. She simply needed some encouragement and some good fortune. And Joe was going to be all that and then some. God willing.

"Lily baby," Samantha said through tears. "I was so worried about you. I was *so* worried. Are you okay?"

"I'm fine, Mommy. But you should have seen it. I had quite an adventure. You really missed out."

Samantha couldn't help laughing as she glanced at Joe. Her look said *we had quite the adventure, too.*

"I'd say so," Samantha told Lily.

The girl wiggled free of her mother and then scampered over to the bed, hopping onto it even though her mother told her to be careful.

I just died. What're you worrying about?

Lily wrapped her arms around him. He could feel her soft little face against his prickly beard. It didn't seem to bother her.

She pressed her mouth against his ear and then whispered a secret that she'd obviously been wanting to tell him.

"You were right," Lily said. "The jar worked. I got my wish."

When he saw those bright eyes again, Joe could only smile. Now he was emotional and he didn't want them seeing such a big, strong man crying. No way. But he knew something.

Lily wasn't the only one getting her wish.

God was good. Even when—especially when—He didn't have to be.

The heavy darkness of the night hovered outside those hospital walls, but inside we stared at a tiny miracle. We stood in
the corner of the natal ICU in the maternity ward of the hospital,
watching Faith. I held Grace, and we simply looked at the tiny
baby hooked up to tubes and sensors. A lamp above her illumi-
nated incubator glowed like some kind of tanning machine. She
had curly hair, just like her mother had.

This was the first time we stood there, though we didn't know
it would be the first of many times. It didn't seem right, yet it all
felt like some kind of divine plan. Taking the broken and imperfect
and making it right.

I remember standing there, holding on to Grace, thinking of
Maggie, then thinking of Faith. Then pulling the cross from my
pant pocket and gazing into it.

I was reminded again of that full, perfect story. The one that
began when God became man, born in a stable so many years ago.
The one that nearly ended when all seemed lost on the cross.

I realize now that life can often give us reminders of that perfect story, even though our stories are so marred and imperfect.

Now, in the quiet of my study, finishing up this chapter in this
story, I know more details now. And I see things that stick out so
clearly.

Reminders of that perfect story.

The gift of life in a newborn baby, like the child Maggie had. A baby named Faith. A toddler now, the daughter Grace and I love more than we ever imagined possible.

There's the blood that was shed. The night of the accident, the people who were wounded. People like J. D. Newton.

There's the feeling of the abandonment, like the kind I heard about from a young woman named Lacey. She recently started attending church with her boyfriend and his relatives.

There's death. The kid named Pretty Boy who came into my office with a bag of money. The mother named Maggie who took her last breath in front of me.

Then there's the miracle. The resurrection. A man coming back to life just like Joe Philips had in the hospital.

I see it now, and all I can do is sit in humility with tears streaming down my cheeks.

That full, perfect story.

Jesus, born as a frail human baby.

Jesus, who shed blood.

Jesus, who cried out to know why his Heavenly father had forsaken him.

Jesus who gasped his last breath.

Jesus who came back to life with a message and a promise.

Jesus arriving at the cross and conquering it.

I know there are doubters. Skeptics. Cynical souls who prefer to see the dark scars instead of the sunrise. Those who say it's too simple, too silly, too saccharine for their taste.

But who would make up a story like this? About a God who gave up everything to become man and die for the very people who refused to believe in Him?

The cross is not too good to be true. The blood stained it. Death hung on it. Grief left it. But Jesus rose above it.

Every day people pass by the cross. I did, too.

All it can take to change a life is a simple question. That's all it took for me.

EPILOGUE

WE BELIEVE

I'm not sure any of us ever gets to see the whole picture. The God's-eye view, so to speak. It would be easier if we could. It would help us for the long road ahead. Yet we have to battle on and let love invade those dark and despairing places.

CLUTCHING THE CROSS in a hand cuffed to the side of the hospital bed, Kriminal looks down and remembers. He stares at it and sees his brother and vows to change. To change *everything*. To stop what he was doing regardless of where he goes beyond this. To finally do what Pretty Boy told him to do. To be the man G-Ma always wanted him to be.

When the police come, they ask him whether he's the guy calling himself Kriminal. All he can do is hold this cross in his hand. He pauses before answering.

"I was," he says.

• • •

IT'S LIKE WE'RE little children, sitting on the floor. Gazing up at the backside of a tapestry that's being woven. To our eyes, it sometimes looks ugly. The colors are a jumble, and none of it makes much sense.

CARLOS AND LACEY sit in the booth across from each other, their plates of food from the all-night diner barely touched, their eyes barely moving.

Neither can believe that they're here. Smiling at each other.

After telling the story about the crash on the bridge and the miracles that unfolded, Carlos listens to Lacey talk about her own miracle, about her prayer.

"This is crazy," Carlos tells her.

"Didn't I tell you that before?" Lacey says.

"So what do we do now?" he asks.

Lacey doesn't respond for a moment, thinking, staring around them in the crowded restaurant.

"Pray," she eventually says. "I think that's the starting point. And then—yeah."

Her eyes move to the cross that sits in the center of the table. Belonging to both of them.

BUT ONE DAY, we'll no longer be sitting on the floor. We'll come around to the other side. And the genius of God's handiwork will become clear. At the center of it all, we'll see the cross.

GUIDING HER PERSISTENT and stubborn husband down the hall-way in the wheelchair the nurse reluctantly gave him, Teri pushes toward the mother and daughter waiting for them outside the hospital room.

The joy on Lily's face. It's the kind of childlike glow that the world will eventually dull. But Teri and J.D. actually mirror that smile. And even Samantha has a look of overwhelming relief on her face.

"See, Mommy?" Lily shouts. "God really *does* love us."

The faith of a child.

Samantha finally releases her own joy as she holds Lily in her arms. "Yes, He does, baby. He really does."

They open the door to Joe's room. He's waiting for them.

BUT IN THAT immense tapestry, we'll also see the single, unique thread—the only one of its kind and color—that our own life has added to the piece.

BOBBY TURNS THE knob and nudges the front door open while Elena follows, stepping into the quiet shelter of the living room. He guides the door back and turns the lock. He aches from exhaustion and the minor injuries from the crash. Yet most of the hurt comes when he thinks about the young mother who lost her life tonight. He knows she's in a better place, and yes that's good to know, but the sadness will still shadow his days for some time.

He and Elena take their time to be quiet in the kitchen. Before heading upstairs, Elena stops him.

"I want to see the boys."

They're surely asleep in the room they share, just like Elena's mother, who sleeps in the guest room.

"Sure," Bobby says.

He follows her up the stairs and into the boys' room. The orange glow of the night-light in the corner of the room is enough for them to see both boys in their bunk bed.

Elena stands and stares at them. Smiling and thinking and then closing her eyes to pray again. Bobby stands watching this, momentarily surprised, then moving closer to her and putting his arm around her.

"I want them to know," she says in a whisper. "I want them growing up and knowing."

"Me too," he answers. "Me too."

THE ONE THREAD, without which the whole thing would somehow be incomplete.

MATTHEW WATCHES AS the nurse gently hands the baby to Grace. Of all the surprises and unexpected blessings, this almost tops them all. The tragedy that gave this gift—it's too much. But for the moment, he sees his wife holding Faith with this deep look of comfort on her face.

He doesn't say anything. He can't. For someone who is always full of words, either for a sermon or for encouragement or help— Matthew simply can't find any of them.

"What are you thinking?" Grace finally asks him.

He starts to say something, but then shakes his head and wipes tears away from his eyes.

The words will eventually come. For now, Faith is enough.

THAT ONE THREAD in that immense tapestry . . .
Personally, I can't wait to see His masterpiece.

ABOUT THE AUTHOR

TRAVIS THRASHER is the bestselling author of more than thirty works of fiction in a variety of genres—from love stories to supernatural thrillers and nearly everything in between. These works include collaborations with filmmakers, musicians, and pastors, such as *Paper Angels*, coauthored with Jimmy Wayne, and *Letters from War* with Mark Schultz. He has also written several novelizations, including *Home Run* and *The Remaining*; collaborated on a series of books with the Robertson family from *Duck Dynasty*; and cowritten a nonfiction work called *The Brainy Bunch*. Before being a full-time author, Travis was the author relations manager at Tyndale House Publishers and worked with many *New York Times* bestselling authors. Travis and his wife, Sharon, live in a suburb of Chicago and have three daughters. For more information on Travis, visit www.travisthrasher.com.